THE SCOUNDREL AND THE SIREN

By Christy Carlyle

PRINCES OF LONDON
The Duke and Lady Scandal
The Scoundrel and the Siren

LOVE ON HOLIDAY
Duke Gone Rogue
Lady Meets Earl
Duke Seeks Bride

THE DUKE'S DEN
A Duke Changes Everything
Anything But a Duke
Nothing Compares to the Duke

ROMANCING THE RULES
Rules for a Rogue
A Study in Scoundrels
How to Woo a Wallflower

ACCIDENTAL HEIRS
One Scandalous Kiss
One Tempting Proposal
One Dangerous Desire

THE SCOUNDREL AND THE SIREN

A Princes of London Novel

CHRISTY CARLYLE

An Imprint of HarperCollins*Publishers*

Without limiting the exclusive rights of any author, contributor, or the publisher of this publication, any unauthorized use of this publication to train generative artificial intelligence (AI) technologies is expressly prohibited. HarperCollins also exercise their rights under Article 4(3) of the Digital Single Market Directive 2019/790 and expressly reserve this publication from the text and data mining exception.

This is a work of fiction. Names, characters, places, and incidents are products of the author's imagination or are used fictitiously and are not to be construed as real. Any resemblance to actual events, locales, organizations, or persons, living or dead, is entirely coincidental.

THE SCOUNDREL AND THE SIREN. Copyright © 2026 by Christy Carlyle. All rights reserved. No part of this book may be used or reproduced in any manner whatsoever without written permission except in the case of brief quotations embodied in critical articles and reviews. For information, address HarperCollins Publishers, 195 Broadway, New York, NY 10007. In Europe, HarperCollins Publishers, Macken House, 39/40 Mayor Street Upper, Dublin 1, D01 C9W8, Ireland.

HarperCollins books may be purchased for educational, business, or sales promotional use. For information, please email the Special Markets Department at SPsales@harpercollins.com.

Avon, Avon & logo, and Avon Books & logo are registered trademarks of HarperCollins Publishers in the United States of America and other countries.

hc.com

FIRST EDITION

Library of Congress Cataloging-in-Publication Data has been applied for.

ISBN 978-0-06-334738-0

Printed in the United States of America

$PrintCode

To Grandpa, for always making sure I knew I was loved and safe, for encouraging my interest in history and archaeology, for gifting me with so many books, and for never being too busy for a good, long talk.

Historical Note

There have been many archaeological finds in Norfolk, but I used a bit of literary license for this story to use the 1939 Sutton Hoo discovery of an Anglo-Saxon ship burial in Suffolk as the inspiration for what Dom and Tess uncovered in 1890s Norfolk.

The Bewcastle Cross in Cumbria and Castle Rising in Norfolk are very real.

THE SCOUNDREL AND THE SIREN

Chapter One

London
May 1896

Dominic Prince shot up in bed, his body eager for escape from the nightmare he'd been lost in. Sunlight streamed with an unrelenting gleam through the curtains of his flat above his family's antiquities shop, and he lifted an arm to block the light.

His head weighed a thousand pounds and his throat burned as if he'd swallowed sand. Flexing his hand, he winced at the pain, then glanced down to see flakes of blood clinging to his knuckles.

He was sore all over, as if he'd rolled his way home over the roughest cobblestones in London. And yet none of it had eased the emptiness in the center of his chest.

The night before had been too much—too much liquor, too much carousing, too much pain and anger to hold inside. Memories flashed and flickered in his mind. He couldn't even say for sure who he'd punched. Probably Hemphill. He was always game for a night of revelry, but he liked to provoke too, and Dom had been in no mood for provocation. Whoever it had been, it seemed they'd landed a few blows of their own. His side ached and pain from his jaw reverberated into his neck.

As he shifted to collect his trousers from the carpet, he let out a groan. Bloody hell. Maybe there had been more than one opponent landing blows. His back was a mess of knots and aches.

Crossing to the wardrobe to collect a fresh shirt, a ball of white caught his attention out of the corner of his eye. He sneered at it, though the sneer was truly directed inward.

The crumpled letter lay at the edge of the fireplace grate. He hadn't even been able to dispose of the loathsome thing properly.

The letter's author, a lady cousin of his longtime friend, had written a lengthy, rambling missive with one salient point. Sharp enough to cut Dom to the quick—Peter Caldecott was dead.

They'd been friends for as long as Dom could remember. The Caldecotts had owned a jewelry and silversmith enterprise on Oxford Street, not far from Dom's own family's antique shop. Dom's father had been a restless soul, always off on an adventure somewhere far from home, often taking his mother along with him. But the Caldecotts had been like the ledgers Peter kept for the family's shop with such meticulous care: balanced and dependable. And Peter had been the steadiest of them all.

Dom had wanted to take after his father and traveled with him as soon as he was old enough. Those absences had cost him friends and lovers aplenty, but when he returned to London, Peter was always there. Unchanged and steadfast.

Dom had pitied him. Who could bear such cloying domesticity? He imagined Peter envied him, the one who would never settle and had no other aim than constantly seeking the next thrill.

When Peter married, Dom had thought him a fool for succumbing to wedlock so young. Then he'd seen Peter and his bride together and known that his friend had found a contentment Dom couldn't fathom. A contentment that, for the merest of moments, he'd yearned for too.

And then, two weeks ago, some bloody drunken fool had crashed his carriage and ended Peter's steady, contented life. And Dom's own life had become too much of a chaotic mess for him to even read the letter for a week.

For years, he'd been living out of traveling cases. When he did return to London, he preferred the cramped flat above his family's shop to his elegant rooms in the town house his family owned. His bedchamber at the Prince town house was too comfortable, too warm and inviting. It reminded him too much of the domesticity he did not want.

He kept his life busy, always moving, to keep monotony at bay.

It was no wonder he'd ignored his post for weeks. Who could bother sorting letters when one was planning the next expedition, the next hunt for treasure, the next daring feat that would get him a mention in the papers?

But now Peter was dead, and learning of his loss had forced Dom to stop and take stock of his own life.

He loathed self-examination. Hated acknowledging that there wasn't a great deal to show for his decade and a half of chasing his father's acclaim. A few yellowed clippings from the newspapers. A map of scars on his body. A trunk full of journals and photographs cataloging his travels to lands far and wide. And dozens of lively stories to tell at parties. Everything else in his life was changeable. No woman stayed long, friends found him unreliable, and he'd never met anyone he'd even considered asking to share his unpredictable life.

Restlessness gnawed at his belly like hunger. God, he longed to depart London. Only a few more days, and he and Eve, his sister and partner in the excavation project they'd begun in Norfolk, would head north again.

He couldn't wait. If he had his way, they'd depart today.

Since reading that damnable letter and learning that Peter was gone, he'd needed to escape. He'd been stagnant too long. After their promising dig a few months past, he and Eve had barely ventured beyond London. Their patron, American tycoon Gordon Van Arsdale, was working behind the scenes to arrange for further exploration, though the landowner involved was apparently a challenge to maneuver. Eve, the studious Prince, was busy presenting papers, doing research, and writing about Anglo-Saxon history. She relished all of it. Dom had always preferred action, so the weeks of waiting had all but driven him mad.

Learning of Peter's death had pushed him over an edge he hadn't even fully realized he'd been perched upon.

He'd been on the go for so many years of his life that he no longer knew how to sit in discomfort, how to savor a moment, how to feel at home anywhere. Though it wasn't until contemplating Peter's loss that he'd realized his insatiable wanderlust might keep him from ever feeling anything like contentment.

Admitting as much made him angry—at himself for chasing so doggedly in his father's footsteps, at his father for leaving a legacy that was so bloody hard to live up to, and at Peter for reminding him what mattered most in life.

"Do you think you'll ever marry and have children?" Peter had asked the question the last time Dom had seen him, while still in the first months of marriage to his pretty bride.

Dom scoffed at the question, bristling at the expectation

that he fall in line with what all the other boring gentlemen in society did. But Peter asked because he cared. Because he somehow sensed the moments of loneliness Dom hid with a procession of paramours and travel to far corners of the globe.

"Hello?" Eve's voice echoed up from the hallway stairwell. "Dominic?"

"I'm here."

His oldest sister's determined footsteps grew louder as she approached.

"Are you alone?" she whispered from the other side of the door. "Shall I avert my eyes?"

Dom scoffed and ran a hand through his hair. The presumption that he used this flat above the family's shop for debauchery usually amused him. Today, he found it grating.

"I'm alone." After donning the clean linen shirt he'd retrieved, he opened the door.

"Good morning," Eve said the minute he faced her. Her color was high, her blue eyes alight, and she was all but bouncing with joyful energy.

"Good morning." Dom lifted a brow. "What's happened? You look like Father when he found the queen's diamond."

"Do I?" She giggled.

Dom's brow shot higher. "You'd better tell me before you erupt."

She clutched something in her arms as if it was a rare treasure, and yet as far as he could tell it was the same leather-bound folio she often toted about to collect her notes and writings in.

"I've received an invitation." She dipped her hand down and lifted an envelope out to him. "Professor Albrecht has invited me to speak at a conference of historians in Berlin. Scholars are coming from all over the world to discuss historical and archaeological subjects for a whole week."

"Excellent." Dom only glanced at the letter before smiling and offering it back to his sister.

Reasons and rationales for declining a request to join her on the journey flickered through his mind. As much as he longed for travel, sitting in on a series of lectures for the entirety of a week sounded hellish, especially in his present mood.

And then there was the potential delay. "What of our progress in Norfolk? Are we not commencing our trip north?"

She darted her gaze away from his, scanning the narrow confines of his room. His sister would be a dreadful poker player. Her tells were far too obvious.

"What's the part you don't want to tell me, Eve?"

If the trip had been cancelled . . . His heartbeat thrummed louder, faster. He needed to get away from London.

"You may not like it."

"Tell me."

"Van Arsdale doesn't want to delay."

Dom let out such a sharp exhale that his head spun for a moment. "Thank God."

"I thought you might spare a moment to be pleased for me." Eve's brow crimped and she perched a hand on her hip. "You only care about the dig."

"Of course I care about it." He knew she did too. "It's what we've both been preparing for since we left Norfolk in October."

"Then you won't mind going alone." She stared at him now, expectantly and yet with a bit of hesitation.

"Alone." Dom swallowed hard, imagining carrying the

weight of all the responsibilities on his own shoulders. It shouldn't have daunted him. The papers presented him as a fearless swashbuckler, as they had his father.

But he and Eve were better as a team. He relied on her to take care of all the paperwork, the details that he found tedious and mind-numbing. He far preferred to have them summarized by her than wading through it all himself.

"Does Van Arsdale want me to do this alone?" Dom didn't want to delay, but he sure as hell didn't want to disappoint the man either.

"No." Eve shook her head. "You know that his ambitions will take a team. We've discussed hiring as many as five or six local men," Eve reminded him.

"Of course." Dom tried to push away the emptiness Peter's death had opened up in him and focus on the task at hand. He could be strategic. Organized. He could do this. "So he's recruited local men?"

"Oh no, not at all." She bent her head and rifled through her folio, slipping her finger along the edge of one particular sheet. He could only see that it was entirely covered in her neat cursive. "The landowner remains resistant, and Van Arsdale wants us . . . er, you to meet with him. A Lord Fenbridge. And as for a liaison with the locals, Van Arsdale has located and hired a local historian who is familiar with the site, the village, and Fenbridge."

She collected several pages behind the one she'd read from and lifted the thick, neat pile out to him. "These are my notes on the Norfolk project and also the letters from Van Arsdale and his man in London."

Dom took them and willed away the quiver in his belly. "Perfect."

Eve studied him, and he knew that she, much like Peter, could often see what he thought he was a master at concealing.

"I'm not going to ask about the blood on your hand or the bruise on your jaw."

"Best you don't." Dom cracked one of his signature grins and tried not to wince when his jaw protested.

"I know you're eager to start moving again. Dominic Prince remaining in London for nearly six months is nigh unheard of." This time she grinned, but it was soft and carried a hint of sadness. "I don't like seeing you like this."

"Like what?" He was curious, as he always had been with Peter, to know what she saw that others missed.

Eve gestured toward him and then swung her arm to encompass the spartan, narrow bedroom. "You close yourself off from the rest of us at home and end up looking like a trapped animal. It's as if you won't allow yourself any ease."

"There's no point in calcifying."

A muscle tensed in her jaw. "Must we forever parrot what Papa used to say?"

"Perhaps he had a point."

She pulled her folio against her chest, and he could all but see her mind whirring.

She hadn't had the rapport with their father that he had. While their father had mentored and molded Dom, he'd always been a bit put off by Eve's intelligence and diligence. He'd wanted to marry her off to a nobleman to improve their family's cachet in polite society, not watch her stack up a pile of academic papers and accolades for her research and writing skills.

"I don't think he did," she finally said, the words spilling from her as if she'd been holding them in a long while. "He was a man who could not be bothered with the day-to-day tasks of fatherhood and family life. He was so absorbed in his own wishes, he barely had time to consider Mama's. Or ours."

"Eve—"

"You don't have to be a facsimile of him, Dom. You can decide what you want, and what makes you happy."

His heartbeat ratcheted up again. Peter would wholeheartedly agree with his sister. "If you start talking about getting leg-shackled—"

"I wasn't going to, but . . ." Her eyes widened. "Have you met someone?"

"No! Not at all." Bloody hell, he wanted to end this conversation. He lifted her notes still clutched in his hand. "Thank you for these. I hope you know I'd much rather you were coming too. We started this together, and you should be there if we find what we both hope we will."

"Oh, don't worry. I'll come as soon as the conference in Berlin ends." She nodded at her notes. "In the meantime, hopefully Van Arsdale's man in Norfolk proves a good partner."

Dom hoped so too. Van Arsdale liked to manage every little detail from New York, or Mr. Worthy, his man of business, did so from London. It would be far better to have someone with local connections.

"Wish me luck." She wore the same vibrant smile as when she'd first greeted him. His sister didn't need luck. He suspected there were few women in England as confident and competent as Eve.

"You'll impress them all." He leaned forward to buss her cheek. "Safe travels."

"Oh, there's one more thing."

"What's that then?" He steeled himself for more talk of their father or questions about his amorous pursuits.

"Before you depart for Norfolk, could you do me one tiny favor?" Her tone had softened to the lilting cadence his sisters used when trying to persuade him, but there was an undercurrent of hesitation.

He had the distinct feeling it would be a task he'd loathe.

"Lady Goddard—"

Dom groaned before she could say another word.

"She has some books she'd like appraised, and, frankly, I think she'd rather have your opinion. She's very fond of you."

"That's . . ." It was an enormous bloody understatement. He'd met the lady at a society soiree, and she'd invited him to assess some items she'd inherited from her mad collector uncle. But the moment they'd stepped into her opulent library alone, she'd all but accosted him.

He wasn't opposed to liaisons with widowed noblewomen, but there'd been no spark of attraction with Lady Goddard, and he didn't fancy being in the same room with her ever again. Though he hardly wished to explain why to his sister.

"Please. It shouldn't take long. But she's determined to flog any books that might fetch her a good price."

Dom nodded in the middle of Eve's explanation. "Very well. I'll go."

"Thank you." She beamed and he could all but see her shoulders rise as if a burden had been lifted from them. "I'm off then."

He rested his hand against the doorframe after closing it.

"Steaming hell and bollocks." How could he determine a time to visit Goddard House when her ladyship was not at home?

Even if he had felt a glimmer of attraction to the lady, the last thing he needed before departing for Norfolk and a dig that could put him in the annals of notable discoveries next to his father's name was some ill-fated flirtation.

Best get this favor done posthaste so that he could focus on the dig.

Chapter Two

Tess Hawthorne's first sign that the day would not go as she'd planned was the stopping of her pocket watch. The bevel-topped, etched-case heirloom had ticked along comfortably for all the years since her late father had gifted it to her, urging her to conquer her tendency to overcommit and stop showing up tardy to one of her many charity events or to the house of someone in the village who she'd promised to visit.

Since taking short-term employment in London, it had become a daily reminder of home, not to mention a useful device to ensure she got to Lady Goddard's elegant town house on time.

This morning, like every day of the past week, she'd rushed out of her boarding house, caught the omnibus heading toward Hyde Park, and glanced down half a dozen times at the watch's face, as if it was more talisman than timepiece and could somehow help her get to Mayfair at precisely the right moment.

But the last time she'd glanced down, the clock's hands had stalled where they'd been minutes before. She'd wound it this morning as she always did. The watch had never failed her. She shook it as forcefully as she dared, considering its age and preciousness to her. All to no avail.

The stopping of the watch felt like an omen of events to come, and despite her aim to be logical in nature, she couldn't help but give in to a bit of the superstition that her twin, Tristan, and those back in her village were prone to.

Yet the moment Mr. Newby, the kindly white-haired butler at Goddard House, bid her good day and took her coat and gloves, she felt a bit lighter.

London was flush with watchmakers. She'd get her watch looked at and hopefully repaired, but now that she'd arrived, her mind was fully on the task at hand.

Lady Goddard had hired her to catalog a vast collection of books and documents inherited from an uncle who'd fancied himself an antiquarian. Tess relished the task, never knowing what she might uncover. Secretly, she hoped to find something that would further her father's life's work—penning a history of Norfolk, which she and her brother continued writing whenever they could.

Nothing had popped up yet, but she held out hope. After all, the county had seen habitation by the Romans, the Angles, the Danes, and been subject to Viking raids, so its history crossed paths with that of many others.

Though she realized her ladyship's goal was to pare down the collection and discover any pieces that might fetch a substantial price with a book or antiquities dealer, Tess found something interesting in every book, every scrap of paper the noblewoman's uncle had collected.

So, after parting from Newby, she strode eagerly toward the library, ready to immerse herself in the day's work. But as she neared the door, she slowed, a frown tugging at her brow. The door was ajar.

Tess always made sure to pull the door shut when she left each afternoon as Lady Goddard entertained in the evenings. Her ladyship had mentioned a desire that none of her guests visit the library until Tess had put the whole jumble she'd inherited into some kind of order.

But even more disturbing than the half-open door were the

noises emanating from the room. A clattering thwack interrupted the quiet of the town house. And then after a brief silence, the same awful sound again.

Tess pushed the door open and her heart dropped to her boots. She clutched at her stomach as a sudden queasiness took hold. She struggled to make sense of the sight before her. Books—a horribly disorganized pile of those she'd organized over the past days—lay on the rug in the center of the library. As she stepped inside another flew down to join the heap. *Thwack.*

Looking up, she saw a tall, broad-shouldered madman on the rolling oak staircase above her. He loomed overhead, one foot perched on the high rung of the stairs and his long arm reaching up to snatch another volume from the shelf. He was dark-haired and wore no suit coat, as if he was quite comfortable at his dastardly task of dismantling all she'd worked to put in order.

After retrieving one of Lady Goddard's books, he flipped through its aged pages roughly and then reached out his arm as if to drop it down to join the jumble in front of her.

"Stop!" Tess's shout echoed up to the high ceiling, and yet it still didn't seem like enough. She reached out her arms, palms up as if she could push the book back up onto the shelf by sheer force of will. "Cease this instant!"

She'd startled the man with her shout. After a quick glance at her, he weaved on the staircase, then clutched its railing for balance.

All she cared about was the book and let out a tiny puff of relief that he still held it pressed against the frame of the staircase.

"What the bloody hell do you think you're doing?" he barked down at her. He'd braced himself and shifted, subjecting her to a direct glare. "I could have fallen to my death." He gestured toward the book-strewn carpet.

Tess glanced back at the open library door, debating whether to seek Mr. Newby's help to remove the intruder.

"Have you nothing to say for yourself?" the miscreant shouted from his high perch.

"Me?" she scoffed, struggling to form thoughts in the face of the man's turpitude. "You come into this room and defile Lady Goddard's property, and you question me? How dare you, sir."

One dark brow arched, and his square jaw hardened. But there was no apology. No regret. Not even an ounce of shame seemed to trouble him.

Something reared up in Tess then, a spitefulness that was usually not at all part of her nature, but this . . . this . . . book abuser, with his thick biceps and dark tousled hair and extraordinarily broad shoulders, had sparked it in her.

"Maybe you deserve to fall to your death for how you've mistreated her ladyship's property."

Her heart beat a frantic and somewhat guilty tattoo. She wasn't cruel and never wished real harm on anyone. This man brought out the worst in her.

Then he shocked her completely.

His reaction to the most heinous declaration she'd ever made to any individual in her six and twenty years was to smile. Not just a flicker of amusement. Not a flash of mirth. A genuine, toothy grin.

He suddenly looked impish and unbearably handsome all in the same moment.

And she no longer felt guilty for being mean to him.

"You find me amusing?" she rasped, for the man had so much audacity that it had all but taken her breath away.

"Are you a housemaid?" he called down as if they were now going to engage in a pleasant chat.

Tess made a sound that she'd never heard emerge from herself before. Somewhere between a squeak and a splutter.

A housemaid? She ducked a quick glance down at her day dress. It wasn't the height of fashion by any stretch of the imagination, but it was well-tailored and of decent quality.

"I," she said with a proud notching up of her chin, "am a librarian."

Or at least she had been hired as such two months ago and would be for the next several weeks. Though Lady Goddard might offer an extension, now that she had to undo the mess this man had made.

His grin had eased into something less excessive but was still somehow potent.

"A librarian," he murmured as he stared at her.

Then he shifted, stepping down closer, then closer, his gaze never leaving hers.

Tess sucked in a sharp breath and a trace of his scent came with it. The man smelled like pine trees and fresh air and—

Heaven help her, what did it matter what he smelled like?

No, no, she was not that foolish, gullible girl anymore. She'd given in to a rogue's charm once and paid the price. Never again.

She turned away from him. She'd tell Mr. Newby or Lady Goddard, if she was at home, about the man's atrocious treatment of her books.

"Wait." A large hand brushed Tess's upper arm.

She turned but flinched away as if she'd been singed. Then she laid her hand against the spot where he'd touched her.

"Don't you want to know who I am?" he asked in a warm, deep voice that held far too much humor for the matter at hand.

"Who are you?" Tess said, irritation causing her to tap the toe of her boot against the carpet. She cast a mournful glance at the jumble of books on the floor and was angry all over again.

"You don't recognize me?" he said, now resting quite casually on the stairs with his thick arms crossed over his chest. He seemed to be posing, as if waiting for some artist to capture all the sharp angles and brooding beauty of his face in oil paint.

What he looked like was a rogue, a man who knew his own appeal. He was an impressive specimen of manliness, even if he was an abuser of books. She tried thinking of an occupation that seemed the least likely for a man such as himself.

"The chimney sweep?" she offered dryly.

He chuckled and flashed that irritatingly appealing smile again.

"You're not very good at being snappish, Miss Librarian." Leaning toward her, he whispered, "But I admire the effort."

Tess made the splutter-squeak sound once more, and the man managed to look the slightest bit contrite.

"Now stop hissing at me and tell me your name," he said softly.

"Tell me your name first so that Lady Goddard can pass it on to the police for—"

He reached out and hovered two fingers over her lips. She felt the warmth of them, but he did not touch her. "I was invited here to assist Lady Goddard. Seems that you were too. So we might as well be allies. Now tell me your name."

DOMINIC DIDN'T KNOW WHY he was determined to flirt with the young woman who'd stormed into the library and looked at him as if he was the worst sort of villain. She was a beauty with sunbeam-gold hair and eyes as bright green as spring's first leaves. Most distracting were her lips: a too-perfect Cupid's-bow mouth. Sharp little peaks but with a full lower lip lush enough to be a mighty distraction.

Of course, he'd bedded beauties aplenty. Yet there was something about the fiery spirit of the petite librarian glaring at him that he found himself determined to explore.

Coming to Goddard House, even when the lady of the residence was thankfully out, had made him irritable and on guard. The lady librarian's presence changed all of that. She'd altered the whole energy of the room when she'd swept in and shouted at him.

"Apologize first," she demanded, one delicate brow arched high.

Dom's brow shot up too. "To her ladyship?" He shook his head. "Not necessary. She asked me to come and have a go at . . ." He flicked a hand toward the discard pile he'd started. "Sorting the wheat from the chaff, if you will."

That information shocked her. Her thick lashes fluttered as she blinked. She was dismayed, maybe even disappointed. There was the slightest tremble of her chin, and he immediately wanted to take back what he'd said.

Seeing even a bit of her righteous fury dimmed made him feel like the miscreant she seemed to think he was. If she was Lady Goddard's hired librarian, he *had* made a proper muck of her efforts. All of the volumes he'd pulled down had been arranged alphabetically by author, and now that he thought of it, they'd been grouped by topic as well.

"None of it is chaff," she said, regaining a bit of her vehemence. She cast her gaze over at the pile and her expression softened, as if she was looking at objects that deserved reverence and care. "A book is such an effort to produce, for the writer, the binder, those who set the print. And while some of these may not fetch much from a bookseller—"

"They won't fetch much of anything, Miss . . ." He gave her a faux frown, then shrugged. "I still don't know your name."

She took a step closer. "Even if no one wished to buy them, they could be donated. Many who cannot afford fine leather-bound books would love to have one to read."

Color rose in her cheeks as she warmed to her subject. She leaned closer, lifting a finger to point at him.

"And," she said, that damning finger of hers almost touching his chest, "if Lady Goddard asked you to assess the books, I highly doubt she wished you to treat them so carelessly. You may have damaged spines, bent pages, ripped the thread in the binding. They are her inheritance, sir, whatever you may think of them."

Dom looked down at her finger and felt the oddest flash of disappointment that she wasn't touching him. He was tempted to lean toward her but knew she'd balk. Yet he wondered if her touch would electrify him. If all that fierce emotion of hers could jolt the parts of him that felt deadened and bring them back to life.

Her finger was ink-stained, he noted. Had she penned some fervent letter to a lover or set about writing a list of every little way she intended to conquer Lady Goddard's library today? The latter, he decided.

When he looked up again, he studied her face. She was close enough for him to see freckles spread across her cheeks in a delightfully disarrayed pattern. The flashes of sunflower-yellow in her green eyes. The little wisps of hair that had escaped pins to frame her smooth cheeks. Then his gaze fell to her mouth. Good lord, such a lush confection.

He'd wanted to kiss plenty of women upon first sight. Lust had never been anything he avoided. And despite the debacle with Lady Goddard, it was usually effortlessly mutual. Women were attracted to him, and he rarely minded living up to the roguish reputation he'd acquired.

"Do I have something on my face, sir?" she asked, her words sharp and laced with irritation. A spark lit her eyes.

He'd taken it for heat, for a simmer of interest much like he felt for her.

"You're staring quite rudely," she added with a bit less ire.

He was staring like an addlepated fool. Good grief, it wasn't like him to tip from flirtation straight into boorishness. He'd been treated rudely by her employer in this very room, and he had no interest in subjecting any woman to that.

"Forgive me," he said with true regret. "You're lovely, and I—" He stopped because she made that noise again. That odd squawk she'd emitted a few times already. Then she scoffed as if he'd made the most outlandish claim she'd ever heard.

Miss Librarian was not used to being complimented, it seemed, and for such a beauty, that was a mystery.

He'd miscalculated badly. The last thing he wished to do was cause her embarrassment.

She was breathing fast, though a bit of her fire toward him seemed to have ebbed. Now she was simply looking at him warily, as if trying to anticipate what he might do next.

Dom stepped away from her and went to retrieve the books he'd tossed onto the carpet. Perhaps that had been badly done of him. He'd taken his dislike of Lady Goddard out on the innocent volumes that were, as Miss Librarian pointed out, the product of a great deal of work by wordsmiths and craftsmen.

He hadn't gotten far with sorting through the collection, but he'd had enough of ruffling the feathers of a pretty librarian and dreading the appearance of Lady Goddard at any moment.

"What are you doing?" she asked, as quietly as she'd said anything to him thus far.

"I made a mess of your efforts at organizing." After he'd stacked the dozen or so volumes onto a table in the center of the room and collected his suit coat from where he'd tossed it on a chair, he glanced back at her. "I'm sorry for that."

Those pink lips of hers fell open a bit.

"See those on the left edge of the top two shelves? Those will fetch her a fine price, and there's a seven-volume set of Shakespeare from 1733 among them that I could take on consignment at Princes if she likes. I know a bard enthusiast who'd snap them up. Tell her that, will you?" He gestured to the rows of books in Lady Goddard's library. "I'll let you get back to your work."

The urge to reach for her hand or some other form of leave-taking that would give him an excuse to approach her once more nearly overwhelmed him.

But he'd unsettled the young lady enough. He needed to forget about her vivid green eyes and perfect lips.

He had a Viking hoard to find in Norfolk.

Chapter Three

The encounter had been so strange, so unsettlingly provocative, that Tess stood frozen after the man departed, her gaze fixed on the doorframe his broad shoulders had barely squeezed through.

It took far too long to catch her breath and tame the wild beat of her heart. Even then, she felt overheated and utterly frustrated because the room seemed shockingly empty now that he'd gone.

Mercy, the way he'd looked at her, as if she was some fascinating creature. As if he found her all but irresistible.

Her. Tess Hawthorne. The scandalous spinster of Wiggenstow.

For a moment, he'd stared so fixedly at her mouth, she thought he might kiss her. And for one terribly brazen moment, she'd wanted him to.

One word he'd said echoed again in her mind. Princes.

She swung around and went to retrieve her satchel, pulling out the notebook she always carried with her. It had become a compendium of notes about her father's research and then her own, as well as her other interests and preoccupations. A few pages in, she found what she sought—a clipping cut from a local Norfolk news sheet several months ago.

And there he was—all that magnetism, wavy dark hair, and square jaw. The artist had even captured the cleft in his chin. The article featured sketches of both Dominic Prince and his sister Eveline, along with details about the dig they'd conducted at a mound near Tess's village back in October.

Her twin brother, Tristan, had drawn a heart above Mr. Prince's head to tease her, as Tess couldn't help commenting on his handsome face. But they'd both been most interested in the details. The Princes were doing the sort of work that Tess had often dreamed of undertaking. Though their father had been a historian and had long speculated on what sort of treasures the mounds in their county might hold, he'd never had any desire to organize a dig himself.

Tess had actually attempted to do just that once, planning out the whole undertaking and convincing Tristan and a few young men in the village to help. But the one person she could never convince was Lord Reginald Fenbridge, the greatest landowner in the county. The mounds on his land were tantalizing, yet he'd allowed no one to fully explore them.

Tess couldn't fathom why the old nobleman did not wish to know if ancient gold and silver lined those hills. His own ancestors might have left a trace of their lives and personal histories under the soil.

She ran her finger over the image of Dominic Prince and remembered the warmth that rippled through her when he told her she was lovely.

What nonsense.

The man's reputation as a charmer and rogue was now completely understandable. He was silver-tongued and far more appealing than anyone had a right to be.

She tucked the clipping into her notebook and turned back to Lady Goddard's books. Now it made sense why he'd been here. The Princes were renowned antiquarians, though it still rankled that the dowager countess would employ him to rifle through the collection without telling her.

Why engage two people to work at cross purposes?

Tess inspected each book Mr. Prince had tossed onto the carpet, trying to ignore the scents of pine and clove that wafted up from the volumes he'd touched. None seemed to have suffered any significant damage, but what was she supposed to do with them? Would her ladyship truly wish to discard perfectly good books?

Her organizing efforts had been going so well until Dominic Prince appeared, disturbed her orderly system, and left her breathless.

Good heavens, if Tristan knew he'd never let her live it down.

"Miss Hawthorne?"

Tess jumped at the sound of the countess's voice. She was usually busy making social calls during the hours when Tess came to work on the library.

Pasting on a smile, she turned to face her employer.

"Yes, your ladyship?"

The countess seemed to take in everything in one sweeping assessment—the gaps on the shelves, the pile of books on the table, and then Tess.

"You look overwrought, Miss Hawthorne."

"Not at all."

She narrowed one dark eye at Tess. "I take it you met Dominic Prince."

"Yes." Tess stifled the urge to say more.

"Newby says he heard raised voices and that Mr. Prince left abruptly."

"I . . ." Tess fumbled to explain what had taken place with the tall dark man whose scent still lingered in the air.

Lady Goddard didn't wait for Tess to say more. "I was expecting Miss Eveline Prince, you see, but I was most pleased when Newby informed me that Mr. Prince had appeared instead."

Something flashed in the countess's expression when she mentioned him that Tess thought looked a great deal like giddiness.

"But now I find that he's already departed." Her lower lip jutted out a bit, like a child who'd just had their favorite toy plucked from their hand. "Why ever did you send him scurrying off so quickly?"

"I didn't."

Lady Goddard narrowed her gaze on Tess further, studying her.

Tess prayed her blush had faded, that her eyes gave nothing away, that none of the whirlwind of feelings Dominic Prince had evoked were apparent under the noblewoman's keen inspection.

Lady Goddard stepped closer. If she had a quizzing glass, Tess didn't doubt she'd be using it to assess her. "What exactly occurred between you and Mr. Prince?"

Tess cleared her throat, struggling to construct the simplest explanation with the fewest words. She didn't need another scandal in her life. She wasn't that reckless girl anymore. Yet when she recalled the way he looked at her, the heat that had zinged through her at his words, the way her body responded to his nearness . . .

"Out with it, Miss Hawthorne, or I shall assume the very worst."

How could she tell the woman the truth? *The man looked at me like he was starving, and I was a jam tart.*

"He was sorting through the very books I spent the last week organizing."

Lady Goddard nodded. "Yes, that is precisely what I asked his sister to do, and for some reason, he came in her stead."

"I did not know that, my lady, so I was surprised to find him here." Tess heard a tinge of annoyance in her tone and regretted it.

The countess was already peeved at the man's departure.

"I may employ whoever I please, Miss Hawthorne, and do with all of this"—she flicked a hand at the cluttered library—"as I see fit."

"Of course."

She harrumphed and crossed her arms. "I want him back."

Tess pressed her lips together and cast her gaze at the carpet. What on earth could she say to that? Especially considering that the exact same sentiment had filtered through her mind the moment he'd left the library.

"I think we shall put an end to your organizing, Miss Hawthorne. Please do not return tomorrow or thereafter."

Tess snapped her gaze to her employer's. "Your ladyship? You're dismissing me?"

"I shall pay you the whole sum we agreed upon," she said as if Tess should be grateful for her magnanimity. "My uncle's friendship with your father demands that at least. But yes, I appreciate what you've done so far, but I think I prefer to have Mr. Prince here to finish the task."

It was on the tip of Tess's tongue to tell the countess that he'd done nothing like what she had done. She had been organizing the collection, as she'd been asked to do. He'd been throwing books on the floor, for heaven's sake.

But if six and twenty years of life had taught Tess anything, it was that some battles weren't worth fighting. The determined set of Lady Goddard's jaw told her that this wasn't one she'd win, even if she tried.

"Very well, my lady. I shall finish up and—"

"Yes, do, Miss Hawthorne. Then collect your things and see Newby, who'll provide you with the amount we agreed upon." She nodded as if quite pleased with her decision. Then she swept from the room, the beaded fringe of her day dress rustling as she went.

Tess bit her lip and fought the frustrated tears that threatened to fall. She'd never been dismissed from employment in her life. And she'd done nothing to deserve it now.

But then relief swept in too. She wasn't losing out on the much-needed wages that had drawn her to London and this opportunity in the first place, and she had been missing home. Whenever she was away too long, she began to worry about what Tristan might be getting up to. Her twin seemed to stumble into trouble effortlessly.

After penning a note regarding what she'd done, what she thought still needed to be completed, and Mr. Prince's recommendations, Tess collected her satchel and then took one last look at the library and all the items Lady Goddard's uncle had collected over a lifetime. She hoped that wherever the books and pieces ended up, they'd be treasured.

Then she strode into the hall to find Newby waiting for her.

"Wishing you the very best, Miss Hawthorne," the butler told her as he handed her an envelope with her wages inside. "It will be odd not to greet you tomorrow."

Tess smiled. "I was thinking the same, Mr. Newby."

Once she was out on the pavement, and Newby had closed the door behind her, Tess calculated how long it would take to return to the boarding house, pack the few items she'd brought with her to London, and catch the train headed north. Habit caused her to lift her grandfather's pocket watch to check the time.

It was still stuck where it had been on her omnibus ride. Apparently, it had been a portent of bad tidings after all.

TESS SECURED A TICKET and made the journey in time to step into Foxdene, her family's cottage, just as the orange wisps of sunset began to sweep across the horizon.

"Oh, dear Tess, you gave me a fright, you did." Mrs. Wells, the family's longtime housekeeper, cook, and staunchest defender, paused a moment, eyes wide, before bustling forward and giving Tess a warm hug. "We'd all expected you to be in London at least a fortnight longer."

"As did I." Tess drew in a breath and smiled at the familiar scents of fresh baked bread, roasting vegetables, and the lavender Mrs. Wells always favored for the ointment she made herself and claimed cured all sorts of ailments. "But I'm glad to be home early."

With a warm hand on Tess's cheek, Mrs. Wells assessed her, both silver brows arched. "Always pleased to see you, dear girl, but you're not unwell, are you?"

"Not a bit. I simply . . . finished my work for Lady Goddard early."

"Mm-hmm." Viola Wells didn't miss much, and the thoughtful sound indicated she knew there was more to the story, but, bless her, she asked no further questions.

"Where's Tristan?" Tess asked, noting that the cottage was quiet. Her brother was rarely present without making noise.

Mrs. Wells lifted a hand to pat at her hair, then checked the buttons on her high-necked day dress. A stalling tactic that sent a little shiver down Tess's spine.

"What has he done?"

"It's really the Bromley brothers you should be vexed with."

Tess closed her eyes for a moment and tried to temper what she truly wanted to say to their beloved housekeeper.

"So he's back to toying with Justine Bromley's heart again, is he?"

Mrs. Wells frowned at that. "Now, now, she might be his heart's true mate."

Tess scoffed. "Where is he?"

"I can only guess he's—"

"At the pub."

Mrs. Wells gave her the tiniest of nods as if she didn't truly wish to admit as much.

"Don't be too cross with him," she called to Tess as she headed out toward The Black Swan.

Tess offered a wave and a smile and then gritted her teeth the whole march to the village public house. She'd had this talk with Tristan many a time. Young ladies were drawn to him like bees to a field of wildflowers, caught up by his effortless charm and handsome face. Their protective brothers and fathers weren't nearly as susceptible to his charm.

Music wafted on the breeze the closer she got to The Black Swan, and when she strode inside, heads turned her way.

"Miss Hawthorne!" Mr. Cardwell shouted, cutting short whatever he'd been playing on a battered piano in the corner and then starting into a rousing little ditty, as if to please her.

"Tess," Old Tom the publican called, "we've missed that pretty face of yours."

"There's my girl." Alice, the barmaid who Tess had known since girlhood, gave her a wink and a grin. "Thought London might snap you up and not give you back."

"Not a chance." Tess returned her wink. Then she spotted Tristan and groaned.

Her brother was, to put it mildly, in his cups. He was sitting at his favorite table and yet swaying as if on a ship at sea. A smile spread across his lips, and he lifted bleary green eyes and a tankard toward her.

"Sishter dearest, what a sweet shurprise." He waved her over, his arm swinging wildly.

"Aren't you even curious why I'm back early?"

He frowned as if just realizing that was the case.

"I was dismissed, Tris, and you'll love hearing why."

His eyes lit. "Oh, I do love a good story." He held up a finger as if to bid her to wait. Then he shoved his hand in every pocket—shirt, waistcoat, trousers—and finally frowned as if he'd failed to find some lost treasure. "I've something to tell you about too. Must have left it at home."

"Well tell me about it anyway." When he lifted his cup, Tess reached for his hand. "Tell me before you drink yourself into a stupor."

"A letter came. For Father, actually." Tristan eyed his beer longingly. "The great American titan did not hear of his death, it seems."

"American titan?" There was only one American they ever discussed in such terms. "Gordon Van Arsdale?"

Tristan tapped the tip of his nose. "The very one. He's asked for Father's aid on a dig. Hoping for a hoard for his museum in New York."

"So we find it, and he takes it. Lovely," Tess said bitterly.

Tristan shrugged. "He who pays keeps the loot."

"Whatever's in those mounds should remain in Norfolk. In England, at least."

"By that logic, someone should let Elgin and Petrie know there are a few items in England that need returning."

"Perhaps they should be." Never mind that Elgin was long dead.

"Good luck with that, Tessie."

"Let's say one of those mounds on Fenbridge land gives up its treasures. Imagine how people would flock to Wiggenstow if a museum could be established here."

"I think it would take a bit more than a few bits and bobs to put our village on the map." He nudged her elbow where it rested on the table. "We could use the funds Van Arsdale's offering."

"Offering to our late father."

"You know as much as Father did." He caught her gaze and looked momentarily clearheaded. "And you've long wanted to be part of a dig like this. Write him. Offer your services in lieu of Pater's. Don't turn him down."

"I'll consider it."

"He sent a check," he said with a hopeful arch of his brow. The money was needed. Foxdene was let, not owned by their family. Lord Fenbridge owned the property, much as he owned so many other acres in the county.

"I could offer my tutoring services again or teach at that school in Norwich. My friend Magda says they're in need of more teachers."

"It's a sizable check, Tess. And whatever's found might help us finish Pater's book."

She sighed. "I said I'll consider it."

"Good. Now tell me why you got sacked."

"In sum, Dominic Prince was the cause." Might as well just blurt it out and not prevaricate. But even saying the man's name made her pulse pick up speed. She felt heat rush into her cheeks and willed Tristan not to notice.

But of course he did. Then he leaned closer. "Did you have a dalliance in the city?"

Tess's warm cheeks went furnace-hot and she shot her twin a glare. "Don't be daft. I've had my share of scandal, thank you very much." She crossed her arms. "The man got me dismissed."

"Did you kiss him first?" he teased.

"I should have kicked him." But of course, she'd thought of kissing Dominic Prince. How could she look at a man so beautiful and not think what his lips might feel like on hers? Regardless of all her vows about becoming the most respectable spinster in England.

"There he is," a man barked.

"Drunk, of course," another replied.

At the deep, angry voices, Tess stiffened. She knew those voices, and a sinking feeling told her she knew exactly who the *he* in question would be.

"Ignore them," Tristan murmured, keeping his gaze fixed on the tabletop.

Tess couldn't ignore them. The Bromley brothers were massive, angry, and no doubt headed straight for her brother.

She let out a sigh, gave Tristan one long-suffering glower, and stood to face them.

"Gentlemen, how are you this evening?"

Even with all their bluster, their expressions softened.

"Not as well as could be, Miss Hawthorne," the younger Bromley said with a nod and a half-smile. He was as tall and intimidating as his brother, but he'd always seemed kinder.

"Tess," the elder, Bill Bromley, said, his dark gaze boring into hers, "you can't protect him forever."

He'd been one of her father's tutees, a childhood friend, and she empathized with him entirely.

"I don't know exactly what he's done, Bill," Tess admitted. "I only just returned from London."

"It's Justine. As soon as he comes around, her hopes rise again," the younger explained.

"So he'd do well to stay away." Bill, the elder, took a step closer, and Tess laid a hand on his shoulder. "I'm here to make sure he stays away."

"I'll see that he does," she vowed to him.

He narrowed dark eyes on her, but she felt no fear despite how he towered over her. Tess counted his wife a dear friend, and Sarah would never forgive him if he did Tess harm.

"After all you do," he said quietly, "it's not much of a man who makes his sister his protector."

Tess heard Tristan shift and pivoted to stop him from whatever drunken impulse had prompted him to intervene. But she was too late.

He thrust his arm past her and it connected with a sickening thwack against Bill Bromley's cheek.

The elder Bromley was hardly jostled by the blow, but his brother lunged forward and grabbed Tristan by the shirtfront. Tristan wheeled an arm up again, bringing his forearm down hard.

That's when Tess saw local bully Nigel Hardy stand to join the fray. The Bromleys were well-liked by all, but Hardy relished a good fight.

Tess pushed Nigel back, both hands on his chest. He'd been one of her father's tutoring students too. Most of the boys in the village had been. She didn't fear him, but she trusted him far less than the Bromleys. When he tried to wave off her hands and push into the fray, she slammed her boot down on his, and he let out a roar.

Behind Hardy, two men stood from the drinks they'd been

sharing with him, their matching scowls pointed in her direction.

Tess knew how quickly such tussles could get out of hand. She shot a pleading look at Old Tom. The barman had a club he kept on hand, which he used as more of a threat than a weapon to return order at moments like this.

But before he could step out from behind the bar, Wiggenstow's magistrate emerged from a corner where Tess hadn't even noticed him.

"Who threw the first punch?" he bellowed as he marched toward them, his barrel chest leading the way.

In chorus, the Bromleys shouted, "Tristan Hawthorne."

"Might've known." Magistrate Darnley waved a hand at Tristan. "Come, son. A night in the lockup will do you good."

"Magistrate, please," Tess cried. "I've only just returned and seen my brother for but ten minutes before all this." She waved a hand to encompass the riled men standing in an uneven circle around them.

The balding, gray-browed man, a friend of her late father's, assessed her, and she thought she saw pity flicker behind his spectacles. A mischievous little smile pushed up the edges of his mustache.

"You're welcome to join him, Miss Hawthorne."

Chapter Four

Dom had traveled to points around the globe. To Egypt so many times that a part of him felt homesick for its glorious sunsets and ancient ruins at times. To Greece and Italy, where the wine and food were incomparable. To France for pleasure more often than for work. And once, the year before his father died, they'd ventured together to Japan.

And yet despite his lifelong sense of wanderlust, his soul's urgency to always be on the move, something about the green fields dotted with spring flowers on the train ride up to Norfolk almost managed to charm him. He'd headed north soon after leaving Lady Goddard's and packing his usual kit back at his flat. Now, he stared out at the bucolic landscape. He hadn't taken much notice on the previous journey, as he and Eve were likely in discussion about their plans. But now, on his own, he could almost understand why men yearned for a home in the countryside. Almost.

Find a lady as lovely and tempting as the one he'd met this morning and make a life. Wasn't that what other men did? Wasn't that what Peter had urged him to do?

Of course, being the sort of man he was, all he could think about was how he should have kissed the blond library beauty senseless.

The train arrived at East Winch in the early evening, and it was a short ride in a hired cart to deposit him in the village of Wiggenstow. He and Eve had stayed at the local inn during their previous venture north, and she promised she'd once again make all the arrangements for this trip.

Dom wondered if she would leave Germany and join the dig as she'd vowed, or whether she'd get swept up in connecting with other academics. That side of things always interested her most—poring over books, writing about what she'd found, and hypothesizing about the past. He admired her knowledge and had needed it on every venture they'd undertaken together.

He opened the leather-bound journal he had tucked under his arm and found the details about Van Arsdale's local man. He hoped—he squinted down at the man's name—T. S. Hawthorne proved as helpful as Eve would be if she were here.

After his bags and equipment were settled into his room at the inn, Dom headed down to the taproom. It was sparsely populated, and he knew a more lively crowd could be found at The Black Swan up the lane.

"Good evening," he said to the innkeeper, who stood with his wife preparing trays of food that would no doubt be taken up to lodgers.

"Mr. Prince, is the room to your liking?"

"No complaints whatsoever." Dom had found the rooms as tidy and cozy as during his last visit when he and Eve had each rented rooms. "I'm wondering if you might know a T. S. Hawthorne and where I could find him."

Mr. and Mrs. Randall exchanged a look.

"There's a Tristan Hawthorne who all but resides at a table at The Black Swan," Mrs. Randall finally offered. "Bit of a troublemaker, he is."

Dom arched a brow. That didn't sound promising. "I believe my patron, Mr. Van Arsdale, selected him for his knowledge of the history of the area."

"Oh yes," the couple said in near unison and apparent understanding.

"All the Hawthornes know this land's history," Mr. Randall opined. "But take care with that young man."

The Randalls' warnings rang in Dom's head as he walked the short distance to The Black Swan. It was as lively as he recalled from their previous stay, and when he stepped inside, the publican tipped his head in recognition and welcome.

Dom beelined straight for the man and felt the perusal of the barmaid and a few others gathered around the pub's scattered tables.

"Hello, sir. Welcome back to Wiggenstow." He glanced over Dom's shoulder, noting the empty space. "No Miss Prince this time?"

"My sister will arrive soon, I hope." Dom cast a gaze around those gathered in the warm, low-ceilinged space. "I'm seeking a Mr. Hawthorne."

The publican's eyes ballooned. "Are you now? Doesn't owe you money, does he? 'Fraid you won't get it. He and his twin sister are skint ever since their father died."

Dom chewed on that additional detail. Did anyone in the village have a single good thing to say about Mr. Hawthorne?

"Is he here?" Dom said with more wariness now that he'd learned a bit about the man.

The publican wiped at the bar with a cloth and seemed to ponder his answer far too long. Finally he looked up, a bit remorsefully. "Sorry to say you'll find him in the village lockup." He turned his gaze toward a back corner. "Magistrate, we've a gentleman who needs directions to the lockup."

Ten minutes later, Dom had learned even more about Mr. Hawthorne's nefarious reputation. Apparently, the man had terrible luck at cards, but grand success with the ladies. According to Magistrate Darnley, who whispered behind the shelter of his cupped hand, Hawthorne had swived half the unmarried ladies in the village.

Dom was beginning to form a picture of the man that reminded him a little too much of himself. He swept a hand through his hair. "But he's been hired for his historical knowledge. He has that at least, doesn't he?"

"Suppose that's a talent the whole family possesses," Darnley said amiably. "Ah, here we are, sir."

The older man had led him to a structure shaped a bit like a large stone beehive with a few openings to serve as crude windows. From those windows, Dom heard the distinct sound of two people laughing—a man and a woman.

"Good God, he can even attract a woman while he's in the lockup?"

The elderly magistrate chortled. "In this case, it's just his kin. Man's blessed with a sister far more loyal than he deserves."

"Indeed." Dom couldn't imagine either Eve or his younger sister Allie being willingly incarcerated with him if he'd done something as stupid as attempting to start a drunken brawl, which according to the magistrate is what had landed the young man in custody.

"There's someone coming." A blond man's face appeared in one of the openings as his words floated to Dom on the breeze.

"Mr. Hawthorne, I presume," Dom said to Darnley.

"Aye, the very one," the magistrate confirmed.

"Have you decided on mercy, Magistrate?" a lady's voice called out.

Dom swallowed hard. Something about the timbre was familiar. Anticipation flared in his chest, though he wasn't entirely certain why.

Darnley unlocked a wooden door with aged iron hinges on a flat side of the beehive, and a woman ducked her head as she stepped out into the cool spring evening. Light from the lantern the constable held high gilded her face as she arched her back and stretched her arms toward the early evening sky.

Dom's mouth went bone dry, and the anticipation in his chest bloomed into something fierce and fiery. Pleasure rushed through his veins at the sight of her.

Miss Librarian. He'd never imagined he'd see her again, and yet she stood before him as if he'd evoked her with his thoughts.

She was too busy thanking the magistrate before the man trundled off to even notice him at first, but her brother did. He'd stumbled out after her and approached Dom, blocking his view of her.

"Well, well, well. Look who it is, Tess." The young man was nearly as tall as Dom, with darker gold hair than his sister's and the same green eyes. "Come to apologize, have you?"

When Hawthorne turned back to check his sister's reaction, Dom got a clear look at her again.

She stood unmoving, her lips parted, eyes wide. "Why . . . ?" she started and then fell silent. "How did you . . . ?"

Dom stepped past her brother. He understood the young man was the one he'd come to find, but she was the only thing that interested him at the moment.

"So this is how I discover your name," he said softly, only for her ears. "I had to come all the way to Norfolk to do it." He grinned at her, but she still looked stunned, and not a little annoyed, as she tried to work it all out in her mind.

"Good to meet you, Miss Tess Hawthorne. Again." Dom held out his hand and dearly hoped she'd take it. The desire for that simple point of contact was intense.

She did. Her warm fingers slid against his, and then they were joined palm to palm. He resisted the urge to stroke his thumb against the back of her hand. He found himself wary to overstep or cause her to withdraw.

"She fired me, you know," she hiss-whispered to him, clutching his hand with surprising force. "You, sir, got me sacked. Lady Goddard decided she wanted you back instead."

Anger welled up to dim some of the pleasure of touching her. He clasped her tighter, and she immediately loosened her hold.

"I'm sorry. That's outrageous. I never would have allowed her to do such a thing."

She arched a brow at that. "Do you have such powers of persuasion over her?" There was a note of suspicion, perhaps accusation, in her tone.

"I would have damned well tried." He meant every word. The notion that the noblewoman had dismissed her made his gut churn. He hardly knew Miss Hawthorne and yet every protective instinct made him furious she'd lost her post because of him. "I can send off a telegram first thing tomorrow."

"No, please don't. I'm happy to be home. But now . . . you're here," she said, her hand still in his. "Why?"

"I know why," her brother said from behind them in a singsong tone. "It's to do with what I told you in the pub, Tess. He must be Van Arsdale's man on the scene, though the letter said a Miss Prince would be returning to Norfolk."

At that, Miss Hawthorne pulled her hand from his.

"Of course, you've come for the dig." A bit of annoyance

entered her voice, much like he'd heard every time she'd addressed him this morning.

Good grief, had they only just met this morning? It felt as if she'd been on his mind much longer than that.

"I've come to hire your brother." Dom cast one glance over his shoulder.

Mr. Hawthorne immediately approached and clapped a hand on his shoulder as if they were old chums. "No, Prince, your Van Arsdale wanted my father, but Pater's no longer with us. Though Tess will do the job nicely."

Dom turned to him, forcing Hawthorne to remove his hand. "You're not T. S. Hawthorne?"

"T. O. Hawthorne," he said with a hand over his heart. "Though Tess is a T. S. Hawthorne, just like our father was. You see how convenient this all is."

Dom didn't know about convenience. The whole thing seemed a bit of a muddle, and all his body knew for certain was that a lovely woman was nearby and he wanted to know her better.

"Then you're the one Van Arsdale wanted," he said to her. "Has he written to you about engaging your help for this dig?"

"He wanted my father, as Tristan said," she told him, her arms crossed over her chest. "I haven't yet seen the letter, but I don't think I can help you."

"Tess . . ." This emerged from her brother in a whine that reminded Dom of the way he and his sisters would have spoken to each other when trying to wheedle something.

She stared up at Dom, studying him. He tracked her gaze as she took in his face, the width of his shoulders, his mussed hair. He could usually guess what women were thinking when they looked at him. Their eyes lit, or their cheeks flushed, or the tilt of their lips gave it all away. Yet Miss Tess Hawthorne was inscrutable.

And that only made him more determined.

"Is there a place we could discuss the matter?" he asked her. Alone, preferably, though he dared not say it.

She let out a sigh, lowered her arms, and cast a glance at her brother.

"You might as well come home with us," she said with more resignation than eagerness. "I want to have a look at this letter the American titan sent."

MRS. WELLS RUSHED OUT the door as soon as they were at the wooden gate in front of Foxdene, as if she'd been watching for them. Tess felt a pang of regret that they'd caused her to worry.

"Oh heavens, I heard you were in the lockup," she said as she joined them. "I was just on my way to see for myself."

News traveled fast in Wiggenstow.

She scanned them both from boot to brow. "Are you injured?"

The question was mostly directed at Tristan, who grinned and bent to kiss her cheek.

"Not a bit of it, Wellsy. I ducked every blow," he boasted easily, though none of it was true.

"I stopped it before there was more than a single blow," Tess corrected.

Mrs. Wells just looked pleased to find them both in one piece. Then she clutched her chest and let out an utterly female sound of delight.

"Oh my. Good heavens, who's this?" She took a few steps

closer to Dominic Prince and looked up at him as if peering up at a colossus. "Mercy, aren't you tall and dashing?"

"I'm not exactly short," Tristan put in with faux outrage.

"How do you do?" Dominic Prince's warm-as-syrup tone made a little shiver tickle down Tess's spine.

She understood why women succumbed to his charms. The moment she'd seen him outside the lockup, she'd had the urge to rush toward him. As if he were an irresistible magnet and she was some lump of very susceptible metal. And then she'd touched him and found she couldn't stop. He'd thrust out his hand and she'd taken it, but they didn't shake hands as two people who hardly knew each other might. They'd held on to each other until she could feel her body listing toward his, yearning to melt into the tall, warm enticement that he seemed to exude like a scent.

Thank heavens she'd pulled away before breaking all the rules she'd set for herself. As if him finding her dirty, disheveled, and in the local lockup with her mischief-making brother wasn't sufficiently embarrassing.

He and Mrs. Wells made small talk, speaking of his train journey.

Tess just yearned for a washcloth and to fix her hair before she had to face him in a well-lit room.

"Shall we go inside?" she asked the three of them as dusk began to darken to night.

"Come right along, Mr. Prince," Mrs. Wells urged. "A spot of tea after a journey will do you wonders. And there are fresh biscuits too."

"Never fear," Tristan whispered to him as they walked side by side toward Foxdene's wisteria-edged front door. "There's whiskey too, if you fancy it."

At the threshold, Mr. Prince turned back to look at her.

Tess licked her lips and time seemed to slow. The lights from inside the cottage lit all the beautiful aspects of his face—those full lips, that square jaw, the dark amber depths of his eyes. She imagined heat in those eyes. She thought she saw him swallow hard, his gaze flicking down to her mouth as it had in Lady Goddard's library.

"Don't dally, love, there's a nip in the air now the sun's down," Mrs. Wells called.

The moment broke, and Tess came back to her senses. Mr. Prince had gone inside.

She reached up to try to right her hair, then button the top button of her shirtwaist that she'd loosened because the lockup had been warm and confining.

There was nothing for it. She looked a fright, and now she had to welcome Dominic Prince into her home.

By the time she stepped inside the cozy warmth of Foxdene, Mrs. Wells already had biscuits plated up and a teapot and cups on the tea tray, which she carried into the room, her eyes flicking to Mr. Prince every now and then.

His eyes, to Tess's dismay, were trained on her.

"The letter, Tris, where is it?"

Her brother had already slumped onto his favorite overstuffed chair, one leg flung over its arm. At her question, he got to his feet and collected a small pile of post from the mantel.

"On the top, as you'll see." He winked at her as he handed them over, and she could tell he was sobering up. He seemed to be suffering no ill effects from the night's hijinks.

Tess turned away from everyone and faced the window that looked out on the old oak that had stood sentry on this land for ages. Something about it grounded her, comforted her. When everything inside her felt topsy-turvy, the old oak stood strong and unwavering.

The typed letter was brief and to the point. Van Arsdale had definitely intended it for her father, as he referred to the previous letters they'd exchanged. The American had first reached out to her father years ago, and his knowledge was given freely. Even eagerly. It had never required much urging to get Papa to speak of the Celts and the Anglo-Saxons and Vikings who came after them to Norfolk.

I herein enclose a check for the sum of 500 pounds. The same sum upon completion of the project will be forthcoming.

"Get the smelling salts, Wellsy," Tristan called in a teasing tone.

Tess heard him approach. "You knew I couldn't refuse," she said, still staring out at the wide trunk of the oak and the rolling fields beyond. "A thousand bloody pounds."

Tristan chuckled.

"So you'll do it?" Even from across the room, Dominic Prince's voice affected her.

She turned to face him, the letter and check clutched tightly in her hand. "Do you think he'll mind that I step in for my father?"

Mr. Prince set his teacup on a table near the settee and stepped closer.

Anticipation glittered in his dark eyes, and that confident smile of his curved his mouth. "I know he won't, and if he did, I'd persuade him otherwise."

Once again, so certain of his ability to persuade. What would he be able to persuade her of in the coming days? Nothing, because she'd learned that lesson all too well. Once burned, now determined to never be a fool again.

And yet a rogue brazen shiver made her bite her lip.

"It's all settled then," Tristan said, clapping his hands merrily. "This calls for whiskey."

"You've had enough," Tess murmured to him before brushing past to approach her new partner in this endeavor of Mr. Van Arsdale's. "You should know," she told Dominic Prince, "that I don't relish the notion of digging up our history to have it shipped off to America. We could start a museum here."

Tristan let out a little groan at her return to the topic.

"Perhaps Van Arsdale could be persuaded to leave some of what's found here," Mr. Prince opined.

Tess blinked. "Do you think he'd do that?"

Mr. Prince shrugged. "He likes credit for his good deeds. As long as you slapped an etched plate on the museum crediting him, he might be persuadable."

"Would you speak to him about it?"

After a moment of hesitation, Mr. Prince, a soft smile playing at his lips, said, "For you, I would, but I can't make any promises."

"Understood, but I'd appreciate the attempt." Tess no longer believed in promises made by rogues anyway.

"But he'll want the finest finds to go to America," Tristan added, sounding terribly practical and not at all bothered by the truth of his words.

Tess wouldn't have any sway with the American at all if she refused to help Mr. Prince. And heaven knew they sorely needed a thousand pounds.

"Very well. I'll assist you," Tess finally said, confident in her decision, her chin notched up a tinge.

She was immediately gifted with a beaming smile from Dominic Prince. Not one of his sultry grins or cheeky smirks.

This smile was boyish in its enthusiasm, bone-melting in its sincerity.

Tess knew this land's history as well as her father had, but whatever was happening between her and Dominic Prince was entirely unknown, dangerous territory.

"Where do we begin?" she asked, forcing her voice not to quaver.

He took a breath, a smile still lingering on his lips. "I think we should start tomorrow by speaking to the landowner, Lord Fenbridge." He reached up and gripped the back of his neck before meeting her gaze again. "Apparently, he's still not entirely in favor of this project. Van Arsdale hoped that with a Hawthorne's help, we could convince him."

Tess seamed her lips together to keep from scoffing the way she had when he'd called her lovely, but a wave of wariness blotted out how tempting it was to have his dark-honey gaze on her.

What Van Arsdale and Mr. Prince didn't know was that Lord Reginald Fenbridge loathed nothing in the world more than a Hawthorne.

Chapter Five

Dom awoke to birdsong and in a far softer bed than his one above Princes.

Ah, Norfolk. Part of him missed the clatter of horses in their traces and the smoky waft of coffee from the coffeehouse next door to his family's shop. Yet something savory was baking, the linen was soft and clean, and the beds at this inn were ridiculously spacious and comfortable. He sat up and scrubbed a hand across his face.

The same hand that held Tess Hawthorne's last night.

He'd enjoyed that simple contact far too much.

A knock sounded at the door, and he quickly dressed in trousers and a rumpled shirt. He'd almost forgotten this part from his previous stay when he and Eve organized an exploratory dig nearby. The innkeeper's wife seemed to have impeccable timing, delivering breakfast the moment her inn's occupants stirred.

"Mrs. Randall, you—" His greeting died on his tongue, and for a moment his brain couldn't muster any other words.

"Good morning, Mr. Prince." Tess Hawthorne stood in the inn's narrow hallway, looking fresh and lovely and smiling warmly at him as if she'd stepped right out of that not-so-proper dream he'd had of her during the night.

"Is that for me?" he finally managed, though his mind still felt sluggish and his eyes kept straying to her smile. Still there. Not a figment of his imagination.

"Indeed." She offered him the cup of steaming coffee on a little tray with a scone, a crumpet, and some sort of biscuits. "Mrs. Randall said you prefer this to tea, and the rest is freshly baked."

Dom took the tray, and his stomach rumbled.

"I know it may seem early . . ." She swept her gaze around his room and the bed he'd just rolled out of. "But Lord Fenbridge is extraordinary among aristocrats in that he prefers early calls. He might be less prickly if we seek him out this morning."

"Then I'll wash and dress quickly and we can set off."

At the word dress, she flicked her eyes down to the spot where his bare chest was exposed by his half-buttoned shirt.

Dom tried not to grin. Maybe he hadn't misread her reaction to him yesterday entirely.

"I'll . . . wait downstairs."

"I won't be long."

Dom rushed through washing, shaving, and dressing in one of the finer day suits he'd brought along with him, all while stealing bites of Mrs. Randall's buttery baked goods. As Fenbridge's agreement was crucial to the success of the whole endeavor, he decided the nobleman was worth the effort of donning his best. Yet Dom was also intensely aware that Miss Hawthorne waited for him.

Twenty minutes later, he descended the stairs to find her assisting Mrs. Randall to set out small vases of fresh flowers on each table in the taproom.

"There you are," Tess said as soon as she spotted him. "And well-polished too." She took in his suit, cravat, and waistcoat, and seemed to find him wanting.

She approached with a little pinch between her brows. When she was close enough for her floral scent to surround him, she fixed her gaze on his neckcloth.

"May I?" she asked, gesturing to the silk cloth.

"Yes," Dom replied a little too quickly.

He had no doubt he'd made a muck of tying his tie. He hated the bloody things and wore them as infrequently as possible.

After only a moment's hesitation, she took the cloth in her hands and pulled it loose.

Dom studied her face—the soft peach flush in her cheeks, the plump fullness of her lips, the quiet focus in her eyes, the scatter of copper freckles across her nose.

When the back of her hand brushed his chin, she glanced up. "Stop staring, Mr. Prince, and tip your head back."

He bit his lip against a teasing retort and obeyed. But with his gaze off her face, he became acutely aware of her nearness, the warmth of it, her simple floral scent. Lavender, perhaps. It shouldn't have been so enticing.

"There." She stepped back, tilting her head to survey her work. "Much better."

"Thank you." He offered her a smile to match the one she'd offered upon greeting him, but she didn't return it.

"Shall we head off?"

Dom nodded, and Tess waved a goodbye to Mrs. Randall.

"Thank you for the help, Tess dear. Bless you."

They walked in silence for a mile, and Dom wondered what he'd done to burst the momentary amity between them.

"So he's not an amiable sort?" Dom tried, keeping his tone light and his gaze from lingering on her.

She looked ridiculously lovely in a pale peach day dress. No gloves. No hat. She'd forgone the starched shirtwaist and ink-black skirt he'd seen her in the day before and seemed lighter, more at ease. Or at least she had been until she'd tied his tie.

Perhaps she was simply pleased to be back home. The whole of Wiggenstow seemed to adore her. They'd been greeted warmly by half a dozen villagers as they made their way down the lane and past a few cottages before heading toward Fenbridge Hall.

In reply to his question, she slid him a sly smile and let out a knowing little chuckle. "Van Arsdale didn't forewarn you at all? You'll soon see."

Dom knew she was worried about their meeting with the curmudgeonly nobleman whose estate he could glimpse in the distance, but he was so pleased that her smile had returned that he couldn't worry about Fenbridge.

Miss Hawthorne's smiles set something in him alight. Warm and sweet, and every bit as provoking as the scowl she'd given him in Lady Goddard's library. He didn't want to examine the why of it too closely, didn't dare snuff it out. But she affected him in a way no woman ever had.

"When did this row between Fenbridge and your father start?" Dom asked, recalling her insistence that the nobleman maintained a grudge against the Hawthorne clan.

"Oh, there wasn't a single disagreement. They rowed constantly, and then they'd make amends, and then something would set them off again." She shrugged. "They were sometimes friends, sometimes enemies."

"And now Fenbridge has transferred his ire toward your father to you and your brother?"

She shook her head and a tendril of honeyed-blond hair slipped across her cheek. "I think he misses my father, but Tristan and I asked him about digging on his land, and that set him off."

"Your father never pressed him on the matter?"

"I don't know. Papa preferred books and historical documents to digging up antiquities. It all interested him, of course. He read of Schliemann's excavation of Troy, Petrie's digs in Egypt, and he knew what might be in those mounds . . ."

"A hoard," Dom finished for her when her voice trailed off as her eyes fixed on the broad, long mounds dotting Fenbridge land. One was more pronounced. As if some giant had tucked his largest loaf of bread under the green field.

"So your American has mostly persuaded Fenbridge?"

"Van Arsdale offered him a fortune, but he's yet to sign for his permission." Dom tipped his head toward her. "Your assistance, well, your father's, was meant to be a final enticement."

Miss Hawthorne reached out a hand and pressed back against his chest. Dom stopped and was a bit disappointed when she immediately ceased touching him.

"My assistance might displease him," she insisted. A flash of worry put a crimp in her brow. "Do you have an alternative plan if he doesn't sign?"

Dom shook his head.

"Isn't that a wee bit presumptuous of the American? And you?"

Dom couldn't help but smile.

"Why do you look so pleased, Mr. Prince?"

She was why, but he could hardly tell her that. Whether they were sparring or chatting amicably, he was enjoying himself. And it was a feeling he hadn't felt in . . . if he was honest, a good long while.

"We'll convince him. A bit of that spirit of yours and my undeniable charm—"

She scoffed, but it immediately turned to a chuckle. "You do not lack for confidence." Her hand came up and tucked that stray lock of hair behind her ear. "The difficulty is that Fenbridge is not fond of my spirit."

Without explaining further, she turned and began walking again, her stride long and determined.

Dom's longer stride brought him to her side in a few steps.

"He once told me I should cease my meddling and marry. That I needed taming."

"Old fool," Dom said, though a more colorful condemnation danced on the tip of his tongue.

"You don't go in for the taming of ladies?" she asked teasingly.

"No, I bloody well don't." Dom felt his own temper rising and took a deep breath to tamp it down. His father had been given to angry outbursts, and it was one aspect of the man he never wanted to emulate.

But the idea of breaking ladies' spirits struck something deep inside him that railed at the notion that anyone must diminish themselves to fit into society's strictures.

"Ridiculous," he added with a glance her way.

A tiny smile flickered on her lips. "Well then," she finally said.

Dom wasn't certain if it meant he'd grown in her estimation, but he hoped it did.

Not long after, they crossed from grassy field to gravel drive and started toward the enormous country house that sat on a small rise, higher than all the mounds nearby. It had been designed to impress, but the years had taken their toll. Though the worn stone and swaths of ivy covering the hall's face only added to its character.

"Lady Fenbridge has been gone for over a decade and his lordship never remarried." As their footsteps crunched on gravel on their approach to the front door, she added, "I suspect he must be very lonely. Perhaps that's why he's so cross with everyone and everything."

When they'd almost reached the polished wooden front door, Miss Hawthorne stopped and turned to him.

"Do I look presentable?" She swiped a hand at the loose hair at her ear again, tucking it into neatly pinned hair that had been pulled back into a knot at her nape.

The ruffled fabric at her neckline had become untidy during their walk, particularly near her shoulder.

He approached, lifting a hand. "May I?"

She shot him a wary look, studied his expression a moment, and nodded.

Dom reached up gently and ran his fingers along the fabric across her shoulder, laying it so that the ruffles were folded neatly.

"There," he said, stepping back and catching her gaze. "Eminently presentable, Miss Hawthorne. One might even say lovely." He wasn't sure how it would land, but he kept his tone light, felt his mouth tipping in a smile.

She smiled too, and he felt as if he'd won. Passed some very important test.

"You're incorrigible," she whispered.

"I promise not to be to Lord Fenbridge. I can play the proper gentleman when necessary."

Miss Hawthorne's brow shot up, but she said nothing as she lifted the polished bronze knocker affixed to the massive front door.

It slid open a few moments later, and a tall, austere white-haired man looked down at them through a pair of silver-rimmed spectacles.

"Dominic Prince and Miss Tess Hawthorne to see Lord Fenbridge," Dom told the man, presumably the butler.

At mention of Tess's name, the old man jolted.

"Miss Hawthorne?" The man's cold, thin-lipped expression melted into a genuine grin. "My goodness, it's been too many years." He leaned a bit closer. "The spitting image of your dear mother, you are."

"It's good to see you, Teague."

"Come." He reached out an arm, and Tess laid a hand on it as she stepped into the house.

Dom followed her inside.

"Is he awake?" Miss Hawthorne asked the butler, who she seemed to know well. "He will be expecting a visit from Mr. Prince, but he doesn't know I'll be accompanying him." She and the butler exchanged a look that Dom couldn't decipher.

"Very well." Teague nodded. "Wait here, and I shall prepare the way."

The high-ceilinged entry hall was dim, with doors of nearby rooms closed and no lamps lit. The only light filtered in from a half-moon window above the door's lintel. The house felt as if it rarely admitted visitors.

"This way," Teague called from a spot near the stairwell.

When they joined him, he directed them to a room near the end of the hall. Dom heard the groan of a chair's springs and footsteps as they crossed the enormous library's threshold.

"We had no appointment, Mr. Prince. You've told my retainer a lie."

"Forgive me, Lord Fenbridge," Dom offered in a warm tone, determined to win the gruff-looking man over. Though he had no intention of groveling and suspected Fenbridge wouldn't like him much if he did. "Mr. Van Arsdale would have apprised you of my arrival via letter. Have you not received it?"

The gaunt, broad-shouldered man with overlong silver hair swiped an arm through the air. "He did not indicate the day of your visit, Mr. Prince. Do not prevaricate."

"Regardless"—Miss Hawthorne stepped forward, positioning herself at Dom's side—"you did know Mr. Prince would show up on your doorstep. Though my presence may be a surprise, here we are."

Lord Fenbridge's eyes, which had been squinted in irritation, opened wide at the sight of Miss Hawthorne.

"Teague did not exaggerate," he murmured as he stepped out from behind a massive desk and approached her, his gold-tipped cane thudding on the carpet with every step. "You are quite like her, but, most of all, I see your father staring back at me through those green eyes. So sharp. So knowing. As if you're as ready to find fault with me as he was."

"My father visited you nearly every day, my lord, so he must not have found you too distasteful."

"Pert-tongued too." The merest hint of a smile seemed to twitch under his mustache. "That is very much like your mother."

"I appreciate that you find traces of my parents in me, but I come on my own merits," she told him with a boldness Dom couldn't help but admire. "I've agreed to serve as advisor to Mr. Prince during his time in Norfolk." She gestured to the messy pile of documents on his desk. "Will you sign the agreement from the American and allow us to dig on Fenbridge land?"

The nobleman swung his gaze at Dom, and he felt the scrape of it. It was as if Lord Fenbridge was attempting to weigh his very soul. His father had a similar way of sizing up the merit of a man. Dom had always felt unnerved under such scrutiny. But unlike his gregarious father, Fenbridge had a grim air about him. The old man's miseries seemed to fill the air around him with an oppressive weight.

Dom wondered if it was the weight of regrets.

"You'll be heading this dig? Octavius Prince's boy, are you?"

"Boy" was no doubt meant to provoke him, but Dom merely nodded. "Did you know my father?"

"Know him personally? No. Know of him? Of course. The man was a treasure seeker. Acclaim seeker. Prince had a craven need for fame, it seemed." Fenbridge swept his gaze over Dom again. "Is that same hunger in you, boy? Is that why you want to dig up my hills?"

Dom felt Miss Hawthorne's gaze on him as Fenbridge waited for an answer.

It was rare to not be eager to claim his father's treasure-lust or admit how much they were alike, but this was one of those moments. The Hawthornes cared about the history of this swath of England, and Fenbridge cared about the land that had likely been in his family for many generations. He sensed his own shallowness in how clearly he could envision the write-up in the London papers if they found the hoard he and Eve suspected was buried under Fenbridge's fields.

"Any antiquarian worth their salt would wish to find something of value when they dig into the earth." The words didn't satisfy the old man. They sounded thin to Dom's ears too.

"And to have the Prince name associated with it is a boon indeed, yes?"

"Yes," Dom admitted through a clenched jaw.

"Mm-hmm." Fenbridge's murmur was knowing and dismissive, and he seemed pleased to finally be able to turn his attention back to Tess Hawthorne.

"You want to help a fame chaser such as this Prince whelp?"

She hesitated for a breath. "I have agreed to. Yes."

"Your seal of approval will carry great sway in Wiggenstow, Miss Hawthorne." He slid one narrow-eyed look Dom's way. "Indeed, that is precisely why Hawthorne assistance was desired to achieve the American's aims."

After one glance at the thick carpet below their feet, she tipped her gaze up. "Will you agree, Lord Fenbridge?"

"You wanted to find it yourself, girl. Why have you given up your aims to help this glory chaser?"

"Because you refused me, my lord." She hitched up her chin and shot him a look that would chill most men's bollocks. "Will you sign Van Arsdale's papers or not?"

The old devil drew out the suspense, his dark eyes flitting from Miss Hawthorne to Dom and back again. Fenbridge's gaze finally held on hers, and then the edges of his mouth inched up in a smirk.

"On one condition." He lifted a gnarled, bony finger. "I will be apprised of your progress."

"Of course," Dom agreed.

"No," Fenbridge all but shouted. "Apprised by Miss Hawthorne. You will come visit me, young lady. Daily. In the morning. As your father used to do."

Dom watched her, trying to read her reaction. If she refused, he'd back her. The man's demand struck him as overreaching.

"Very well," she finally said. "I shall come each morning while the dig is underway."

Fenbridge turned back to his desk, brushing a hand across

the piles of papers until he snatched up a particular document. With dramatic flair, he swiped up his pen and signed his name in a messy black scrawl. As the ink dried, he shot a look back at Miss Hawthorne.

"The dig is underway now. As soon as you take this document away with you and I take the lucre Van Arsdale sent my way. And you, Miss Hawthorne, will begin visiting me on Monday."

Chapter Six

Teague ushered both of them out of Fenbridge Hall and they stood for a moment, drinking in the fresh air after the closeness of the hall's dark rooms.

"We did it." Mr. Prince shot her a boyish smile, then clapped his hands together, rubbing them against each other as if he could not wait to start. "We should begin immediately."

Tess grinned, catching a bit of his exuberance, though she couldn't resist reminding him, "You haven't yet shared any details of your plan, Mr. Prince. Surely, there's a great deal of preparation to undertake first."

"Oh, there is, but . . ." His face fell a bit, growing serious. "Can we begin with you calling me Dominic?"

"I don't think—"

"We'll be working together for weeks, perhaps months. I suggest it for practical reasons." He lowered his gaze, almost sheepishly. "I do understand when formality is necessary, as with Fenbridge, but surely we can do away with it while planning."

She'd known the man for all of two days, and yet she had agreed to assist him. It seemed a simple request. "Then you may call me Tess."

"Tess," he said as if testing how the single syllable felt on his tongue. He drew it out softly, almost reverently. He made her feel as if something as simple as calling her by name was an honor.

Tess swallowed hard and hoped he didn't notice.

Ridiculous. She was being utterly ridiculous. She was getting drawn in, and she knew better than to let her guard down.

"Where should we convene?" He looked off toward the village. "At the inn?"

Tess thought of the rumpled bedclothes she'd spied behind him this morning. She knew the dangers of meeting a gentleman alone in his rooms, and it was a mistake she would never repeat again.

"There's a public room upstairs," he offered as if to reassure her. "A sitting room of sorts. That's what I meant."

Could the dratted man read her mind?

"That might do, or you could come to the cottage. Father's study is surprisingly spacious." She didn't know why she was inviting him home again, but it seemed a better option than the inn. She could imagine the village gossip and speculation.

"Hmm." Those amber-brown eyes of his sparked. "And there's the added enticement of whatever Mrs. Wells has baked."

Tess didn't bother telling him that Mrs. Wells had mentioned him half a dozen times that morning. After all that had happened, Mrs. Wells was generally as wary of attractive young men as Tess was, but somehow Dominic Prince had already charmed her.

"Shall we?" He started off and turned back to make sure she was following.

"What's first in your mind?" Tess asked as she kept pace beside him.

"Help with the dig. We need men. I'm thinking ten." He glanced over at her. "Too many?"

"Not at all. I was thinking a dozen. They could work in shifts."

He nodded. "Exactly. Will it be hard to round up that many?"

"I shouldn't think so." Tess thought of the Bromleys. Beyond the brothers, there was a passel of cousins. And there were a few other young men in the village who often sought extra work. Tristan would know, and The Black Swan would be the perfect place to spread the word.

Tess was on the cusp of suggesting they go there first when she heard someone call her name.

"Miss Hawthorne." The feminine voice rang out in an unmistakably husky tone.

They both turned toward the sound, and Tess repressed a groan.

Miss Priscilla Walcott had been a rare young female student among her father's tutees. The young woman's father, Sir Owen Walcott, believed his daughter should be educated as well as his son. Since they were of a similar age, Tess had tried to befriend the girl, but Priscilla had always insisted on seeing them as rivals, or perhaps seeing herself as Tess's better. All Tess knew was that they'd never gotten on as well as she'd wished.

Rumor had it that Miss Walcott had once been as taken in by Mr. Shaw as Tess had been, but they'd never spoken about it. As if they each wanted to keep their regrets to themself.

"How could you fail to tell me of Mr. Prince's arrival, Miss Hawthorne?" Priscilla asked teasingly, though there was more irritation than warmth in her tone. "I had to hear about it in the village."

"I only arrived yesterday," Mr. Prince—Dominic—told her

with a friendly smile. Not quite his usual smoldering charm, but it seemed to work its appeal on Miss Walcott, nonetheless.

"Then I suppose you can be forgiven." Her coquettish smile was legend in Wiggenstow, and Tess understood why.

"Miss Priscilla Walcott, may I present Mr. Dominic Prince." Tess stepped back when Priscilla strode closer, planting herself in Dominic's path.

"We missed you during your last foray into Wiggenstow, Mr. Prince. Father and I were traveling, but we're so glad you've returned. You must come tomorrow evening and dine with us." She beamed at him, waiting for his acceptance.

He cast a questioning gaze at Tess.

Sir Owen was pleasant enough, but the prospect of Priscilla fawning over Mr. Prince for an entire evening held little appeal. In fact, Tess found herself irrationally irked by the prospect.

"Oh," Miss Walcott said, noting his hesitation, "you must come too, Miss Hawthorne. Father and I wish to hear about your grand endeavor. Fenbridge may own much of the land in the county, but my father is the man to speak to if you need any sort of real assistance."

"Thank you," Tess put in, though most of Priscilla's words had been directed at Dominic.

"Say you'll come, Mr. Prince." She waved a gloved hand in Tess's direction. "And Miss Hawthorne."

"I look forward to it." Mr. Prince offered her a little bow, then took her hand and deposited a kiss atop her glove, all the while training his amber-brown eyes on Miss Walcott.

"Wonderful," she said a bit breathlessly. "I shall go and tell Father. He'll be most pleased."

She glided off down the lane in her elegant walking gown, and when she was far out of earshot, Dominic turned to Tess.

"Tell me about Sir Owen. Is he someone who could prove helpful with the dig?"

In an instant, he'd utterly altered from charming rogue to practical treasure seeker. Could all of that potent charm be nothing more than a tool he wielded? It made her wonder about the true Dominic Prince. It wasn't just the distrust of charming gentlemen that had become second nature now. She wanted to know who Mr. Prince might be when he felt no need to perform for others.

"He is," she admitted. "Sir Owen is the richest man in Norfolk, perhaps one of the wealthiest in England. He invests widely and knows every businessman and government agent in the county. If any permits are needed, he'd be a good man to know."

"Excellent." He nodded. "I'll return to the inn and collect the documents I've brought along about our last dig. When shall I meet you back at Foxdene?"

She suddenly regretted asking him to join her at home. Their relationship must remain professional, and she couldn't afford to be drawn in by his charm.

"I have a few calls to make, and then I'll begin making inquiries about workers for the dig."

He looked a bit crestfallen.

"I could send a few your way at the inn, and you can decide whether they'll suit."

"Then I'll review my plans and await them."

"Why don't I come later in the afternoon? We can review those plans in the public sitting room you mentioned."

"I look forward to it, Tess."

Tess didn't go to the inn to meet with Mr. Prince—Dominic. Instead, she sent him eight men who were eager for employment and willing to work on the upcoming dig. After announcing the opportunity at The Black Swan, a handful came forward and said they had brothers or cousins who'd be interested too.

Tristan planned to help, of course, and promised he could rustle up a few more men willing to offer their labor without much difficulty, even if he had to venture to the neighboring village's rowdy pub. He said the last with a suspicious glint in his eye. There were, of course, several young ladies in said neighboring village who were very fond of her brother.

An hour before it would be time to depart for the Walcotts' dinner, Tess stood in front of the cheval mirror in her bedchamber, arguing with herself about which dress to wear.

"Though you've not asked, I have an opinion to offer," Mrs. Wells said, her voice warm and gentle, from where she stood on the threshold.

"All of them are out of fashion," Tess told her.

She would not fool herself on that score. Though she visited others in the village often, there were rarely any opportunities to attend fancy social gatherings.

"Nonsense. Several of those"—she gestured to the pile Tess had built atop her bed—"are quite becoming." Bustling forward, Mrs. Wells sifted through the pile, straightening and laying the dresses out more neatly. "Besides, you will be wearing whichever you choose, and you're pretty enough to make a potato sack look fetching."

"You're too kind." Tess laughed, despite how wretched she'd begun to feel after sorting through her evening gown options. And it wasn't just that she had nothing truly spectacular to wear. It was the silliness of caring so very much. Fashion had never mattered to her. She lived most of her life within the handful of miles that comprised Wiggenstow, and there was no one she wished to impress.

But somehow, tonight mattered a great deal to her. She told herself she was not in competition with Priscilla Walcott. In truth, she'd always wished they could become friends.

No, the butterflies careening in her belly were about him. And that made her angry at herself for being so easily taken in—again—by charm and a handsome face.

"Perhaps it is time for a visit to the dressmakers."

"Even if there were money for dresses, I certainly don't have the time. The dinner is tonight."

"Oh?"

"I'm sorry, Mrs. Wells. I forgot to tell you. I've been invited to dine at the Walcotts'."

"That's wonderful, my dear. Are you and Miss Walcott finally warming to each other?"

Tess shot her an arched brow look. "Not as such. She invited Mr. Prince, and my invite was likely out of courtesy since she encountered us while we were together."

"Ah," Mrs. Well said in her usual knowing tone. "Miss Walcott has set her sights on your famous visitor, has she?"

"It seems so."

"Many of the ladies will want his attention." Mrs. Wells shrugged as she continued to sort through Tess's rejected gowns. "And it makes a good deal of sense. He's a curiosity. For a while, he'll be the most interesting man in Wiggenstow."

And then he'll go back to London, Tess thought. The notion, which should have brought her relief from all the ridiculous attraction she felt for the man, was oddly unsettling.

"How about this one?"

Tess turned to find Mrs. Wells holding up a dress that had

long been one of her favorites. The flattering design with a square-cut neckline was made of violet silk with darker plum velvet panels around the bodice and skirt.

"You look stunning in this one," Mrs. Wells insisted.

Tess shot her a dubious look as she took the dress and held it up in front of her at the mirror. "I'm not sure I've ever pulled off looking stunning in my life."

Mrs. Wells drew closer and tipped her head to the side. "What's come over you, Tess? It's not like you to think poorly of yourself."

"I don't think poorly of myself." Tess swallowed hard.

"And why should you? You're the kindest, cleverest young woman I know."

Tess knew her worth. What she doubted was her judgement.

"Tell me what's troubling you," Mrs. Wells pressed in a soft voice.

"I must dress or I'll be late."

Mrs. Wells shot a glance at the clock on the mantel. "Ten minutes with me before the fire won't make you late." She slid her arm around Tess's.

"Very well. Perhaps five minutes."

"You drive a hard bargain," Mrs. Wells teased.

They settled into the two worn but comfortable chairs before the fire, and Tess laid the purple gown gently over the chair's arm.

"I can tell you're fretting." She smiled warmly at Tess. "There's two wee lines that form between your brows when you fret. What is it?"

Tess nibbled at her lip, debating what to confide. Debating with herself about whether her worries were silly.

"He disturbs me," she finally admitted.

"Mr. Prince," Mrs. Wells concluded without a moment's hesitation. "Or are you thinking of the past?"

"Both. It's impossible not to. He's so very much like—"

"Is he?" Mrs. Wells drew in a long breath, then leaned forward. "You've known Mr. Prince all of a few days. Is it not too soon to cast such judgement?"

"I know you're quite taken with him." Tess smiled. She meant no castigation in the observation. How could she when he had such an effect on her too?

Mrs. Wells shrugged. "He was polite and complimentary and respectful when he visited last evening. As first impressions go, he makes quite a good one."

Tess couldn't argue with her. She'd been ready to have the man bodily removed from Lady Goddard's the moment she met him and then wished he'd stayed longer by the time he departed.

"May I admit something to you?" Mrs. Wells asked.

"Of course. You may tell me anything. I always appreciate your opinion and value your advice."

Mrs. Wells only smiled in reply because they both knew Tess was hardheaded, and Tristan was much the same.

"That man who weighs on your mind from the past did not make a good first impression."

Tess snapped her gaze to the woman who'd become like a mother to both her and her brother over the last decade and a half. She'd been so deeply affected by her feelings for Mr. Shaw before introducing him to her father or Mrs. Wells that whatever impression he'd made could not shake her feelings for him.

"He was a bit rude. Arrogant."

Mrs. Wells had never been fond of him, and Tess's father

had gently expressed his own reservations. Yet she'd still been shocked when Shaw shattered her heart.

"Why didn't I see it?"

"Because he didn't wish you to. The man was a pretender. He treated you well enough, I suppose, so it was hard to see who he was beyond those moments. Many were taken in by him."

"And what if I'm blinded by a man's charm again?"

"You're too clever for that now."

"I was clever then too."

Mrs. Wells laughed. "You were indeed, but you fell in love."

"Does love make us all fools then?"

She shook her head. "Perhaps there's a poet or two that says as much, but I think it's more that love is a risk."

"I don't want to take that risk again."

"Oh Tess, I hope you do."

"Why? You saw what it did to me. And how poorly people think of me as a result."

"Who thinks poorly of you?" Mrs. Wells sat up in her chair, squaring her shoulders as if prepared to take on anyone who dared to look at Tess askance. "Send them directly to me, if you like, and I'll set them straight."

Tess chuckled. "I don't wish to be pitied again."

"You did nothing wrong, my dear." Mrs. Wells reached out and took Tess's hand, holding it gently between her own. "You do know that, don't you?"

"I trusted a deceiver."

"As did Priscilla Walcott, if the rumors are true. The man was convincing, and he'd perfected his vile game." Mrs. Wells gave Tess's hand a squeeze. "Trusting others is not a fault, my girl. Deceiving others is. The fault lies entirely with Mr. Shaw."

Tess didn't disagree, and yet once he'd been exposed, she'd felt somehow deserving of the heartbreak and shame.

"Please don't let what one awful man did mar the course of your life or cause you to wall yourself off from love and companionship forever."

"Spinsterhood seems easier."

"And lonelier. You have so much love to give, Tess."

Tess bit back tears. "Thank you."

Mrs. Wells scooted to the edge of her chair. "Now, let's get you into that pretty gown, and I'll do your hair."

Tess reached up to touch the messy knot she usually pulled her hair into. "Oh, we needn't fuss. It's just the Walcotts."

Mrs. Wells tsked. "Nonsense. You should wear those amethyst earbobs of your mother's. It's been too long since you've had a proper evening out." Mrs. Wells stood. "Come, Tess. It's time to enjoy yourself a little."

"All right, Wellsy. Do with my hair what you like. Make me stunning."

Chapter Seven

Dom tugged at his neckcloth and ran a hand down his waistcoat to ensure every button was fastened. Yet none of it distracted him from the lady sitting a few feet across from him in the finely turned-out carriage the Walcotts had sent around to fetch him.

When the vehicle wheeled up outside of the Wiggenstow inn, he'd climbed in expecting to find it empty.

What he'd found was Tess Hawthorne, and she was once again transformed. She was no longer the irritated librarian, nor the at-ease country gentlewoman she seemed to be earlier that morning. She looked regal, elegant, and thoroughly bewitching.

He'd climbed inside to sit opposite her and had been thunderstruck. All but speechless. He'd given her a nod, which she'd returned.

And now as they rolled toward the Walcotts', he snuck glances at her, enchanted with this version of her—bejeweled and garbed in a gown that accented her every curve.

He wasn't entirely certain what the hell was wrong with him.

In the last decade, he'd been acquainted with—and bedded—his share of beautiful women. When he wanted a woman, he'd never had trouble conveying that desire. And God's teeth, he wanted her.

But Tess Hawthorne wasn't like any of them. She was something else entirely. She'd challenged him the first moment he met her, and attraction, at least for him, had flared into flame immediately. Now that they were partners, he sensed that she wished to maintain a professional, if not friendly, rapport between them.

He should accept that and look forward to the next beautiful lady to cross his path. There would always be another. His life was transitory, his amorous liaisons temporary. Yet he could not deny the effect Tess Hawthorne had on him.

And now he'd seen her family home. He'd met her brother. He'd won over her delightful housekeeper. He'd felt oddly comfortable in that cozy cottage of theirs, almost enough to make him appreciate the desire to make one place a haven—a home. That was a feeling he'd never understood. Lodgings were meant to be as temporary as lovers, no matter how appealing they might be.

But each time he saw Tess, his craving for her grew. Indeed, he'd even dreamt about the damn woman, but he couldn't sate his hunger. He could not seduce her. He could not bed her. Theirs was a professional partnership now, and he needed her assistance with what might prove to be the most significant dig of his life.

"You look well," she finally said, breaking the silence in which he'd been twisting with the conundrum of how to stem the ache he felt whenever she was near.

God, what an arse he'd been. He'd yet to tell her how gorgeous she looked, and she certainly deserved every compliment.

"Thank you." He licked his lips, let himself look at her, felt his heart skitter in his chest. What in the blazes was wrong with him? "You look dazzling," he finally managed.

She quirked a brow at that. "Do you always do that?"

"Do what?"

"Effusively compliment ladies?"

"Believe it or not, I tempered my compliment to you just now. I wished to be much more effusive."

She huffed out a breath as if the answer disappointed her. "There you go again. Charming. Flirting." A hand came up and she laid it against her chest.

Dom adored the neckline of her gown. He stared at the juncture between her neck and shoulder and his mouth watered. He wanted to taste that spot, and the hollow below her throat where a simple pendant hung.

Perhaps it was the fact that he could not bed her that stoked this mad craving.

"Your reputation would certainly dictate that you behave just as you do," she continued. "But is any of it genuine, I wonder."

A flirtatious response came instantly to mind, but he quashed it. Perhaps charm was a reflex. Did he do it because it was expected of him? Perhaps. Or in order to live up to the reputation that he'd crafted for himself? Possibly.

Yet even if any of that was true, it had nothing to do with his reaction to Tess.

If only she knew that he had to contain himself when he was near her.

"You doubt my sincerity. Are you trying to tell me that you don't trust me?"

"I hardly know you."

"Then I hope the dig takes a while so that you can get to know me."

"Why ever would that matter to you? You don't need my approbation, Mr. Prince."

"Dominic," he reminded her softly. "And I want it just the same."

"I'm not sure I understand why." She gestured toward the carriage window. "You'll get plenty of it from Miss Walcott this evening, I'm sure."

"Miss Walcott is not someone I'll be spending time with in the coming days. She's not my partner in this endeavor. You are, and your opinion matters a great deal." He swallowed hard. He heard the vulnerability in his own voice and loathed it. Yet every word he'd said was true.

Tess grew quiet, contemplative. She craned her neck to gaze out the window, as if hoping they'd arrive soon, and she could be free of him.

That was entirely new. Ladies liked his company. Adored it, in fact. She wouldn't let him get away with charming her and it rankled.

When she looked back at him, he was on tenterhooks. Waiting for what, he wasn't certain.

"In that case, can I ask something of you?"

"Anything." He leaned forward, readying himself.

He liked that she was asking something of him. It would give him a chance to prove himself to her, and he wanted that opportunity.

"Be honest with me. You needn't charm me or flirt with me or seduce me." The merest tremor seemed to run through her, and then she dipped her head as if considering her next words. "I'd ask that you tell me the truth, even if it's difficult. Even if it's not the charming rogueish thing to do."

She spoke with such passion that he sensed it was born of pain. He wanted to know where the vehemence had come from. Who had lied to her and made trusting so hard?

Damn it all. He rarely wanted to delve into the pasts of the women he was attracted to. Learning about another's pain created a sense of responsibility, of obligation, and he avoided such entanglement at all costs.

Once again, his impulses with Tess were singular.

"Be yourself," she said softly. "The genuine Dominic Prince. That's who I wish to work with. That's who I hope to know."

A simple request, and asked so gently. So why did he feel the urge to jump from the rolling carriage? His heart thrashed behind his ribs.

Be honest. Be himself. Why the hell did it seem so much more perplexing than merely seducing her as he longed to?

He wasn't sure he even knew how to be himself, or who that man was.

"Very well," he finally told her because now that she'd asked something meaningful of him, he damned well had to try.

"Good." She tried for a smile but still looked at him warily. She then fussed with her evening gloves, tugging them up on her arms.

A moment later, the carriage rolled to a stop.

"I suppose we're here." She didn't sound particularly pleased.

And as he helped her down from the carriage, he sensed the tension in her.

"You don't like Miss Walcott," he surmised.

"She doesn't like me," Tess corrected.

"I find that hard to believe. Everyone seems to adore you."

She tsked. "Honesty, Mr. Prince. We agreed on it."

He couldn't help but chuckle. "I am in earnest. Each person we encounter seems drawn to you."

"Well, Priscilla is somehow immune."

Before he could learn more, they were assailed by the Walcott staff. A footman came forward to guide them up the path to the front door, and a butler stood on the threshold.

"Good evening, sir, and Miss Hawthorne." The man, like everyone else in town, seemed to know Tess.

Once a maid had taken his overcoat and Tess's cloak, they were directed toward a drawing room teeming with people.

"Mercy," Tess murmured under her breath.

It seemed she, like Dom, had expected that they were attending an intimate dinner, just Tess, himself, Miss Walcott, and her father. Instead, there were at least a dozen people inside the spacious drawing room.

"Apparently, a few more were invited than just the two of us," Dom said, as if Tess couldn't see the gathering herself.

"Half the unmarried ladies of the village have been invited."

His attention had been mostly on Tess, but now that she'd pointed it out, Dom felt the gazes of a room filled with colorfully garbed ladies turned his way.

He was used to catching the notice of ladies wherever he went. It was what was expected of him, as Tess had pointed out. And he was damned good at playing his part.

"I don't see Priscilla." Tess scanned her gaze around the assembled group, and the lady herself appeared as if summoned.

"Mr. Prince, how glad we are that you've come." She approached in a crimson gown that glittered with a thousand faceted beads and placed a hand lightly on his arm. "May I present the members of my ladies book club, and a few others from my Ladies Charitable Society."

As an afterthought, she beckoned Tess forward with her free hand. "And you all know Miss Hawthorne, of course."

Almost as one, the assembly of ladies nodded at Tess.

"My father and a few of his friends are in the smoking

room. Ghastly habit, but gentlemen will do as they please." She smiled up at Dom coquettishly. "But before they join us or the dinner gong sounds, do regale us, Mr. Prince, with tales of your exploits."

"Tell me what would please you, Miss Walcott, and I'll oblige." He smiled down at the diminutive young lady, who now had her arm entwined with his as if they were about to promenade in Hyde Park.

"Oh well. Hmm." She tapped her lip with her gloved fingertip, and he realized it was as much a performance for the assembled guests as what she was going to ask of him. "How about one short tale now, as a sort of aperitif, and then a far juicier story after dinner as our dessert?"

Dom inclined his head, offered the watching crowd of women a dazzling smile, and launched into a truncated story of his visit to Japan. It was the trip with his father he was asked about most, if only because access for Westerners was so tightly controlled.

As he spoke, he couldn't help but notice Tess had taken up a spot in the corner, observing his performance.

The other ladies around him seemed rapt, hanging on his every word. Not Tess. She'd crossed her arms, even cocked one pretty blond brow.

What's the true story? her look seemed to say.

Because, of course, he was embellishing, leaving out the illness he suffered on the trip, the frustration of bureaucratic delays, the fact that his father got so soused on rice wine that Dom had to all but carry him back to their lodgings.

When he'd finished his tale, the ladies moved toward him until he was surrounded. They peppered him with questions, touched him blatantly as they leaned in to speak to him, and batted their lashes. Normally, he'd be quite content to be drowning in feminine company, but it was a strange kind of torture tonight.

The only lady's attention he truly wanted stood with her back to him, examining a painting on the drawing room wall.

As they went through to dinner, he thought to catch her notice. He wanted to escort Tess to the table, but of course Miss Walcott, as hostess, expected to take his arm.

Inside the spacious dining room, each table setting was labeled with a name, and Dom cursed silently to see that Tess was to be seated practically in the next county, at the farthest end of the table from him.

It was going to be a long bloody evening.

He'd gone missing.

After dinner, the whole party had gathered in the drawing room. Though Sir Owen entertained his own gentlemen friends in the billiards room, Priscilla insisted that Dominic Prince join the ladies.

He'd seemed eager to do so. Indeed, Tess had never observed such a potent performance of ongoing charm in her life. No matter how many times he was asked similar questions, he answered with a colorful tale and flashes of that dazzling smile he wielded so well.

The ladies were enthralled after the first story, nearly spellbound as the next ones unfolded. Mrs. Wells was absolutely correct. Within a few hours, Mr. Prince had become the most fascinating man in Wiggenstow.

Yet after the second parlor game, when the entire party stood and the staff wound through the gathering to refresh drinks and offer delicate petit fours, he slipped away.

Tess immediately counted the ladies, wondering if he'd be so brazen as to engage in a tryst during the dinner party. But all of Priscilla's friends were accounted for and busy conversing.

"I suspect we've overwhelmed him," Priscilla whispered after she broke away to approach Tess.

"Perhaps." Tess suspected she knew where he'd gone. "Would you like me to have a look for him?"

"Would you?" Priscilla arched a brow as if surprised by the offer. "I fear if I leave the gathering, the ladies may panic."

"Of course." Tess wondered what that boded for the moment he'd actually depart for the evening.

"Thank you for bringing him, Miss Hawthorne." Priscilla's smile seemed genuine.

"Oh, I don't determine where Mr. Prince goes." To Tess, he seemed a man who would balk at the notion of any lady directing his actions or interfering with his wanderlust ways.

"Perhaps not, but word is that you two will be working closely together on the excavation of Fenbridge land, and he immediately looked to you when I invited him." Priscilla leaned an inch closer. "Not to mention seeking you out with his gaze continually this evening."

"There's nothing between us," Tess hurried to insist. Her stomach wobbled at the prospect of rumors about her rushing through the village.

"No, no, I never meant to imply such." Priscilla reached out and laid a hand on Tess's arm. "I'd never subject another woman to that after my own folly."

"Thank you." Tess nodded.

"Bring him back if you can," Priscilla told her, then returned to the fray of chattering ladies.

Tess sat her drink on a low table and headed for the Walcotts' billiards room.

To her surprise, a quick peek inside told her that Dominic

had not joined Priscilla's father and his friends as she'd suspected. Her next guess was the terrace. She strode toward the rear of the enormous manor house and stepped out into the cool night air.

She immediately drew in deep breaths, scanning the wide stone terrace for him, but spotted no dark-haired, broad-shouldered gentlemen lurking about. Still, she took another moment to savor the fresh air after hours spent among so many fawning ladies.

When she finally turned back toward the house, she noticed the lights lit in the ground floor library. It seemed odd that he'd seek solitude in such a room, given his treatment of books on the day they met. Still, Tess reentered the manor house determined to check.

The doorway to the library stood ajar, and she glimpsed him through the gap. He'd found the drinks cart and knocked back a snifter of amber liquid. Then he went to the cart and filled it again before running a hand through his hair and staring out the long library windows into the moonlit gardens.

Tess slipped inside the room, leaving the door cracked as she'd found it.

"I promised Miss Walcott I'd find you."

He stiffened and drank deeply from his glass before turning to face her.

"I'm surprised you noticed my absence," he said. "You were the only lady entirely uninterested in my travel tales, Miss Hawthorne."

"I . . ." Tess didn't wish to admit that she was as intrigued as every other lady present, but she didn't want to be taken in by his appeal. She refused to be. They were partners in a business matter, and she was not the foolish girl she'd been at nineteen.

"You think I'm a fraud." He lifted the snifter and emptied it.

It wasn't a question, and Tess didn't know how to deny the accusation. But she couldn't stop the question on the tip of her tongue. "Are you?"

A laugh rumbled up and erupted into a deep, amused chuckle. "Of course, sweetheart."

The use of an endearment he had no right to shouldn't have made her pulse race, but it did. And when he took a step closer, she should have retreated, but she didn't.

His eyes were bright in the fire glow, and a flush of color, no doubt from the drink, deepened the olive hue of his skin.

"No one wants to hear the real stories," he told her as his eyes fixed hungrily on her lips. "They all relish the drama, the adventure, the tales where I make myself out to be—"

He stopped when she licked her lips. She hadn't meant to do it, but the longing in his gaze made her breathless. Foolishly so.

"A scoundrel? A rogue? A rapscallion?" Tess offered, trying to distract him and her own ridiculous yearning for him to take a step closer.

He nodded. "They want that. They're starving for it." And then he did it. He took the step that brought him so close she felt the tickle of his breath on her skin, the heat of his body nearly pressed to hers. "And yet all I wanted tonight was your attention."

"Why?"

"Oh Tess." He reached up and tucked a lock of her hair behind her ear, his fingers dancing over her skin, lingering at a spot along her neck that made her shiver. "Don't you know?"

"No." Heaven help her, her body listed toward his, and she couldn't seem to stop it.

He dipped his head.

Mercy, he was going to kiss her. And she was going to let him.

But he didn't. He hovered his mouth near a spot by her ear that he'd just stroked.

"You're damned beautiful. Fierce and clever and—" His breath caught, and she heard him swallow hard. "And you want to see beyond the facade."

Tess reached for him because it felt as if she'd fall into him if she didn't. Just one hand on his chest. Her fingers curled around his lapel and she felt the strong, insistent thud of his heartbeat.

"Are you sure you want to see?" he asked, his voice raw and husky.

"Yes." She turned her head, needing him to look into her eyes so he knew she was in earnest.

But then his mouth brushed hers, and she reached for him without hesitation, her palm at his nape, fingers sifting his dark hair. He knew just where to touch her—a hand at her hip, the other at her back—to fit her perfectly against the muscled heat of his body.

He kissed her tentatively, exploring. Asking rather than taking—so unlike anything she'd ever experienced before. He tasted and teased as if there was no rush, no party to get back to, no one but her to give himself to.

At the squeak of hinges, they both froze. Dominic pivoted, but with an arm behind him, still holding her close so that her body was shielded by his.

"Forgive me, sir." Tess recognized the voice of the elderly butler who'd admitted them earlier. "Miss Walcott asked me to find you, Mr. Prince."

"I'll return to the drawing room directly." Dominic's voice emerged in a forceful rasp.

Tess dared not move or breathe, even when she heard the

man's footsteps retreat. She had no doubt the watchful servant knew Dominic was not in the library alone.

Dominic released her slowly, letting one hand linger on her arm as if determined to keep her steady until she took a step away from him.

"Which of us should go back first?" he asked softly.

"You," Tess told him immediately. "You're the one they want." She hadn't meant to snap or be harsh. That kiss had shaken her, left her breathless and stunned, but it had been mutual. She would not deny that.

"And yet all I want is to stay here with you." He leaned in and added, "That's the truth."

"If you don't go, they'll send a contingent to find you." Tess could imagine the ladies would soon be queueing outside the library door now that the butler had found him.

"I'll go." He looked as if he wished to say more. Instead, he dipped his head and left her.

Flushed and tingling from his kiss, Tess hugged an arm around her middle and reached her other hand up to her mouth. Her body trembled at how good it felt to be in his arms—so warm, so tantalizing. She licked her lips to catch the trace of lingering brandy.

How had she given in so easily? She knew better.

But what terrified her most was how much she wanted to kiss him again.

Chapter Eight

Two days later

Dom sat in the taproom of the village inn, awaiting the breakfast that the kindly innkeeper's wife insisted on making for him. Thankfully, the coffee was dark enough to match his mood.

The one lady in all of Wiggenstow he actually wanted to see and speak to was avoiding him. Though, of no real interest to him, two of the ladies he'd met at the Walcotts' had already sent invitations. One wished him to join her family for tea, and the other quite boldly asked him to squire her to the village's spring fair, which was apparently imminent.

He'd set both invites aside, wishing he'd never agreed to attend the blasted dinner.

No, of course, that wasn't true. Those few stolen moments with Tess that night had made all the smiling and boasting and forced magnetism worthwhile.

Dom drank down a swig of the hot brew to distract himself, but it was too late. He was already hard at the mere memory of the lush sweetness of her mouth. He wasn't sure she'd even realized the sounds she'd made when he swept his tongue against the seam of her lips, or the way her body arched into his, but he'd noticed everything. Every breath. Every slide of her fingers against his skin. Every erotic little mewl she emitted as he tasted her.

His lust for Tess Hawthorne blazed far beyond what it should after only a few days' acquaintance. Hell, it wasn't appropriate at all, given their agreement to work together for Fenbridge.

What he hoped most is that she didn't regret it.

He'd thought of calling at her family's home when he'd heard nothing from her on Saturday, but as it was now Sunday, he didn't wish to invite himself and intrude. But he had sought out her brother via a note delivered by a local lad.

Even as he awaited Tristan Hawthorne's arrival, Dom had already decided that he would apologize, if that's what it took to make amends with Tess. He didn't regret a damn thing. Hell, it was all he could do on their carriage ride back from the Walcotts' not to touch her. But she'd kept silent, seemingly lost in thought, and he didn't want to give her more to fret about. So, he'd say he was sorry if it allayed whatever regrets she might have.

He'd vow not to touch her again, not unless she invited him to. He groaned, hating that idea, suspecting he'd be tempted to break the vow as soon as he was near her again. Yet he knew it was the proper and gentlemanly thing to do.

He shook his head and swigged more coffee. When the hell had he ever been concerned with being a proper gentleman?

That part of him that didn't give a toss about propriety whispered possibilities in his mind. He wanted her, whatever the cost. Her kiss, the way she'd tucked herself against him, confirmed that Tess was attracted to him too, at the very least.

Would it be so bad if they gave in to a craving that was undeniably mutual?

"Good morning, Prince," Tristan Hawthorne called in greeting. "I was surprised by your summons. Thought you'd be seeking out Tess rather than me."

Dom stood to greet the man, taking his offered hand and giving it a firm shake. "Call me Dominic."

"Tristan."

"I'll apprise Tess of everything I'm about to discuss with you, or you could. But I was hoping you'd agree to serve as foreman among the men we've hired for the dig."

Tristan blinked as if surprised by the offer and then smiled. "I'd be happy to."

"Good." Dom pulled out a document he'd prepared for Tess's brother. It was a copy, more or less, of the cross section Eve had drawn during their dig the previous fall. It also included estimated measurements for the trench they'd dig to begin this excavation.

"As you see, we'll likely need to remove around five feet of soil before we begin to find anything of value."

Tristan nodded. "Understood. We could start as early as today if you like."

"Are you certain?"

The innkeeper's wife approached with a mug of coffee for Tristan, and he thanked her with a roguish wink.

Dom waited while the man took a sip, seeming to savor it as much as he did.

"Most of the men we've engaged work other jobs during the week. They're expecting to devote hours on weekends. I can't promise all would be willing to start today, but I could likely gather a group of six or so."

"Excellent." Dom felt that familiar churn of anticipation in his gut. His fingers itched to touch the treasure they were going to find in Fenbridge's field. "I've had new supplies sent from Norwich and delivered to Fenbridge's groundskeeper. The man has cleared out some space in a shed at the estate."

He handed over a pouch filled with coins. "We can pay the workers daily or weekly. You decide."

"Daily will keep them happier and will draw more workers, no doubt." Tristan took the pouch, jangling the coins inside. "We have tools at Foxdene too if they're needed. Tess and I were keen to dig and have our own little collection from excavating the back garden. We just made do with whatever we could find." He chuckled and then shook his head when he saw Dom's brows shoot up. "We found nothing of value, I assure you. Some interesting rocks, a coin or two, a bit of dinnerware a former mistress of the cottage must have chucked out."

When Mrs. Randall came by with Dom's breakfast plated up, Tristan declined to order any for himself.

"I'll go and let Tess know the plan and then begin gathering the men," he told Dom. "We'll get a few feet down before sunset, I wager."

"I'll join you at the site within the hour."

Tristan gave him a mock salute and made as if to stand.

"How is Miss Hawthorne?" Dom couldn't stop himself from asking.

"Ah," the lady's brother said knowingly.

Dom didn't know what to make of the man's inscrutable expression. "Is she unwell?"

"Tess is always well," he told him. "Or at least she pretends to be. She keeps a great deal to herself." Tristan took another sip of his coffee and set the mug down, then flicked his gaze up to look at Dom straight on.

"I considered inviting her today but . . ." Dom stumbled out, but he loathed volunteering anything to Tristan if Tess hadn't told him about the night at the Walcotts'.

"Look," her brother began, "Tess would have my bollocks for prying, but what sort of a brother would I be if I didn't?"

"I take it you plan to pry."

Tristan looked off into the distance a moment. "I may play the fool, Dominic, but I'm not blind or unobservant."

"I never thought you were. I wouldn't hand a full bag of coin to a fool."

Tristan dipped his head in acknowledgment. "I suspect something happened at the Walcotts'."

Dom opened his mouth to speak, and Tristan stopped him with his palm out.

"I require no details. My sister is a grown woman and needs no approval or permission from me for her actions."

"I agree," Dom told him.

"You fancy her." Tristan didn't ask or even sound accusing. It was a mere fact. Dom had no doubt that anyone within ten feet of him when he was near Tess could sense his reaction to her.

But what could he admit to her twin?

"Any man would." The quip was too blithe, too flippant. "Yes," he rushed to add. "Though we are barely acquainted."

Tristan frowned. "Time doesn't factor into such things, does it?"

"No," Dom admitted.

Tristan took a deep breath, gripped the back of his neck, and then finally blurted, "Tread lightly with Tess."

"Lightly?"

He stared up at the inn's ceiling. "I know the Almighty is chuckling right now that I must be the one to explain this. I, who have caused more heartache than I have a right to."

"I would never—"

"No," Tristan cut in. "I never intend to either, but it happens all the same. Matters of the heart are never without risk. Not truly. Even when it seems like nothing more than scratching a carnal itch."

Dom swallowed hard. There had been a few ladies who'd sought more from him than he'd been able to offer in return. But, with his reputation, most understood that any liaison would be fleeting.

"Are you warning me to steer clear of your sister? At least in that regard?" Dom asked the young man. "State it clearly if you are."

Eve had attracted undesirable suitors, and Dom had considered stepping in more than once, though she'd proven quite adept at putting them off herself.

"I won't ask your intentions because Tess must make her own decisions." He leaned across the table closer to Dom. "She doesn't trust herself, you see, and the last thing she needs is a man like me judging her choices or pontificating."

Dom leaned closer too, shoving his cold plate of food aside. "Why doesn't she trust herself?"

"She's been burned, man."

"Burned?"

"By a blackguard, of course." Tristan edged back, settling against the chair as if stunned that Dom could be so thick. "The man wooed her, then hied off when he got what he wanted." He ducked his head and mumbled, "He was a charmer. A libertine, not unlike me."

Then he lifted his head and gave a hard stare back at Dom. "Not unlike you."

TESS SHOVED HER FOOT into one long boot and then searched for the other in her wardrobe, all the while mumbling curses at Dominic Prince under her breath.

The riding skirt that Wellsy had sewn into trousers fit inside the boots, so she was careful to put them on just right, despite how angry she was.

Once she found the other, she made short work of slipping into the boot, then swiped up her straw sunhat from where it hung by her bedroom door.

When she emerged, Wellsy watched her warily as she cleared the table where they'd shared Sunday lunch.

"You're storming over there then?" she asked as she wiped the table.

"They've started without me!" Tess huffed out a breath and tempered her tone. "This is high-handed nonsense, and he needs to know it's not acceptable."

"Tristan did explain—"

"I know." Tess resisted the urge to curse her brother too, though he was just as complicit as Mr. Prince.

And it would be *Mr. Prince* from now on. She'd made a mistake by allowing herself to be as drawn in as one of those panting ladies at the Walcotts' party. So what if one look at him made her belly flutter and he kissed like a dream?

He would never have an ounce of respect for her if she could not maintain a professional distance. And that's what she intended to do going forward.

"They just wanted to get down far enough that your work tomorrow would be fruitful."

"Do you think me incapable of digging a hole, Wellsy?"

She shook her head decisively. "Not a bit of it." Then she turned an amused look Tess's way. "But do you want to dig a hole, Tessie? Hasn't this American hired you for your knowledge of the history?"

Tess closed her eyes, inhaled and exhaled thrice, willing her anger to ebb. "He did," she acknowledged. "But Lord

Fenbridge wants to know what happens on his land, and it's my duty to report to him."

"Could they not note it all down and share it with you?"

Tess sighed. "I want to be there. I want to be a part of every step. And if he thinks that just because he—"

Mrs. Wells arched a silver brow. "Just because he . . . ?" she prompted.

Tess had told no one about the kissing, which was a small miracle in and of itself, seeing as she'd hardly gone an hour without replaying every single second in her mind.

"I'm going to the dig site." Tess shoved her hat on her head. "Enjoy the rest of your Sunday, Wellsy."

"Be safe, my dear."

Tess cut straight across the back garden toward Fenbridge's field, not bothering with the village lanes. It slowed her pace, as she pushed through tall grasses, but the movement eased a bit of the tension in her body and the sun on her skin did wonders for her mood.

Then, within a few minutes, she caught site of them in the distance. They'd already made quick work of removing the sod and the first layer of soil. The men stood in a line, stretched out at nearly equal intervals. An organized dig, and she had to admire that at least.

She kept marching toward them and gasped when she saw him.

He stood speaking to Tristan, the wind whipping at his dark hair. He'd rolled his shirtsleeves up high and even from the distance where she stood she could make out the corded muscles of his sun-kissed skin.

Her mouth went dry when he turned her way, gesturing as if directing Tristan. His shirt . . . was not buttoned all the way to his neck.

All that resolve she'd just summoned seemed to wisp away on the spring breeze.

Then she noticed what was in Tristan's hands and everything in front of her became tinged with crimson.

She stomped toward the two of them, and it took them an irritatingly long while to even note her approach.

Tristan spotted her first. Eyes wide, he waved at her tentatively.

Oh yes, he had good reason for that guilty dip of his brows. Tess pointed at the map in his hands. Her map. The one she'd prepared when they went to Fenbridge nearly a year ago to ask for permission to dig.

She'd worked on the plan for months, gathering together any details she could from public records, studies of the region, and her father's own writings about the history of the village. Measuring and plotting and theorizing had taken up so much of her time that she'd barely slept, sometimes forgot to eat. She felt so certain of what they'd find on Fenbridge land.

She had given some of those documents to Mr. Prince already, mostly the historical studies her father had completed, but the map held special meaning. It was their dream—hers and Tristan's—all laid out in graphical form.

They saw her now, Tristan looking uncharacteristically sheepish and Mr. Prince watching her approach with one of his roguish grins tipping those lips she now knew the taste of.

No. Stop. Ignore his tempting mouth.

She didn't miss how his gaze lowered to take in her trousers before looking up at her face again.

"You started without me, Mr. Prince," Tess shouted when she was close enough to ensure they heard every word. "I consider that a very poor play from a man who said we would be partners in this endeavor."

"Tess—" Tristan tried.

"No." She lifted a hand up toward her brother. "Do not *Tess* me when you come out here with my map yet without me." She plucked it from his fingers. "This is my plan, Mr. Prince." She held up the document but did not release it to him. "Do you not have one of your own?"

He scrutinized her a moment, his eyes sparkling with much more amusement than he had any right to.

"Of course, Miss Hawthorne." He reached into a leather satchel on a battered little table they'd set up at the edge of the dig area. After pulling out a sheaf of papers in a folio, he handed it to her.

Inside the folio, Tess found meticulous notes about the dig the Prince siblings had conducted the previous fall, as well as a projected plan for how the current dig should proceed. All were written in the same neat hand, though a few pages were typed.

"My sister prepared much of that," he admitted while she flipped through each page.

"All of it, it seems." Tess arched a brow and looked him square in the eye.

He managed to look the slightest bit chagrined. "Eve is better at the planning. I tend to be better at . . . digging in and taking action."

"I'm prepared to dig in, Mr. Prince, I assure you." Tess only had the little digs she and Tristan had conducted on the fields next to Foxdene as experience, but she'd conducted them methodically, documenting every step.

When Tristan stepped away to oversee the village men who continued to dig into the top layers of soil, Mr. Prince stepped almost scandalously close.

"Are we to be foes again, Tess?"

"Someone needs to document everything that's happening," she told him, struggling not to reveal how his nearness unnerved her. "Who's doing that?"

He pulled out a folded sheet of paper from the pocket of his trousers and offered it to her. It was warm from being pressed against his body. Tess tried to ignore that as she held the sheet in her hands.

He'd noted the start time, added a grid drawing of the area, and listed the name of each gentleman who'd begun working this morning.

"I'm sorry," he said quietly while she perused his notations. His voice was low, a bit rough, as it had been the night before last. "I didn't mean to leave you out or exclude you."

But you did, she barely resisted blurting.

"I wanted to spare you the boring bits," he said, rocking on his heels and swaying a bit closer. She caught the scent of his shaving soap, the smoky allure of coffee.

"None of it is boring to me. I've wanted to do this for years."

He lifted a hand as if he wanted to touch her but then lowered it.

"I'm sorry," he repeated. This time his expression matched the warmth in his voice. He looked genuinely contrite, as if disappointing her truly troubled him.

Was it real? She'd asked him for honesty and then watched him put on the greatest performance of charm and colorful storytelling about his adventures for hours.

Still, regardless of her doubts, Tess found herself listing closer. "You're forgiven." The words emerged breathless, and it only got worse when he beamed at her in response.

"Thank you." He stepped back a bit, creating a respectable foot of distance between them. He then gestured to a pile of tools he, or perhaps Tristan or one of the other men, had assembled. "Want a shovel?"

"Yes." Tess strode over and chose one.

"When we get down to the more careful work, you're welcome to borrow my set." He pointed to an assembly of hand tools tucked into a leather pouch that lay spread out on the grass. They included a brush, a small trowel, even a magnifying glass, and a tiny pickax.

"What will you use?" she asked him.

"I have Eve's set with me too."

Tess bent down and ran her fingers over the tools. She'd never had a proper set, but she'd always wanted one. That he was offering her his made her want to believe him—that he hadn't meant to exclude her today. That the kiss had been real too.

No, no, she wasn't going to think about kissing him. This work they were undertaking mattered more.

"We may not get to use any of those for days." He spoke from behind her, and when Tess turned back, he swept a hand through his thick dark hair. "This is the part where patience is a virtue." He grinned. "I'm always short of it, I'm afraid."

Tess was too, but she was determined to take this opportunity to dig on Fenbridge's land and do it right. Not for Van Arsdale's money, though heaven knew they needed it. But more importantly, this was a chance she'd always wanted.

She stood and pointed to the pile of larger shovels and spades. "If we're impatient, we should help dig. The faster we dig, the sooner we find it."

He bent to retrieve a shovel. "You're certain we'll find treasure."

"I'm certain," she admitted. "The size of that mound means something. If it's not already been looted, we'll find a hoard."

"Then let's dig." He lifted a shovel out to her.

She reached for it and their fingers brushed. That single touch was like a bit of flint striking that steely part of herself she'd built walls around, threatening to spark it into flame.

Tess had avoided this for years. Avoided gossip. Avoided temptation. But now she would be spending much of her day with this man who made her insides tremble.

Chapter Nine

On the third day of the dig, the weather took a turn. Dom had squinted up one moment into a cloud-filled blue sky, and within an hour, the breeze had grown in strength and storm clouds swept in across the horizon.

"We should begin preparing to cover the dig site," he called to Tristan, who was on the far side of the trench they'd worked to carve out over the past days. They'd assembled a small but reliable group of men from the village who'd made excellent progress.

Tristan tipped his head up. "We'll collect the tarpaulins," he shouted back.

Dom approached to assist. The chandler in Norwich, who'd produced the enormous oilskin coverings, assured them that they'd keep out the rain. It would be the first test of the man's vow.

As they rushed to stretch the first length of waxed cloth, Tess appeared at the trench's edge, an enormous basket in her arms.

"I saw the clouds and brought some stakes from Fenbridge's groundskeeper."

Each morning, he looked forward to her return from visiting the grumpy nobleman. And each morning, his pulse kicked up like he was a besotted schoolboy the moment she appeared.

"Stakes?"

"To secure the edges of the tarp," she said as if it was the most obvious thing in the world.

"Of course." Somehow his foresight had extended only to stretching the tarpaulins across the site, but the stakes would be crucial if the wind kicked up.

As she did the past few days, Tess immediately joined in. The lady was not interested in merely advising. She seemed to relish digging, sifting, or doing whatever was required to help move the excavation along. Like Dom, she was not content to sit on the sidelines and watch others work.

Within a quarter of an hour, they had the largest tarps stretched out over the central trench. Fenbridge's groundskeeper provided them with a couple of mallets too, and Tristan and Dom quickly sank the stakes at the coverings' edges to secure them in place as the soft cool drops of rain began to pelt them.

"Come to the inn," Dom said to Tess as she strode toward him while he pounded in the final stakes. "We can convene about the dig and have an early lunch."

He cast his gaze down the length of the worksite. "Tristan too, and any of the men who want to join us."

"We don't know how long the rain will last." Tess stood with her hands on her hips and looked up into the light drizzle. "Summer rains sometimes pass quickly, and the men won't want to lose a day's pay."

"They'll be paid no matter what." Dom stood and dusted off his hands. "And if it's possible, we'll return to the site."

But even as he spoke, a rumble of thunder rolled across the sky.

"Oh no," Tess murmured in an ominous tone. "Not a quick shower, I'm afraid."

"No?" Dom had dealt with all sorts of weather challenges on various digs. A bit of rain wouldn't daunt him.

Yet the next moment, the gentle, pelting rain turned to a torrent, bucketing down so fiercely that the noise of it seemed to swallow all other sounds.

Dom shucked off his linen sack coat and lifted it, stretching it out above Tess's head.

She'd already been drenched and chuckled. "Such chivalry," she teased. "But a little too late for Mother Nature."

"I had to try." He grinned, loving the easiness of her smile.

They exchanged a few each day, and he never took a single one for granted. Though what they never did was speak of the kiss they'd shared at the Walcotts'. It was as if she wished to forget it. He never could. But he wouldn't demand anything of her. If an amiable working relationship was what she insisted upon, he'd told himself he'd push for no more. Yet it couldn't stop him from hoping, or from how maddeningly attracted he was to his dig partner.

"We let them go for the day?" Tristan shouted in question.

"Let's all head to the Randalls' inn," Dom called to him.

Men turned to each other as the message was passed down the line, and then a few took off walking toward the road that led to town. One scooped up an umbrella. A few broke into a run, but most ambled along, as if they weren't at all bothered by the downpour.

Tristan approached with a couple of the umbrellas they kept at the site for anyone who needed a moment of shade.

He tossed one to Dom, who immediately opened it and lifted it over Tess. She stepped forward, so they could share its shelter.

"We could get the pony cart," Tristan offered.

"Let's walk," Tess insisted. "It's already letting up a bit." She cast a glance toward the trench. "And the oilskin seems to be keeping everything dry."

Indeed, the coverings held tight across the ground they'd excavated, and the downpour had ebbed to a steady patter.

The three of them made their way through the field and to the road that led them into the village. Their hired men had beat them to the Randalls' and the innkeepers looked pleased about the unexpected influx of visitors to their taproom.

Soon tea, coffee, and some of Mrs. Randall's confections had been distributed.

"We're still making good time," Tess said, glancing first at her brother and then at Dom. "Even if we lose the day."

"I'm not concerned about losing a day. We're excavating far faster progress than I'd expected."

"But we've still found little of note." Tristan sounded a bit irked. They'd found some nails, animal bones, a few chips of crockery.

"I'm still hopeful," Dom told him with a glance toward Tess.

She nodded as if she shared his optimism. "We're only a couple of feet down. And there are the soil changes. Those *are* notable."

Tess thought them very promising, though her brother was dubious. Experience told Dom they were a sign, but of what, he couldn't yet say. But for now, he was willing to trust Tess's intuition. As a result, they'd focused on extending the length of the trench rather than the depth over the previous day.

"If you say so," Tristan grumbled.

"Let's stay hopeful," Tess urged.

"I am," Dom told her. That earned him another smile. Her brother arched a brow and flicked his gaze between the two of them.

Dominic Prince's smiles were too beguiling, gradually slipping past her defenses like ivy wound its way up the garden fence at Foxdene: slowly, gently, and yet with determined persistence. Now, she felt the answering tug of a smile each time he looked her way.

She was beginning to believe those easy smiles weren't simply meant to charm but were a genuine reflection of his nature. From what she'd observed, he was good-tempered whenever he was working. In fact, the harder the day's work, the happier he seemed. She sensed his frustration when nothing was found at the end of a day, but he still joked with the others, had built a rapport with Tristan, respected her suggestions, and listened to her observations.

Somehow, the workaday Dominic Prince she was beginning to know was every bit as appealing as the swashbuckler he'd been for the ladies at Priscilla Walcott's party.

No, I am not thinking about that kiss.

The inn's door banged open. A gust of rain swept in followed by a breathless boy in a brown cap and wet boots. His cheeks were red from the rain, and he shouted over the sudden silence.

"Mr. Wilton's barn's come down! Roof caved clean through. Daisy's trapped and she won't come out!"

Dominic and Tristan and a few other men from the dig were on their feet before the boy finished speaking. Tess stood too.

"Come on," Dominic said.

"Can we take your market cart, Mrs. Randall?" Tess asked as the innkeeper's wife stood among them, having just finished topping up teacups.

"Aye, whatever you need," her husband called from the kitchen's threshold. "I've just returned from the village, and Angus is in the harness still."

The group raced out behind the inn and climbed into the wooden cart. Tristan helped hand Tess up to the driver's seat, and Dominic took the spot beside her. She knew the Wiltons well, and it seemed the Randalls' horse, Angus, knew the way too, for the hardworking animal took the path easily. They were at the Wiltons' cottage in but a few moments.

Mrs. Wilton stood outside the barn, her face tear-stained under her wide-brimmed hat. The structure itself was a mess of collapsed thatch, its beams exposed. A man's voice could be heard as he shouted in frustration.

"Still not coming out?" Tristan asked as he jumped down from the horse cart.

Dominic handed Tess down, and they approached to stand beside him. A few of the other men shouted into the barn for Mr. Wilton.

"Stubborn girl, she is," Mrs. Wilton told him. "Must be scared witless. And my mister won't let me inside again. Twisted my ankle when I tried to get to her."

"How old is the child?" Dominic asked.

"Oh—" Tess started.

"No child, sir." Mrs. Wilton frowned at him as if he'd lost his wits. "Daisy's our best milk cow."

"Ah." Dominic shot Tess a look. "Shall we try?"

Tess nodded and started off toward the barn. "Do you think your charm will work on cows too?"

"We'll soon find out."

Tristan and another man from the dig emerged from the barn carrying chickens in baskets. "Be careful if you're going in," her brother told them.

Mr. Wilton stepped out as they approached, leading a calf. "Daisy's the last of them. If we lose her, we lose our earnings."

"Let us see if we can persuade her, Mr. Wilton," Tess told him.

"Kindly of you, Tess." He glanced back at his barn. "We're going to see if we can repair the posts and put canvas over the top."

"Who tends to her most?" Dominic asked.

"The missus has a taking for her, but the stubborn thing won't heed her today."

"She's likely terrified," Tess said. "But will you send Mrs. Wilton round to the edge of the barn near Daisy's stall?"

Mr. Wilton nodded.

Dominic bent to enter the dilapidated barn without hesitation. "Watch your head," he urged, checking over his shoulder as if to make sure Tess was behind him.

Tess dodged puddles, lifting the edge of her skirt, as rain trickled down her neck from the straw overhead.

"Hello, Miss Daisy," Dominic said with all the warmth and charm he'd wielded when greeting Priscilla Walcott that day in the village. "You're all right, girl."

"Part of her stall is damaged," Tess whispered as she pointed to the beam of wood that had collapsed under the weight of the sunken roof.

"Can we get her past it?" Dominic asked.

Tess inched closer from the far side of the stall. "It's not blocking her, but she may not realize that."

"Daisy, love, come out now," Mrs. Wilton called softly through a wood-framed window at the edge of the barn.

The red-coated cow turned its head at the sound of its carer's voice.

"That's it, Daisy girl. Will you come with us?" Tess asked. She looked around, found her lead rope with a slipknot hanging on a peg, and approached slowly. Reaching out, she laid a hand on Daisy's side, letting the animal get used to her nearness. "Nothing to be afraid of."

"Careful, Tess," Dominic whispered.

She reached back to offer him the rope. "You're taller. Can you loop it over her head?"

Wordlessly, he took the rope, then moved up close behind Tess. So close his chest brushed against her back. "She's still scared."

Tess saw the signs too—swishing tail, wide eyes.

"It's all right, girl," Dominic said, his voice low and comforting. "You're safe."

Mrs. Wilton had begun singing a pretty little tune that once again seemed to catch Daisy's attention.

With the cow's head turned, Dominic reached up, his body inching Tess's forward slightly, and looped the rope over Daisy's head.

"You did it." Tess turned her head to glance at him. He stood close, and the heat of his body warmed her skin. "Now we have to hope she'll let us lead her."

Dominic lowered his arm along Tess's side and slipped the rope into her hand.

When he stepped away from her, the loss of his warmth shot an odd sense of longing through her, which she forced herself to ignore.

Gently, she tugged Daisy forward. At first, the cow tossed its head, but as Mrs. Wilton continued singing, and Tess and Dominic offered words of encouragement in soft voices, Daisy took her first tentative step outside of her stall.

"That's it, girl," Dominic said with what sound liked genuine enthusiasm. "A little farther, love."

Tess smiled at his wooing tone and could not deny the appeal of his low, resonant voice.

Daisy wasn't immune either. The cow took two steps forward, and Tess kept the rope's pressure lightly taut but not tight against her neck.

Dominic laid a hand against Tess's back as if to guide her as she stepped backward, her eyes trained on the cow.

"You're doing grand, Daisy," Tess crooned. "A few more steps and I'm sure we can rustle up a carrot for you."

Dominic chuckled. Tess turned her head.

"What?" Tess said. "A treat would motivate me."

His eyes met hers, crinkled at the corners from his smile. "I'll remember that."

"I've got one," Mrs. Wilton called a few moments later. She stood behind them now, near the entrance of the barn, and waved a carrot.

Daisy seemed to understand and took the next few steps with less hesitation. Once she was close enough, Tess reached out and handed the lead rope to Mrs. Wilton.

"Oh, my dear girl," she said as she patted the cow's side. "Thank you both."

"Pleased we could help," Dominic told her.

Once they'd all stepped clear of the barn, Tess noticed the line of men, including Tristan, who stood at the ready to begin basic repairs.

"Thought we'd wait until she was out," Tristan told her. "But we'd best start while the weather holds."

The rain had now slowed to a light drizzle, though the sky remained darkened with gray clouds.

"How can I assist?" Dominic asked her brother.

Tristan handed him a hammer, but Dominic hesitated.

"You'll be all right?" he asked Tess.

"Of course." She offered him one of the smiles that seemed to come easily between them now.

In the past few days when he'd asked after her well-being, she'd initially snapped a reply, feeling a need to prove herself every bit as capable as the men working the site. But Dominic never treated her as if she was unequal to tasks the others engaged in, so now she tried to take his concern as a kindness. The man had sisters. Perhaps his thoughtfulness for the ladies around him was borne of that.

Yet his gaze lingered, reminding her that there was more between them. Something that had been there since he'd balanced on a rolling staircase above her in Lady Goddard's library.

He took her in, rain-soaked and disheveled, eyes flicking down to her mouth, then lower to the damp curls at her neck. The way he looked at her made her skin tingle as if his gaze had left a mark wherever it touched her.

Then he turned away to help shore up the Wiltons' barn, and Tess was left with a warmth unfurling inside her that she tried to ignore. The problem was that the more time she spent with Dominic Prince, the harder it was to dismiss him as nothing more than a seductive rogue.

Chapter Ten

Three days after being rained out, they'd made significant progress uncovering more of the darker tinted soil that Dom now believed, along with Tess, indicated an object, likely composed of wood, which had decayed over time on the site.

The previous day, a cross pendant had been found by Tess at the far edge of the trench that looked to be from the late medieval period. And they continued to uncover bits of animal bone and items that had been used to work the land, such as a weathered iron plowshare.

But the ideas about what might have left the marks in the soil were so debated that some of the men had begun taking bets.

Dom just wanted answers, but he knew patience would serve him best. Memories of Peter reminded him of the value of patience. He worked to summon some of his friend's steady, hopeful nature at those moments when disappointment and frustration crept in at the end of a day with nothing found that could be classified as treasure.

Tess didn't seem to share his struggle. She had a bit of Peter's nature, joining persistence with hopefulness. Dom had never once seen her waver in her belief that the dig was a worthwhile endeavor, even after spending a morning listening to Fenbridge's cynicism about what the mounds might hold.

Tonight, as the men stowed tools and prepared to quit the site for the day, Dom's thoughts were fixed entirely on the sunny-haired beauty making notes at a table set up on the trench's edge. Though he knew it was a special day for her, she'd treated it as any other—as her brother told Dom she would—working diligently, remaining focused on her tasks.

Tristan approached along the trench's ridge.

"You haven't forgotten about tonight," he said in a low voice, his eyes flickering toward his sister.

"Of course not. I'm looking forward to it."

Tristan shot him a half-smile. "She doesn't like a fuss, so it will just be the few of us."

"Thank you for including me."

"See you in a bit." Tristan clapped him on the back and strode toward his sister, who collected her things and offered Dom a wave.

He waved back, and the two headed off toward Foxdene.

Dom made his way back to the inn with a quick, long stride. He washed and took extra care with shaving and dressing, and then collected the item he'd ordered from London as soon as Tristan extended the invitation to join the family tonight.

All the way to Foxdene, he debated whether he should have chosen something else. Perhaps it was presumptuous. Perhaps it was too practical.

Good grief, no woman had ever tied him in knots the way Tess Hawthorne did. She consumed his thoughts when she was near during the day. He admired her insights and her enthusiasm for the work. When they parted at night, she remained on his mind and sometimes even appeared in his dreams.

She'd invited him to dine with them at Foxdene twice, and each time he'd relished the easy conversation between the siblings and Mrs. Wells. The cottage was a place of family and comfort, the kind of comfort he'd been avoiding for years.

Now, he was almost giddy at the prospect of joining them again, though what he really hoped for was a moment alone with Tess. They hadn't had one since she'd found him in the Walcotts' library. He wondered if that was something she purposely avoided. She certainly wanted to avoid the matter of their kiss.

All he wanted was to kiss her again. Once more, and he'd surely get her out of his head. Once more, and he could go back to being the sort of man he'd been before he met her.

Surely, it was the maddening fact that he couldn't touch her, or kiss her, that made him want her with an unrelenting ache.

Foxdene glowed from within, its windows a golden brightness in the dusk, and Dom caught the scent of wisteria on the warm evening breeze.

He didn't have to knock.

Mrs. Wells seemed to be watching for him and opened the door the minute he approached.

"Welcome, Mr. Prince, come in. Come in."

"It's Dominic to you, Mrs. Wells," he said as he stepped inside and was assailed with the scent of sugary, fresh-baked confections.

Tess stood near the fireplace with her brother, and both turned to greet him.

She was all Dom could see.

She wore her hair pinned up, but a single blond curl had come loose to graze her neck. He swallowed hard as his eyes fixed on that spot that he suddenly had the overwhelming need to taste.

She didn't smile—not at first. Her eyes held a flicker of something he'd seen that night in the library.

"Dominic," she said, "Tristan promised me you're the only guest he invited."

"I'm honored."

Her gaze slid down to the gift under his arm.

"This is for you." He offered her the box tied with a satin ribbon. "Happy birthday, Tess."

"Thank you," she said as she reached for the gift with both hands.

"Go on and open it, Tess," Tristan urged before stepping away to convene with Mrs. Wells.

Tess stepped over to one of the stuffed chairs before the fire and settled into it. Dom took the one next to it, sitting on the edge, elbows on his knees, fingers laced tight.

He watched her work at the ribbon on the parcel, and his breath got caught somewhere behind his ribs.

It was absurd. He'd faced vandals in his travels, bartered with grave robbers, and traversed crumbling bridges. But none of that had made his palms itch like they did now as he watched Tess open her gift.

When she edged the lid of the box free, she stilled as she looked inside.

He couldn't read her expression, but she seemed to be holding her breath too.

Then she lifted the leather case out gently, settled it on her lap, and opened it to reveal the tools nestled inside.

"A field set," she said, her voice breathy and low. "But not just any set. This is . . ." She lifted a brush, its mahogany handle polished and smooth. "This is beautiful."

Dom cleared his throat, trying to breathe steadily. "I had it assembled by a gentleman in London, who engraved each piece for you."

Tess lifted the trowel, noting her initials engraved on the brass collar between the blade and the handle.

"I thought you should have your own set rather than being forced to use my blunt old tools, and I wanted you to have the best."

"It's perfect." Her smile lit up the whole room and seemed to ignite something within him too.

His heart drummed in his chest. Relief, he told himself, because he'd chosen well, and she was pleased.

But the feelings were more potent than that. A bit terrifying. What he felt was new. He'd never belonged to anyone. Never wanted to offer a woman more than charm and pleasure. But when she smiled at him—open and joyful—it felt a bit like she'd taken that shiny new trowel of hers and carved her initials on his heart.

"Thank you, Dominic."

He swallowed hard. "You're welcome, Tess."

TESS HAD NEVER RECEIVED a more thoughtful gift in her life, and every time she looked at the man who'd chosen it for her, she felt a blush warm her cheeks.

In that moment before the fire, she'd wanted to touch Dominic. No, she'd wanted more than that. She'd wanted to kiss him. Again.

Not just because he'd given her something precious, but because the gift proved that he saw her aspirations and thought her capable of achieving them.

After dinner and cake, Tristan stood to complete the mortifying birthday tradition of writing ridiculous poems about each other.

He stood, cleared his throat dramatically, plucked a piece of paper from atop the mantel, and began.

"Here's to Tess, my dearest pest, who once declared—at age four—she'd dig up Romans by the score."

Mrs. Wells clapped at that and winked at Tess.

"She knows her kings," Tristan continued, "from Aethelred to the single one who lost his head. May your cake be sweet, your toes never cold. Now you're another year closer to old."

Dominic applauded and burst into deep, booming laughter that Tess felt echo in her chest. She laughed too, and then harder once she saw how much the poem amused him.

Tristan took a bow and then another as if he stood before an adoring audience at the Drury Lane theater.

Mrs. Wells, who'd applauded him the most fervently, stood and began collecting plates and glasses. Tess got up to help her.

"'Tis a full moon tonight, Tess," Mrs. Wells said as they carried the dishes into the kitchen. "Fine night for a wee walk, wouldn't you say? Mayhap to the sacred tree."

A week ago, Tess would have balked at the suggestion that she go out into a cloudless night for a wander with a dangerously handsome man. But now she craved a moment alone with Dominic, and Mrs. Wells had suggested a spot that Tess suspected he would find as interesting as she did.

"Would you join me for a walk, Dominic?"

He stood and shot her a surprised look. "I'd love to."

Mrs. Wells made a little sound of satisfaction, and Tess went to the threshold, where Dominic soon joined her.

For a while, they walked in silence, close enough that their arms brushed.

"I think you'll like this spot I plan to take you to," Tess finally said.

"I'd enjoy being with you even if we had no destination in mind."

Tess said nothing in reply. She didn't dare, for if she did, whatever this spark was between them would certainly blaze. And the thought of it, as tantalizing as the prospect was, made something tighten in her chest.

She reminded herself that he wasn't the other man who'd

hurt her. He'd proven that with his thoughtfulness, by abiding by her insistence that they treat each other in a professional manner, and by never mentioning the kiss that was seared in her mind.

"Tell me about your sisters," she said to stop herself from ruminating and because she wanted to know about his life back in London.

He glanced at her. "Well, they're quite remiss, for one thing. I'm sorry to say that neither writes me a poem for me on my birthday."

Tess chuckled.

"But they're each special in their own way. Eve is clever and confident in her abilities, and she's the most even-tempered of all of us. She keeps the peace. It's hard to truly rile her."

"And the other?"

"Allie is clever too. Fiercely loyal. Almost dangerously inquisitive."

"Is a curious lady a dangerous thing?"

"Not in my opinion, but she took some risks last year while Eve and I were here that I wish she had not."

"Was she injured?"

He tipped a look her way and smiled. "No, thank goodness. It turned out well. In the end, she got a husband and wrote a book."

Tess smiled, then pointed toward the tree in the distance. "There it is."

The yew stood next to the ruins of what had once been a monastery, and perhaps, long before that, a site of pagan worship and ritual. Its long, gnarled limbs stretched wide, heavy with evergreen leaves.

"Good God, that trunk could fit a small cottage," Dominic said, awestruck.

She could sense his excitement. The same she always experienced when approaching this tree that felt sacred in its ancient steadiness.

"Some say it's stood here two thousand years."

As they approached, Tess noted that the air felt cooler near the tree and oddly hushed. One couldn't help but feel the need to show respect for such an elder, the keeper of so many secrets.

"This is the most extraordinary part," she said, lowering her voice to show the aged sentinel reverence. She knelt at the base of the tree.

"A hollow," Dominic murmured, as he knelt down beside her, his thigh touching hers.

"They say it's a wishing hollow," Tess told him, then gestured toward the interior. "See there. Those markings have always looked as if they might be runes to me."

Dom bent to look inside. Even with the bright summer moonlight, the hollow was obscured in darkness. He ran his fingers over the spot she indicated then glanced back at her. "If they are, this yew has stood watch here for many centuries." A smile curved his lips. "An extraordinary thing."

"I knew you'd appreciate it," Tess said with an answering smile. "But the tree has done more than merely stand watch. It's listened too. They say if you press your hand inside the hollow on the full moon and whisper a wish, it will come true."

"Have you ever told it one of your wishes?" he asked softly.

"Yes, a few times."

For a moment, Dominic watched her so intently that she felt herself listing toward him, just as she had in the Walcotts' library.

He leaned nearer too. She could feel the warmth of his breath against her skin. It was coming fast. Just like hers.

"What did you wish for, Tess?"

If she angled an inch closer, she could kiss him as she'd thought of doing back at Foxdene. As she'd thought of so many times since that first kiss.

The breeze blew a loose strand of hair across her face, and he reached up to sweep it back, tucking it gently behind her ear.

"You can't tell your wish to anyone. If you do, it won't come true." Tess looked toward the tree, watching the sway of its heavy limbs, trying to steady the racing thud of her heartbeat. His nearness made her chest tight, not out of fear, but as if all the yearning inside her was too much to contain.

Yes, she'd told her silly, youthful wishes to the tree. Always some version of the same one: a wish to find love. A wish she now kept at bay with rational thoughts and work and the meticulous cataloging of old things.

The last time she'd given her heart, it had cost her that youthful hopefulness.

Yet this man, so appealing he made her mouth water, touched her with such gentleness that it undid her as surely as that one delicious kiss had.

"Shall I make a wish?" he whispered.

"Yes." Tess reached for his hand, and he immediately clasped hers. She bent forward, guiding him toward the tree's hollow. He flattened his palm against the bark, and she held her hand over his.

"You must whisper it," she told him, then stood and took a few steps back.

He looked at her over his shoulder, a little smile tipping the edge of his mouth. Then he bent toward the tree and murmured something low and deep against the hollow.

She was insatiably curious about his wish, of course, but she would keep to the tradition of secrecy.

Dominic stood and dusted off his hands, then he joined her to begin the walk back.

"Did your wishes come true?" he asked as they left the shelter of the yew tree's sweeping branches.

Tess shook her head. "But you'll have to tell me if yours does." As she looked over at him, she stumbled the next step and he reached for her.

When they started off again, he shifted closer and offered his arm as a gentleman would when strolling through a London park. Tess only hesitated a moment before she took it, letting herself relish his nearness and the shift of hard muscles where she touched him.

He tipped his head toward hers and whispered in a low voice, "If my wish comes true, Tess, you'll know it."

Chapter Eleven

Six days later

After twelve days of work, from sunup to sunset, barring their one rained-out day, their rotating crew of men from the local village had made excellent progress.

Dom stood at the edge of the wide trench they'd dug and swiped sweat from his brow. He couldn't keep his eyes off Tess, who'd crouched down at the lowest point amidst the grid they'd laid out. When she'd returned from her visit to Fenbridge this morning, she'd been anxious, almost vibrating with eagerness to get started again.

Over the course of the previous day, they'd found some bits of metal, what Dom suspected was part of a sword, and Tess had detected further changes in the soil. The object that had been sunk in the ground was sizable, based on the pattern of darker soil. Every sign indicated they were getting closer to something of significance.

Unfortunately, they'd also found evidence that they weren't the first to dig into the mound in an attempt to extract treasure. They could see that the robbers' trenches weren't as deep as Dom, Tess, Tristan, and the crew they'd assembled were prepared to dig.

Tess glanced up and Dom flicked his gaze away, loath to be caught staring at her legs and backside—again. Even after nearly two weeks of working with her side by side for much of the day, he found her presence, and her long legs in her very practical trousers, damnably distracting.

"Can you come down here?" she called.

He started off immediately, careful to tread on the boards of wood they'd laid out.

When he got closer, he could see the excited glint in her eyes and the little smile edging up the side of her mouth.

"There's something here."

He squatted down in front of the spot she indicated, noting the spot's distance from the other objects they'd found. She'd carved around her discovery and a hint of metal could be seen through the hard-packed dirt around it.

"I . . ." She swiped her brush from the set he'd given her across the edge gently, then lifted her eyes, as green as the fields around them, up to him. "I think it's gold, Dominic."

His gut clenched. His mouth went dry. His heart began a wild thud in his chest.

It seemed too soon, and at too high a level in the soil, to be anything of significance, but one of the robbers' trenches might have shifted something. They could have churned up items as they dug and yet not discovered them.

"Don't stop," he urged, for her movements had grown slow, almost reverent. He still wasn't convinced. He needed to see it uncovered, cleaned off, and in the bright light of day.

She seemed to be holding her breath as she swept the brush over it again and a piece of crusted earth shifted, revealing a deep, rich red circle that glowed in the sunlight. Like a cabochon. Garnet, he guessed. Possibly a ruby or even a spinel like the one in the imperial crown.

"Breathe, Tess. You've found something for certain. Let's see more of it."

As more dirt fell away, it became clear that the object was

only a broken piece. Perhaps it truly had been struck and damaged and then tossed to higher soil by a robber's shovel decades or even centuries ago.

"Perhaps it's nothing more than someone's lost brooch," she said, a hint of doubt creeping into her tone. "Medieval, do you think?"

She held the broken piece in her hand and offered it up to him.

He pointed with his pinky finger at the edge, still obscured with crusted soil. "Can you clear this bit away?"

When she did, excitement welled inside him like a basin overflowing, and he beamed at her, only barely resisting the urge to sweep her up into his arms.

"That's not medieval. The knotwork, the setting of the gem. This is what we're looking for." He pointed at the edge, which was entirely filled by engraved spirals and interweaving knots. "This style . . . There's an Anglo-Saxon cross in a churchyard in Cumbria with almost the exact same style."

"The Bewcastle Cross. I've never been as far north as Cumbria, but my father had been. He made sketches of it."

"I wish I could take you." The words were out before Dom could think better of it. "You'd find it fascinating," he added, to temper the idea that he wanted to travel with her.

Never mind that he had such thoughts more and more as he lay in his bed at the inn and pondered the days spent with her. He wasn't certain where his next expedition would take him, but whenever he mused on it, Tess would be there with him. Tempting him. Distracting him. Letting him taste her and pleasure her and lose himself inside her.

"Dominic? Where did you go?" she asked in a bemused tone.

He closed his eyes a moment to shake the erotic thoughts

away and then opened his eyes to find her watching him with naked curiosity.

"Woolgathering." He gestured toward the piece of gold in her hand. "Now that we know we're on the right track, we will only find more the farther we go, don't you think?"

Rather than answer him, she got lost studying the object she'd found. She cradled it in the palm of her hand, no bigger than a postage stamp, and used the brush to dust away a bit more soil.

"What do you think it could be?" She looked up at him, flashing a grin.

That simple blink of a smile made his mouth water. That one kiss they'd shared haunted his nights, but it wasn't nearly enough.

He forced himself to focus on their find. Good grief, it was why he was here, and yet the thrill of what it portended didn't feel nearly as powerful as whatever was between him and Tess Hawthorne. Or could be, if she'd let herself have it.

"It's hard to say." The piece was small enough that it could have formed part of a decorative element on any number of objects. "Perhaps a bracelet, or part of a buckle or breastplate. This is a burial trove, presumably, and there might be many decorated elements."

"I wish we could find the rest," she said longingly. "I wonder how much of what's below has been damaged by robber trenches."

"There's only one way to find out." Dom suspected this find was a false lead in terms of its depth, but it was also an indicator that they were digging into a hoard that would ensure his reputation and become the highlight of Van Arsdale's museum.

That treasure-hunting intuition he'd had about this place,

and that he and Eve got a hint of the previous autumn, was proving true.

"We keep digging," Tess said as she looked down the length of the long trench they'd already carved out of Fenbridge's land.

One of the village men seemed to catch her eye and stood to wave his arm and draw them both over.

"Found something," he shouted.

"What is it, Bromley?" The man was one of their most determined workers, though Tess had stressed the importance of keeping him and Tristan a healthy distance apart when they were at the dig site together.

"Found more than one," another village man named Townsend put in.

Bill Bromley deposited an object encrusted in compacted soil that had the shape of a very large pin, almost like a nail. It reminded Dom of spikes he'd seen used on the construction of a railroad line.

"Where?" Dom asked him.

Tristan approached with a clipboard and the drawings with measurements that he'd made and updated each day of the dig.

He eyed Bromley warily and then focused on Dom. "Here, here, and two others approximately equidistant on either side."

"Equidistant," Tess repeated.

Dom's hand shook a bit as he reached for Tristan's drawing, then mentally sketched out what he imagined they might have stumbled upon. "We need to widen the trench," he told them. "Tess, where did you find the soil changes?"

She stepped forward, running her finger along the same line where they'd found the spike-like objects.

"Rivets," Dom breathed, then looked at each of them in

turn. "I think . . . we may have found rivets. And if we did, there will be more to find."

"What are you thinking?" Tess asked. But before he could answer, her gaze snapped wide. "A ship?"

"Maybe."

"And being so close to the river, entirely possible," Tess said. Dom could all but hear her mind churning. "Some prince or king of East Anglia might merit such a burial. The Venerable Bede mentions a King Raedwald and his sons Eorpwald and Sigeberht. Could we have found the resting place of one of those kings?"

"I don't know. We keep digging and find out. And we breathe not a word of this to anyone until our hypothesis is confirmed." Dom shot a look at Tristan. "Let's double security on the site overnight."

"Should we find a dragon to sit atop it too?" Tristan quipped.

"Not quite the level of subtlety I had in mind," Dom told him. "But there's never been more reason to estimate the worth of what we may yet find."

"Won't be easy to gather extra men tonight," Bromley put in.

"Why's that?" Dom would double their wages if needed. Van Arsdale had paid generously for this dig and wouldn't wish to lose any of it.

"The village fair," Tess and Tristan replied in near unison.

"I'll stay," Townsend offered. "I can find another to do the same. The fair goes on for days. Won't mind missing the first night."

"Good. Thank you." Dom waited until Bromley and Townsend departed to turn to Tristan. "We could hire more men too, if you're able to gather them. The faster what's below us is found, the faster—"

"We fill an American museum and you can go on to further fortune and glory," Tristan quipped with his usual easy smile, though there was a bite to his words, highlighted by a knowing glance Tess's way.

Dom found it hard to meet Tess's gaze, but when he finally did, what he saw there cut through him like a blade.

"I'll go and make my notes before heading to the fair," Tristan said. "I'll see you there, Tess?"

She nodded but said nothing as her twin departed.

"I'm sorry . . ." Dom started but hesitated to say more. He realized he had more than one thing to apologize for. They'd still avoided any mention of the kiss, which suggested she regretted it. That ate at him, especially considering that a day didn't pass when he didn't wish to kiss her again.

"For what?" She shrugged and hugged her arms around her body. "You were never dishonest. We both knew who was funding all of this and why."

"I understand why it rankles that whatever we find will leave England."

She frowned. "Do you really care, Dominic?"

God, he loved the sound of his name on her tongue. The first few times she had said it, a lump had formed in his throat. But now the lump was there because he foresaw how she would come to resent him at the end of all this—when he handed the hoard over to Van Arsdale.

Even if she needed the payment the American offered, the reality of seeing all their hard work and discoveries shipped across the ocean would displease her. Hurt her. He didn't know how he'd abide that.

She'd asked him to tell her the truth all those nights ago in the carriage.

"I care because you care." *I care because you matter to me more than you sensibly should.*

She bit her lip but said nothing. "Will I see you at the fair?"

"May I escort you?" He'd been longing for a chance to spend time with her again, beyond the dig site.

"No," she said quickly. "I'll be helping Mrs. Wells, but if you go, I'm sure I'll see you there."

It was as much of a dismissal as he'd ever had from a lady, but no other lady had ever gotten under his skin as she had.

He watched as she gathered her things and prepared to head off to Foxdene. She surprised him by striding back toward him again.

"What should I do with this?" she asked, revealing the piece of gold and garnet she'd found, still sheltered in her hand.

"Do you have some place you can lock it up at Foxdene?"

"You trust me with it?"

"Of course. I trust you entirely, Tess." He could hardly confess how much he wanted that trust returned. Earning it had become his deepest wish—one he'd whispered at the wishing hollow—especially after what her brother had revealed of Tess's heartbreak.

If he could lay hands on whatever rotter hurt her, he'd be more than happy to break him.

"I'll see you tonight," she said, and then rushed off before he could say more.

Even as they'd worked together the past days, when they'd taken that night under a full moon, and today when she'd found the first real sign of the treasure yet to come, he'd sensed a hesitancy in her. A wariness.

He'd never been more determined to win a woman's trust. The hell of it was, he'd never wanted a woman as much either.

Tess favored the village fair in the spring. There was one held in autumn too, and it had once been her favorite—how could one not adore apple cider and pumpkin scones and the smell of crushed fall leaves?

But the autumn fair had been where she'd met Mr. Shaw, and when the spring fair came around the following year, it had been such a bright spot. All the vibrant flowers and fruits had held a promise of a fresh start. A new beginning, even for a feckless young woman with a broken heart.

So the spring fair was her favorite now, and she relished helping Mrs. Wells set up her booth and prepare the treats she offered each season.

But after she'd assisted Mrs. Wells, she approached the main street of the village. Others had already gathered to prepare their offerings and then enjoy the evening's bonfire that would be lit in the field at the edge of town. Tess couldn't help remembering that autumn night years ago and how eager she'd been to fall in love.

And now, despite everything she knew, despite all the rules she'd made for herself, and all the ways she planned to protect her heart, she found herself looking for Dominic.

Whatever she'd thought she found in Shaw was nothing to what she felt every time she looked into Dominic Prince's eyes. His scent, his nearness made her heart race, made her blood feel like syrup in her veins. And in the past days she'd found herself wanting to believe in happily ever after again.

But it only proved she was still that foolish girl.

Nothing about a man like Dominic suggested he was at all interested in ever after or love or any sort of commitment beyond a few nights of passion.

And a seductive and all too brazen voice in her head had begun to ask whether that might be enough this time.

A few nights of passion with a man who made her feel beautiful and desired and who didn't make false promises of anything else.

Could she give herself that? Could she keep her heart from breaking when he left Norfolk?

"I haven't seen you in far too long, Tess." Bill Bromley's wife, Sarah, drew up beside her with a basket full of fresh strawberries.

"Sarah, goodness, I've missed you." Tess smiled and fell into step beside her friend. "Are you at the far edge of the fairgrounds again this year?"

"I am. Will you walk down with me? I could use a hand with Benedict. That boy has a frightening propensity for wandering and a nose for getting into mischief."

Tess laughed. She could just spot the dark-haired boy in the distance, helping his father to assemble their booth.

"So you don't recommend motherhood then?" Tess asked teasingly and with a glance down at Sarah's growing belly.

"I recommend it wholeheartedly, just with the warning that you'll be run off your feet if you happen to have a five-year-old like Benedict."

"Duly noted." Tess had always wanted a family, a husband, children. After all that had happened, she'd wondered if any of the men in the village would ever consider her. It was well known that she'd done more than steal a few kisses with Alister Shaw.

And what if she gave in to her longing for Dominic and that were discovered?

"George Faircross mentioned that he hoped to dance with you at the bonfire tonight," Sarah told her with a wink as if reading Tess's thoughts.

"Did he? He might have waited and said as much to me."

"Oh, he's Bill's closest mate. He meant no harm by expressing his regard for you." Sarah nudged her playfully with her elbow. "He's not the only gent in the village who does—"

Sarah had stopped walking and stared off in the distance. Tess followed her line of sight and her heart began a wild tattoo.

"Is that him?" Sarah whispered as if he might overhear, despite the fact that he was far across the field and still striding toward them. "He's the talk of the town."

"If you mean Mr. Prince, that's him."

"Mercy, I can understand why they're all buzzing like hungry bees. And Bill says he's affable and kind and pays well too." Sarah turned and eyed Tess thoughtfully. "What do you make of him?"

"I'm still assessing." Though he was half a field away, Tess felt his gaze on her.

"Do let me know what you decide," Sarah said cheekily, continuing to watch Dominic's approach, and when he was almost within earshot, she whispered, "It certainly seems as if he's decided on you, Tess."

Indeed, as he stepped closer, his mouth tipped up in one of those grins of his. Though he flicked his gaze down a moment, still smiling, as if amused by how boldly they watched him.

"Good evening, ladies," he said smoothly as he drew up in front of them.

"Mr. Prince, this is Sarah Bromley. Bill's wife."

He took her hand and gave a little bow over it like a nobleman at a ball. "Very pleased to meet you, Mrs. Bromley. Your husband is an incredibly helpful man."

Sarah chuckled. "That's one way to describe him. He has nothing but approbation for you as well, Mr. Prince."

"Then he's very kind too."

Sarah smiled, clearly charmed, and Tess knew her to be a woman who wasn't easily taken in. "You must both excuse me. I was meant to get these strawberries to our stall by now, and heaven knows Benedict will have run Bill ragged."

She turned so that Dominic could not see her and gave Tess a wink.

Tess resisted groaning at her friend's clear glee at leaving her with a dangerously handsome man. Had Sarah forgotten everything?

"I found you." He spoke the words quietly, his voice deep, and somehow they echoed in Tess's chest.

"Yes." She breathed the word and let something in herself loosen.

He stepped closer, and she didn't retreat.

The tension had been building between them since the Walcott party. Not a day had passed when she hadn't thought of kissing him. Not a night passed when she didn't think of him lying alone in his bed at the inn.

She felt as if she was on the edge of a precipice. At her back was a past she wanted to be free of and regrets she wanted to release. Before her was the most tempting man she'd ever met. A man who could lead to even more regrets if she wasn't careful.

Chapter Twelve

Half a dozen men assessed Dom as he proceeded down the row of stalls being assembled for the upcoming village fair. Some took his measure, others shot him jealous glances before more lingering longing ones turned Tess's way.

He couldn't blame a single one of them.

The simple act of escorting her as she pointed out various items of interest gave him an immense feeling of satisfaction. It was a strange sensation. Rarely did he seek feminine accompaniment for anything as simple as a walk.

Yet having Tess at his side, chatting and brushing against him now and then, was enthralling. He enjoyed her nearness. Her voice. Her clear care and appreciation for others in her village.

He felt a swell of pride at being the one beside her. Perhaps because she hadn't sought him out or spoken to him for any other purpose than work in nearly a week. He'd been hungry for this—merely spending time with her.

As the sun set and dusk spread over Wiggenstow, he sensed the villagers' eagerness for the coming bonfire. Everyone seemed to be abandoning the main thoroughfare and moving toward the fields at the far end of town. All except for one gent, who'd passed them twice as they walked and now approached with purposeful strides.

"Pardon me, Tess," he called, stopping their progress.

"Hello, George. How've you been?"

"Very well." He flicked a look Dom's way, then immediately focused all of his interest on Tess. His very ardent interest.

"Looking forward to the bonfire?" she prompted when he said nothing more.

"Indeed, I am, but more so if you'd dance with me."

Dom stiffened, but the young man seemed oblivious. He watched Tess for any sign of acceptance.

"Thank you, George. I'd like that."

Dom bristled, but George, whoever the hell he was, looked over the moon.

"I'll see you there," she told him, her tone more polite than eager.

"You will. Until then." The man didn't seem quite sure what to do as a leave-taking. He raised a hand as if he might reach for her, but Dom instinctively took a single step forward, which stalled the man with his hand in midair.

Then he sketched an awkward half bow, cast a beaming grin at Tess, and scurried off.

"I suppose we should head toward the bonfire," she said once her suitor disappeared from view.

Dom was only willing to go if he could throw George what's-his-name into said bonfire.

She started walking and then turned back to Dom. He couldn't help it. He was stuck there, scowling after the man who'd wheedled a dance out of Tess.

"You're glowering quite fiercely, Dominic."

He sighed, lifting his brows. "Forgive me. I didn't expect to be so unnerved by another asking you to dance. Though I understand the man's enthusiasm."

She pressed her lips together and strode back toward him. So close, he wanted to reach for her, hold her.

"I should have asked you to dance," he said with a rueful smile.

"You still can."

"Dance with me." *And not bloody George.*

Tess stunned him by taking another step closer. Scandalously close. Her bosom brushed his chest. The skirt of the dress she'd changed into pressed against his legs. It still wasn't close enough.

"I have to dance with George first," she said quietly.

"Lucky George."

A chuckle bubbled out of her. "I was being polite." She nibbled at her lower lip a moment. "And you hadn't asked me, so I didn't have a good excuse."

"Then I'm a fool." Dom dipped his head, a hairsbreadth from kissing her. "I won't make that mistake again."

She drew in a breath, flicked her gaze down to his lips. "So you'll claim me for the rest of the night?"

Dom's own breath snagged in his chest. Blood thrummed in his ears. With that one seductive question, she'd made his cock hard and his mind go blank.

"For dancing," she clarified with an alluring smile, as if she understood just how much she'd stunned him.

That allowed a bit of the blood to return to his brain. But he was still shocked. Delightfully so. Was Tess Hawthorne . . . seducing him?

The prospect made his mouth water.

"I'd claim you every night of the week if I had my way," he told her quietly, aware that their nearness was beginning to attract notice.

Not that he gave a damn about anything but whatever was happening between them.

"Dancing every night of the week?" she teased.

"Mmm." Dom bent down a bit further to whisper in her ear. "I'd devote myself to you for any purpose you pleased."

This close, he felt the tremor that rocked through her at his words. But it also seemed to break the extraordinary moment between them.

She took a step back, and then another. Her eyes had widened. Her breath came fast.

"I must go . . . dance with George."

Dom groaned. "Can I at least escort you?" It was a question he'd asked just a few hours ago, prompting an immediate refusal.

But not this time. She nodded, even reached for him, wrapping her arm around his as they had the night of her birthday, as if they were setting out on a chaperoned walk in a London park. But tonight she held onto him tighter than propriety would ever allow, as if he might steady her.

"Are you all right, Tess?" he whispered.

She shot him an odd look. "After I dance with George, I have a question for you."

Dom dared to place his bare hand over hers where she held onto his arm. "Of course. You can ask me anything. I'll look forward to it." And grit his teeth while he watched her dance with that damned blighter, George.

Tess barely heard the music and all but forgot the steps as she danced around the bonfire with her hand clasped in George Faircross's.

As they weaved and turned, she sought a sight of Dominic.

Every time she spotted him standing among those gathered to watch the dancers, his chiseled features gilded in fire glow, her body hummed with a wild hunger for him. Each glimpse of him sparked a warm fizz in her blood, a pulsing need in her core.

It was as if she'd plucked at a bit of ribbon, tugged ever so slightly, and now the whole knot of control she'd kept over herself—her passions and yearnings—had begun to unravel. And she remembered now how fierce and powerful that part of her was. She didn't want to repress it anymore. She didn't want to deny herself or the desire she felt for the first time in such a long while.

This isn't the same. She repeated that to herself like a vow. If she gave in to her feelings for Dominic, it wouldn't be the same. She was going into every moment of it with her eyes open. Not naive and gullible. She was older, wiser, and willing to set rules and boundaries.

It's why she needed to speak to him. She needed to know what the parameters would be. If they could agree to expectations and outcomes, then she could give herself to this . . . hunger without fear that she'd lose herself again. Lose her heart again.

George pulled one way as Tess's body tried to go the other, and she smiled apologetically at him.

Then, past his shoulder, she noticed Dominic and Priscilla Walcott standing next to each other. She smiled as she said something to him, but he only spared her a glance before turning his attention back to Tess.

That was heady. They'd shared nothing but one kiss and yet the attraction they shared was palpable, and she was thrilled at the proof that it was entirely mutual.

When the guitarist and flutist brought the song to an end, Tess offered George a dutiful thanks for the dance.

"Shall we go again?" he asked eagerly.

"No." She tried for a soft tone. "I'm promised for the next dance."

Like an arrow shot straight and true, he turned and pinned Dominic with a look.

"Hope he treats you right, Tess," George told her, his voice tight, his gaze still locked on Dominic. Then he turned to her with a pitying look in his eyes. "Not like the other one."

Tess gritted her teeth and suddenly felt very much like Tristan because suddenly all she could think about was punching George Faircross in the nose.

"Thank you for your concern." She spun on her heel and beelined straight for Dominic.

Priscilla, standing at his elbow, offered Tess a smile in greeting. "Miss Hawthorne."

"Miss Walcott," Tess said with a smile and a nod, but all of her attention was truly on Dominic, as his was on her. He lifted his hand out as she approached.

"Ready for our dance?" he asked warmly.

"I am." She slid her hand into his, and felt a shot of heat up her arm when he clasped it tight, stroking his thumb inside the cup of her palm. "Excuse us," she told Priscilla.

"Enjoy your dance." Priscilla shifted her glance between the two of them and strode off to the food stalls.

Tess led Dominic through the gaggle that had gathered for the bonfire. A few offered them cider, but Tess shook her head and kept moving farther into the field.

They were moving away from the dancing, away from the bonfire, but Dominic didn't seem to mind.

She pressed closer to him as they walked, and he slid his free arm around her waist.

"Don't you wonder where I'm taking you?"

"I'd follow you anywhere." He glanced over his shoulder. "Though people may talk."

"Of course they will." She looked up at him, feeling freer than she had in years. "They already talk about me. I'm a siren in some people's eyes."

"You are a siren." His voice had dropped to that husky murmur that made her shiver.

"Over here there's a bit of privacy." A few more steps and they were in an old apple orchard with trees covered in apple blossoms. The scent was almost as heady as the spice and orange of his shaving soap.

"Why do we need privacy?" he asked her.

Tess stopped when they were far enough in to be unseen and stepped close to him, a hand on his chest. She pushed gently and he immediately understood and backed himself up against the wide trunk of a tree.

She leaned into him, let him take her weight, and he lashed an arm around her waist to pull her flush against him. Tipping her head, she studied his face in the moonlight.

He seemed almost pained, tense, waiting for what came next.

"Tess," he murmured, sliding his hand down to her lower back, then hesitating.

He was allowing her to guide him, to lead, and it seemed to cost him as his breath gusted fast against her skin.

Skimming her hand up his chest, she relished the heat of him, the hard muscles, the thrum of his heartbeat. Then she curled her hand around his nape and arched up to kiss him.

He groaned at the first taste, growled as she stroked her tongue against his.

"I've wanted to do that for a week," she whispered against his mouth.

"Same." He took her mouth, cupped her backside and pulled her closer, letting her feel how hard and eager he was for her. "Every damn night, I dream of you," he admitted breathlessly. He took her lower lip between his teeth, then soothed the spot with his tongue.

Tess bucked against him, shocking herself into pulling back.

"Tess," he groaned when she pulled away. He then ran a hand across his mouth and studied her in the moonlight. "Does this mean I've grown in your estimation? That you've finally decided I'm not a scoundrel?"

"Oh, I know you're a scoundrel," she teased with a smile, "but you're a kind one. An honest one."

"You've asked me for that, and I won't ever lie to you, Tess."

"Thank you."

He bent his head to kiss her again, but she stayed him with a hand against the hard plane of his muscled chest.

"Though I'm not sure I'll ever forgive you for what you did to those books at Lady Goddard's."

He hung his head and slumped his shoulders a moment before offering her a contrite look—or as contrite as a man like him could manage after she'd just divulged how much she wanted him.

"I was in a foul mood that day."

"Why? You seemed quite jovial." An image came to her of that moment when he'd descended the stairs in Lady Goddard's library and then shamelessly flirted with her.

"If I seemed anything other than grumpish, it was because you'd walked into the room."

"You needn't charm me." Tess pushed gently against him again. "Tell me why you were in a foul mood."

She watched as he seemed to weigh what to say, or how much to divulge, even as he'd just vowed to tell her the truth.

"Lady Goddard had . . . propositioned me previously."

Tess recalled how peeved the lady had been to find he'd departed. "That explains a great deal." Tess swallowed and ran her fingers along the buttons of his shirt. "Though I can hardly judge her, considering."

"I cast no judgement on her either. Indeed, I admired her boldness. But it was not something I wished to pursue, nor did I wish to have another such discussion and disappoint her again on that visit."

"So, you're selective as to your . . . lovers?"

He barked out a sharp laugh. "I suppose my reputation would suggest otherwise."

"Are you not fond of your reputation?"

He held her gaze a long moment before answering. "In the past I was. My father was shameless, and I thought I should be too."

"And now?" Tess noticed his jaw had tensed. She lifted her hand and dared to draw her finger along that sharp line.

He grasped her hand in his. She thought he meant to push her touch away. Instead, he laid a kiss against her knuckles and stroked his thumb against her palm.

"I'm not sure I've sorted it out myself."

"You needn't tell me. Honesty doesn't mean we have to declare every thought in our head."

After staring down at the spot where he stroked her palm, he looked up at her again.

"I . . . lost someone who was a genuine friend to me, and now chasing after my father's shadow feels hollow in a way it didn't before." He shook his head and his lips quirked in a rueful grin. "You've brought this out in me, you know? This tendency toward awkward confessions."

"There's no shame in wanting something different for yourself. Tristan and I wanted to be like our father too, studious and history-obsessed, but he encouraged us to be true to ourselves first and foremost."

"Your father sounds like a very good man." He swallowed hard and drew in a sharp breath. "Perhaps it's not wrong to choose something else, but I've wanted to emulate my own father for so long. Any detour from that path feels odd. Ill-fitting."

"Are you afraid of disappointing him?"

"Perhaps. I only know that the more I try to shed his influence, the more odd I feel."

"Does what's between us feel . . . odd?" Tess asked, curious about this man who lived up to everything written about him in the papers, yet at the same time was so completely different.

"God, no." He pulled her closer without hesitation, cupping her cheek, tucking a stray strand of hair behind her ear. "Every day close to you feels . . ."

He trailed off, and Tess leaned in, her breasts brushing the heat of his chest. "Feels?" she prompted.

"You'll say I'm trying to charm you."

"Tell me."

"It feels like a gift." His fingers traced lightly along her jaw, mirroring the way she'd touched him. "Every day that I wake up knowing I'll get to spend my hours with you feels as if I've won some grand prize."

"Oh." Tess didn't know what to say. But her heart, fluttering, twisting, dancing in a way that made her breath catch, did. He wasn't making promises. He wasn't asking for anything. And somehow, that made his raw confession all the more powerful.

"Did I shock you?" he asked softly.

"A little," she admitted. "You surprise me. Continually."

"I hope that's a good thing." He seemed anxious for her reply. "Is it?"

Who was this man who kissed like the scoundrel he was widely known to be and yet spoke to her with such earnestness and vulnerability too?

Chapter Thirteen

Ladies had rarely found him surprising. He played his role so well, and they appreciated that he was precisely as billed. A talented lover. A relentless treasure seeker. A man who'd ask nothing of them, take nothing from them, and yet leave them thoroughly satisfied.

Tess declaring that he surprised her, continually, shot a twist of worry to his gut.

He'd told her the unvarnished truth. Since Peter's death, he'd begun yearning to be something beyond his father's protégé and successor. How had he ever thought it was enough to become a facsimile of a man who, in the end, he'd resented for his falsehoods to Dom's mother, to his patrons, to everyone?

Meeting Tess had only intensified the yearning for more. For her, he didn't want to play a role, or tell her wild tales of his adventures, or seduce her with the intention of having her and then leaving as soon as he was able.

For the first time in as long as he could remember, he felt no urgency to move on to the next exploit or treasure hunt. And it had nothing to do with what they would or would not find in Fenbridge's field. It had everything to do with the lush, lovely woman who'd led him to a sweet-scented orchard and kissed him with an ardent need that made him confess things to her.

"You should not worry," she told him after studying his face in the silver moon's glow. "It's a very good thing."

She seemed to notice how his gaze kept slipping down to her lips. He needed to kiss her again.

"I want to kiss you too, Dominic," she whispered.

Without a moment's hesitation, he bent closer.

She braced a slim hand against the center of his chest and held herself back. "But we must talk first."

"More talking?" He'd already revealed the tangled mess his thoughts had devolved into these past days. What must she think of his confession that he wasn't the man he'd long thought he was?

"Yes." Tess created an inch of space between them, then another, though she didn't step out of his embrace entirely. "I got carried away."

He chuckled at the lovely admission.

"Please feel free to do that often," he urged.

"First, we need rules."

He frowned. "Rules?"

Tess took a deep breath as if trying to untangle her own thoughts. "Perhaps clarity is a better word. Or parameters."

"Parameters."

"Mmm." She nodded as she drew a step closer, her hand still a soothing point of connection against his chest. "If we're to be . . . lovers, I need to know what it will entail, how long it will last, and what will happen when it's done."

He started to smile but then smoothed his features. "You want to know what you're getting into."

"Yes. The limits of it. The shape of it." As she said the last word, her body shifted against his, and she blushed in the darkness at the unintended innuendo.

"Should there be limits to what we do?" He didn't like the sound of that. "Do you mean how often we . . ."

Tess shook her head. "No, that's not what I mean. First, let's begin by you telling me what you want out of this."

He couldn't hold back his grin. If he told her everything he wanted, he'd shock her. But the lovely siren had asked for him to be honest. "I want to kiss every inch of your body, learn all the ways you like to be touched, and pleasure you until you scream my name." His voice dropped lower as desire rocked through him. "And then I want to do it again and again until you're bonelessly sated."

Tess swallowed hard. "I s-see."

"Tell me what you want," he whispered, stroking his knuckles against the edge of her cheek. So warm. So soft. What would she say if he admitted he wanted to kiss her each time she looked his way during the course of a day? "Whatever you desire, Tess, that's what I want to give to you."

"Don't overpromise," she told him with mock sternness. Or perhaps there was nothing mock about it. He did note a bit of wariness in her gaze.

Tread carefully, he reminded himself. She'd been hurt. He would never hurt her. He vowed that to himself then and there.

She'd likely been promised the world once before.

"Very well." He bent and kissed her cheek softly. "I promise only to let your wishes be my guide. How's that?"

"What of your wishes? And please speak the truth."

They were far simpler than she seemed to comprehend. "This, right now, having you in my arms," he told her, "is what I've been wishing for since the moment we met."

"I shouted at you the moment we met."

"And yet I still wanted to kiss you."

Tess's chuckle made him feel lighter, and he pulled her closer.

"I want to be your lover, and I will abide by whatever rules you set. That's how much I want you."

"And we'll always be honest with one another?"

"Yes." He hoped the immediacy of his response reassured her.

"We should keep it secret."

He nodded. "We can do that."

"And we should state now that it is temporary."

"I . . ." Dom understood that she did not want to allow herself to hope as she'd likely done in the past. And he'd never shied from declaring the temporary nature of a liaison . . . until this moment.

"You'll leave and it will end," she went on, "and I'd rather state it clearly now."

His jaw tightened, but he nodded his agreement. If she wanted it, he'd accede to her wishes.

"After all, this won't be some grand love affair." Tess seemed to try for lightness, but Dom heard the thread of bitterness in her tone.

What had that bastard done to her? He wouldn't ask tonight, wouldn't demand she dredge up that pain in this fragile moment. But he'd be damned if he let it keep her from any kind of pleasure or happiness now.

Dominic loosened his hold on her, unease suddenly overtaking him.

"Have I offended you?" she asked in a way that tugged at something deep inside him.

Reaching out, he barely resisted the urge to pull her close again. Instead, he gently set her at a distance and then stepped away from the tree.

"Dominic, tell me what's wrong."

How could he tell her that what he wanted was to find the rotter who'd hurt her and beat him to a pulp? That he wanted to shower her with affection and soak her in pleasure so thoroughly that whatever still ached inside her would heal? That he didn't want to talk of the ways they'd end when they hadn't even yet begun?

Pacing a small path a few strides away from her and then back again, his boots crushed apple blossoms on the path and the sharp, sweet scent of spring filled the air.

Tess waited patiently.

Not a grand love affair? She deserved a bloody spectacular love affair. And more.

He wanted to give it to her, but it terrified him too. Terrified him that he may not be the man who could give her all she deserved.

But God's teeth, nothing in him could even fathom rejecting this gift she was on the cusp of offering him. Yet even now, he knew he wanted more than just her body.

What she was doing, offering to take him as a lover, took courage when she'd been burned so badly once before. He would prove to her that she could trust again, unleash her passion, declare her desires with someone who would never deceive her. Never hurt her.

Turning, he strode back toward her with renewed purpose. A fiery resolve took hold of him. He strode close enough to feel the warmth of her body, yet he didn't touch her. She was the most potent of distractions, and he wanted to make himself clear.

"I'll abide by your limits and whatever boundaries you wish to set. We can sneak about in secret. We can declare here and now that all of what will happen between us will only last for a time, but . . ." He cupped her cheek in his hand, tipped her head so that he could look into her eyes. "What's between us will be bloody grand. I mean to leave you breathless, Tess, and so damned well-pleasured that you'll be without a single thought in your head except of when I will touch you again."

Tess inched up on her toes as if desperate to kiss him.

He was as eager as she, but he worked to steady his breathing and arched back an inch, his gaze boring into hers. "Your desires will guide me. Your wishes will be respected." He needed her to understand at that moment, at the outset, she would be heard. "I do not take what you're offering lightly. I mean for you to feel cherished, Tess."

He stroked his thumb along the satiny curve of her cheek. "Understood, my siren?"

Tess nodded.

"I want to hear you say it." He swept his hand back to grip her nape, and the anticipation of what they were embarking on made his pulse race.

"I understand—"

Before her words were fully out, he leaned forward and took her mouth. He wasn't gentle. He told himself to be, but he was too hungry for her now. He had been for days. There was no coaxing or kissing her gently. He plundered and feasted and stepped her back all the while, his arm around her waist to keep her from falling.

TESS FELT ALMOST RELIEVED when she finally felt the trunk of the tree at her back because Dominic's drugging kisses made her knees feel like jelly.

His body sheltered hers, but he still wasn't close enough. Tess reached for the placket of his shirt, sliding her fingers inside to get a grip and pull him closer.

But the feel of his warm skin was so tantalizing she began

working his buttons free. She wanted to see him, feel him, without barriers between them.

He took her lead and began working the buttons on her blouse. As soon as the edge of her corset was bared, he broke their kiss to pull back and take it in.

Tess felt a moment of embarrassment that it wasn't a terribly frilly thing, lacy and made to entice. But Dominic ran his fingers along the satin edge almost reverently, as if he'd discovered a treasure and wanted to take his time to savor it.

"Since we're telling each other the truth in all of this," he told her, lifting his attention to her eyes, though he flicked a few glances at her lips, "you should know that I've thought of undressing you a thousand times since we met."

Tess laughed and pushed gently against the tantalizing stretch of skin she'd exposed by freeing a few buttons. "Hyperbole is not allowed."

"All right, perhaps more like three hundred."

"I've thought of it too," she breathed when he inched her corset down to free her aching nipples, though they were still constrained by her chemise.

"Of me undressing you?" he asked and then bent to graze his teeth against her nipple. "Or you undressing me?"

"Both." Tess gasped when he edged the neck of her chemise down and took her aching peak into his mouth.

He was wickedly skilled with his tongue, and every time he swirled it against her, a tremor shot straight to her core. She arched her hips toward him, and he made a sound that seemed to convey both understanding and a deep male satisfaction at her eagerness.

While he used one hand to free the tip of her other breast, he bent to reach for the fabric of her skirt, inching it up until she felt the cool night air on her legs.

Then he skimmed his fingers along her thigh, finding her bare skin at the top of her stocking.

"Dominic." His name came out like a plea as she gripped his shoulder, slid her fingers into his hair as he continued to suckle her as he stroked his fingers along her leg, exploring until they dipped along her inner thigh.

When he stroked his finger through her curls, she began to tremble. Not from fear but overwhelming need. She trusted him to touch her just how she wanted him to.

The need to loosen all she'd held inside so long nearly overwhelmed her, and she sensed he understood that too.

He lifted his head and kissed her again, more gently, languidly, as if they had all the time in the world, even as her body impatiently quivered against him.

"You're so deliciously wet," he whispered against her lips.

Then he pulled back until she looked up at him questioningly.

"Please don't stop," she begged.

"I'm not stopping, Tess, but I need to know you won't regret this." His voice was breathy, as if stopping was as maddening for him as it was for her.

But the fact that he was asking, making certain of her wishes, almost brought tears to her eyes. She wasn't naive anymore. He was a man of passion and experience and knew how easily one could get lost in carnal hunger without a single thought of the consequences.

"I won't regret it," she promised him. "I want this. I want you."

He smiled in the moonlight. Not the seductive rogue's smile. This one was wide, joyful, and artless.

"And you'll have me." He slid his hand down to tease his fingers against her. "But first I want to see you let go, siren."

He slipped inside, finding that most sensitive point where all her long pent-up need seemed to have been waiting for his touch. Only his. Mercy, she'd been waiting so long for him. And he was deliciously talented. There was no fumbling, no rushing.

The moment her body began to climb to the peak, he kissed her. Tasting her, stroking his tongue against hers the way he stroked his fingers masterfully.

She forgot everything but him. All her fears and regrets were nothing to how he made her feel—desirable, bold, safe in his arms.

Then, at the pinnacle, she quivered against him, coming back down to the here and now as he held her upright, placing soft, warm kisses along her neck, her cheek.

"Thank you, Tess," he murmured against her skin, then helped her to right her skirt, even assisted her to reaffix a couple of pins in her hair.

She looked up at him questioningly. He'd focused on her pleasure entirely and taken none for himself, and yet he looked at her as if awestruck. As if something about the moments they'd shared had shaken him.

Indeed, he was breathing hard.

Tess leaned in and kissed him, and he reacted instantly, pulling her close.

This moment with Dominic had been just what she'd been waiting for, though before he'd walked into her life, she'd have denied she was waiting for anything.

Somehow, despite his reputation and all the charm she'd seen him wield so adeptly, she'd seen more in him. Glimpses of his true nature that made her feel as if he was a man she could trust, if not with her heart, then with her passion.

Now, she only had to hope her judgement, this time, did not fail her.

CHAPTER FOURTEEN

When Tess went to visit Lord Fenbridge the next day, she took her tiny yet auspicious find with her. She didn't know if Dominic would like her toting it across the Wiggenstow countryside, but if anyone deserved to see what she'd found, it was Reginald Fenbridge.

As demanded by the curmudgeon himself, she arrived early.

What she found most amusing was that he did not seem to like rising early. Often when she stepped into his study, he was still in his dressing gown or his hair was awry as if he'd only just tumbled from bed.

But he did seem to enjoy the morning breeze and looking out on the clumps of daffodils beginning to show themselves in his garden.

Today, he was fully clothed, his hair looked as if his valet had been at it, and he had silver tea and coffee urns set up on a sideboard in his study.

"Avail yourself, Miss Hawthorne. There are crumpets and scones too, if they strike your fancy."

This wasn't the first time he'd pleasantly stunned her by having a sideboard of breakfast treats at the ready, but it had been a rarity. She suspected his lordship struggled with dark moods. Her father had been much the same, especially after her mother's death.

"Thank you, my lord." Tess selected a strawberry scone and poured herself a cup of tea, then added a dash of cream.

Fenbridge lifted his own cup as he sat behind his mammoth desk and observed her.

"What's happened, Miss Hawthorne?"

Tess swallowed a sip of tea and smiled, which only caused Fenbridge's bushy brows to wing up on his forehead. "We've found something."

Silver brows dropping, he crossed his arms. "Have you indeed?"

Tess had expected a bit more. She'd never seen the nobleman anything near gleeful, but she'd imagined the discovery would intrigue him. Perhaps even please him.

Yet as he sat watching her, he looked anything but pleased.

"Aren't you curious, my lord? Isn't that why I'm to report to you each morning?"

"Get on with it, Miss Hawthorne. Tell me what you've found."

Tess had secured the artifact in a box lined with a bit of cloth, and she extracted it carefully from the pocket of her skirt. It felt like such a precious treasure that she couldn't bear to break it further.

She gently eased the lid off the tiny box and set it atop Fenbridge's desk.

He eyed her a moment longer and then leaned in to inspect the box's contents. His brow furrowed. "What in the world is it?"

"We're not certain, but we can reasonably date it to the Anglo-Saxon period based on the designs on the metal."

"Your father would have been very intrigued by this little scrap of metal, wouldn't he?"

"Yes." Tess could well imagine her father's excitement. He'd be breathless, as she was, for whatever they might find next.

Fenbridge didn't seem to share her enthusiasm. "I suppose the American was right after all."

"You didn't want the dig to be successful?"

Fenbridge settled back in his chair and lifted his shoulders in a shrug. "Whatever's under those mounds has been in the earth for centuries. I know others have been keen to have it all up." He stared at her meaningfully. "But, as you well know, I've staunchly refused."

"Until Mr. Van Arsdale paid you generously."

"He did indeed and then sent his famous treasure seeker to do the deed." Fenbridge pointed at the box. "Did Prince dig that scrap up?"

"No," Tess said, suddenly feeling defensive, "I did."

That raised a smile on the man's wizened face. "Now that I quite like."

"Why?" The man was maddening. "I might have dug it up years ago if you'd allowed me to, and then we could keep what we find here in England."

"That worries you, doesn't it?"

"Doesn't it trouble *you*?" Tess retrieved the box and stared down at the burnished gold. "It's not about treasure. Not in the sense of a trove. This is our history."

"Van Arsdale sees it as his own history too."

Tess gritted her teeth. "But it's here now. Has rested here for centuries, as you so rightly pointed out. It should stay here."

At last, the nobleman's eyes lit with interest. "If you're so damned set against the American, why participate in his venture?"

The urge to say something snappish warred inside Tess, battling her understanding of how important it was to maintain

Fenbridge's goodwill until the dig was complete. But the man had thwarted her own ambitions for years, only to yield to Van Arsdale. Could he not understand why she capitulated?

"It was the only way. You refused us and gave way to the American. If I was going to find what was buried in those mounds, this was my only choice."

"And Prince is letting you dig on your own? Does he not fear you might steal the lot of it out from under him?"

"I'm not a thief, Lord Fenbridge." Tess bristled.

He narrowed his eyes at her. "That's not entirely true, is it, Miss Hawthorne?"

Tess barely resisted the urge to roll her eyes. "We were ten, my lord, and it amounted to two oranges."

She and Tristan had found the Fenbridge orangery utterly fascinating and had dared each other to sneak in one evening. They'd both snatched an orange and been so racked with guilt that they'd confessed all of it to their mother the next day.

She'd brought them before Lady Fenbridge, who'd found it more amusing than anything. Apparently, Lord Fenbridge hadn't shared her sense of forgiveness.

"Were they tasty?"

"They were bitter, if you must know."

Fenbridge nodded thoughtfully. "So often, the things we yearn for turn out to be bitter in the end."

If he hadn't seemed lost in thought after that dour declaration, Tess might have thought it some roundabout reference to her personal history.

"But you and Prince are rubbing along well?"

Tess immediately ducked her head and took another sip of tea. She willed her cheeks not to burst into flames, but she wasn't certain she could talk about Dominic without revealing any of her feelings where he was concerned.

"That well, eh?"

"We work together well. Amicably."

A blessed breeze wafted in through the half-open window of the study. The sky had been thick with darkening clouds on her walk over, and she suspected rain was on the way.

"Amicable, are you?"

Tess managed to hold Lord Fenbridge's gaze with what she hoped was a look that gave nothing away.

"Word is that the two of you get on so well that he escorted you to the village fair."

"Gossip, you mean. I didn't think you'd engage with such nonsense, my lord."

"One hears maids whispering whether one wishes to or not."

The few bites she'd taken of the scone turned to stone in her middle. Had someone seen them in the orchard?

A cold chill chased down her back. She did not regret a single moment with Dominic, but she had no wish to be fodder for chinwags again.

"Forgive me, Miss Hawthorne."

Tess snapped her head up and stared at Fenbridge. In all her life, she'd never heard the nobleman apologize to anyone.

"I do not wish to make you fret." He pursed his lips and laid his clasped hands atop his desk, leaning toward her. "I merely urge caution."

"Thank you for the apology, my lord. I'm well aware that I've been the subject of gossip in the past, and I have been cautious. For years."

"You think I judge you, but I do not. I understand better than you know."

"Understand what?"

"That even a very clever young lass can give her heart to a

scoundrel." At his pronouncement, thunder rolled in the distance and raindrops began to patter softly against the windowpanes.

Tess saw more sympathy reflected in Fenbridge's expression than she'd ever expected to see from the irascible man.

After a long moment, he looked away, glancing out into the garden. The rain was coming faster and harder. Tess considered taking her leave early in order to help the others at the dig site secure it. The tarpaulins they'd used the last time they were rained out were large and unwieldy.

"Your mother did once," Fenbridge murmured.

Tess almost dropped the teacup she held. "My mother?"

Fenbridge turned back to face her, settling back in his chair and lacing his hands over his middle. "I take it she never told you."

Tess's mind spun. Her mother had made the same mistake?

As far as Tess and her brother knew, their parents had met in their youth and loved each other steadfastly from that moment until the day each of them departed the earth. And there'd certainly never been a whisper of scandal related to her mother.

"I think you're mistaken, Lord Fenbridge. My mother wouldn't do such a thing. And if she had, how are you the only one who makes such a claim?"

Fenbridge scrutinized Tess a moment and then leaned forward. "Because I was the scoundrel, Miss Hawthorne."

Tess stared back at the old nobleman, but she didn't see him. Her thoughts wheeled like the pieces in a kaleidoscope. Moments flashing in her mind—her mother glancing wistfully at Fenbridge Hall as she'd take them on walks through the countryside, the rows between her father and Fenbridge, the fact that the amity between the two men only took root after her mother's passing.

"My father knew?"

At that question, Fenbridge winced as if pained. "Of course. He was a good man. Told me your mother forgave me." He blinked as his eyes turned glassy. "Hope he told me true."

"He was too honest for anything else."

Fenbridge nodded at that and then cleared his throat.

"You weren't honest?" Tess asked into the taut silence that had settled over his study.

He narrowed one eye at her and his mouth twisted into a grimace. "I lied to myself as much as to your mother. I thought I could ignore duty, my father's wishes, and a marriage contract signed when I was but a boy."

"What happened?" Part of Tess didn't truly want to know. It felt as if she was digging into her mother's secrets, but her curious nature and the likeness to her own mistake made her desperate to know.

"I broke a young lady's heart, and she married a much better man in the end."

Tess pushed against the back of her chair, slumping because it felt a bit as if the wind had been knocked out of her. Fenbridge spoke the words so easily, acknowledged his own wrongdoing with such pained resignation, and she could easily imagine her mother's heartache if she'd truly loved him.

"Why have you told me this?" Everything she'd believed about her parents shifted a bit now, but it made them more human when she and Tristan had idolized them both for so long.

Fenbridge considered a long while before giving her any reply. He reached for his cup, drinking deeply of his coffee before settling it back on his desktop with a thud.

"I wished you to know that the past need not hinder you, Miss Hawthorne. And perhaps I thought it instructive."

"How so, my lord?"

He shrugged. "Great love may be found after heartbreak."

Tess's pulse began to race. She felt her cheeks grow warm.

This won't be some grand love affair. No, great love wasn't what she would have with Dominic Prince, even if part of her came alive in his arms. Even if little pieces of her heart now had his name on them.

She wouldn't get lost in him. She'd promised herself.

Trying to offer a denial to Fenbridge, Tess merely shook her head and looked up to find him watching her with an odd little grin tipping the edge of his mouth up.

Behind him, through the garden window, rain continued to come down in a torrent. She should have gone to help Dominic and the others and saved herself from this far-too-revealing conversation.

Fenbridge turned back at the sound and assessed the downpour. "Not sure you'll be able to dig today if this continues."

"I should go and see the state of the dig site."

Fenbridge stood and Tess got to her feet too.

Normally, a simple leave-taking sufficed. Today, Tess reached out instinctively to shake his hand.

He stared at her outstretched hand a moment as if confounded by the gesture, but then he took it in both of his.

"Until tomorrow morning, Miss Hawthorne." He tipped a glance toward the window. "I can call my coachman to transport you. You'll be soaked if you came on foot."

Tess chuckled. "I am used to spring rains, my lord."

"Have the maid give you a mackintosh at least."

"Thank you," Tess told him, and made her way to the front door.

As if the young woman had heard her master, a maid waited with a mackintosh overcoat at the ready.

"This will keep you dry, miss. Has a hood and all."

"Much appreciated," she told the young woman.

She hoped Tristan had thought to bring a few from home. Otherwise, their whole crew would be drenched by now.

As the young woman helped Tess into the garment, they both jolted at the sound of forceful knocks against the hall's thick wooden doors.

The girl excused herself and went to see to the visitor.

Tess heard a voice that made her body hum to life.

She strode toward the sound and found him, clothes dripping onto the stone floor of the entry hall. Breath tangled in her throat at the sight of him. His dark hair hung damp and curling, a few strands clinging to his temples. His clothes clung to his muscular frame.

"I was just coming to find you," she told him as she stepped closer. Only the maid's presence prevented her from reaching up to brush the raindrop from his cheek.

"And I came to find you." The edge of his mouth tilted up and he took her in from boots to brow as if he'd missed the sight of her despite the handful of hours they'd been apart.

Of course, what had happened between them last night changed everything.

"Good day to you," Tess told Fenbridge's maid. She and Dominic made their way out the front door.

They walked so close to each other that their arms brushed as they proceeded down the steps.

"The site's secured," he told her. "I knew you'd be worried."

"Is that why you came to find me?"

"Yes and no." He looked her way, and his expression was

so intense, it felt like a warm stroke against her skin. "I wanted to see you, and it was a good excuse."

Tess smiled. "Your clothes are soaked through. Are you returning to the inn?"

He stilled her with a hand at her elbow. "Actually, I had another idea."

"Oh?" Tess turned to him but told herself to keep a respectable distance as they were still in full view of the hall's many windows.

"Would you like to join me on a little adventure?"

Dom held his breath as he watched her consider his question and only breathed again when she responded with an arched brow and the slightest of grins.

"What sort of adventure?"

"The sort a lady like yourself will adore."

She half scoffed, half chuckled. "You know my sort so well, do you?"

"I know you love history, and since we're in search of the Anglo-Saxons, I thought a visit to Castle Rising might be in order."

"Father used to take us there." A light sparked in her eyes. "It's not far."

"So, is that a yes?"

"Yes."

Dom gestured toward the pony cart he'd borrowed from the innkeeper. "I've even secured a conveyance."

"There will be more rain." Tess tipped her head up to assess the cloud-covered sky. The rain had slowed to a trickle, but there were more dark clouds on the horizon.

"We can endure a bit of rain. Besides, you're equipped."

He gestured toward the roomy mackintosh coat that obscured all her lovely curves.

"You're not."

"I find the rain invigorating. It's a warm day." A cool, damp breeze whipped at them as if to call him a liar.

Tess laughed again. "Shall we head off now before it turns torrential?"

"Now sounds perfect." Dom led her to the pony cart and she slipped out of the overcoat before climbing into the seat.

As she did each day at the dig site, she wore a pair of trousers that hugged her body, and Dom tried not to stare like a ravenous beast. Yet he felt like one around her now. He knew the sounds she made in the throes of release. He'd turned and tossed all night consumed with thoughts of it and her scent, her moans, the sweet sensual shudders as she melted in his arms.

He settled beside her, relishing the feel of her thigh against his, her arm brushing his as he took the reins.

"Your brother told me the way. I take it you've gone there often."

"Not as often as we would have liked. Our father had to gain permission from the owners to visit, though I think it's open to the public now."

"We'll soon see." He kept turning this head to catch glimpses of her and couldn't help a triumphant smile when he caught her doing the same.

The attraction he'd felt since the moment he'd met her now blazed inside him after her proposal the previous night. One rule she'd set was that any intimacy between them should remain a secret, and yet his thoughts didn't seem to concur. He had the mad notion to pull the carriage aside and kiss her senseless.

They rode in silence for the next couple of miles, sneaking glances at each other like besotted fools.

"This is the lane that will take us there," she said eagerly, placing a hand on his thigh a moment as if to draw his attention.

"Is that it?" he asked, his voice suddenly raspy.

That simple, brief touch of her hand shot an electric ripple of heat through his body.

She sat up straighter in her seat, craning her neck. "It is."

Rain had dappled them off and on as they'd traveled, but it came down in a soft patter as he pulled the pony cart into the field near the fortification that had stood on this swath of Norfolk for over seven hundred and fifty years.

Dom helped her down from the cart, his hands at her waist, though both knew she was fully capable of climbing down on her own. Tess put her hands on his shoulders, and when her boots touched the ground, they held onto each other a moment longer.

"Shall we take shelter in the gatehouse?" she whispered as rain dappled her skin.

In answer, Dom took her hand and rushed up the earthen ring that enclosed the castle grounds and then down toward the remnants of what had once been an impressive forebuilding. It would have impressed visitors or likely given a gatekeeper fair notice of oncoming enemies.

She laid a hand against the stones that comprised the structure. "These stones were laid so many centuries ago and yet still hold fast." She cast a sheepish expression over her shoulder at him. "Though you've likely seen the pyramids, so these must seem young to you."

"Not at all. I can appreciate this history as fully as that of Thebes." He approached to lay his hand near hers against one of the light gray stones. "In many ways, it's easier to feel connected to this history. As if it's not so far in the past that I can't get a vivid sense of those who built this." He looked at the castle ruins. "Or lived inside those walls."

"Queen Isabella lived there."

"Before or after the death of her husband, Edward II?"

Tess smiled. "You do know your English history, don't you?"

"I know my fair share. Knowledge of treasures requires it, but my siblings and I loved the history itself too."

She tipped her head as if assessing him anew. "Here I thought you were only interested in valuable artifacts."

"I'm quite fond of those too." He offered his arm as the rain had stopped again. "Shall we?"

"Watch yourself, the pair of you." The gruff male voice came from behind them, and both Tess and Dom turned to find a stout, older gentleman leaning on a massive walking stick as he observed them. "I'm the caretaker here," he said by way of explanation. "Explore as you please, but the stones inside will be slick from the rain."

"Thank you," Tess called to the man as they proceeded toward the soaring high walls of the castle and keep.

"Do you know the treasure associated with this place?" Dom asked her as they entered through an arched doorway and climbed a set of worn stone stairs to the castle's upper gallery.

"I can think of one."

"A rather important one."

She shot him an arch look. "Go on then, regale me. I sense that you want to."

Dom laughed. "Is there a prize if I do?"

Tess stopped, turned, and faced him, planting her hands

on her hips. "Are you only motivated by riches, Mr. Prince?" she asked cheekily.

Dom stepped closer to her on the narrow walkway, bound on one side by centuries-old stones and the other by a modern wrought-iron rail. They were forced into close quarters along the tight path, but it wasn't close enough.

"The only prize I want, Miss Hawthorne, is a kiss from you."

Chapter Fifteen

Tess wanted to kiss him too. From the moment he'd come to find her at Fenbridge's, it had grown like a deep-seated craving.

"Tell me, then, about the treasure associated with the castle."

He lifted his hand and made a circle with his fingers just touching the inner tip of his thumb. "Imagine a rounded blood-red gem. A crimson spinel from Spain. Imagine a Spanish king challenged by his brother and in need of allies."

Tess listened rapt, the way she used to when her father told a story from history as if he was recounting a tale of Shakespearean proportions.

"Desperate to hold onto power, King Peter of Castile looked to England. To Queen Isabella's grandson."

"The Black Prince."

Dom smiled. "The very one, and he gave his aid . . . for a price. Two of the Castilian king's daughters to marry his sons and one gem as fat as a hen's egg."

Tess knew of the red spinel because it was wrapped up in the history of England's royalty, and those annals had fascinated her father as much as they did Tess and her brother.

"And you know where that big red jewel is now, don't you?" he asked as if fully confident of her answer.

"Since our queen had it added to her imperial crown, I

suspect it's sitting safe and well-guarded in the Tower of London."

"One of these days, we should go see it together, and I'll tell you the full story of my sister's escapade related to the crown jewels."

Tess swallowed hard, and Dom looked immediately chagrined as if he realized he'd misstepped without meaning to.

The notion that they'd go on a visit to see the royal regalia or spend their days in the future together as they often did now was tantalizing. It made her heart yearn for things she knew were foolish. And that she could not allow.

"An admirable recitation," she told him rather than mentioning how wistful his words had made her. Then she turned toward the hollow interior of the castle, imagining the lives lived inside its strong, thick walls.

Dom took up a spot next to her. So close, she felt instantly warmer and could smell his spice and citrus shaving soap.

"I wonder if the gem was ever inside these walls," he said quietly, as if imagining the past noise, colorful people, and finery that would have been a part of the notorious queen's household.

"It's unlikely," Tess told him without looking his way. "The queen died in 1358. The Black Prince was already installed in his own castle in Hertfordshire."

"You're encyclopedic," he said with an undisguised admiration. "I always struggle to recall precise dates, though I realize that's a dreadful thing for Octavius Prince's son to admit."

"I forget dates sometimes too, though my father encouraged memorization," she admitted. "Tristan and I read whatever history books he'd lend or gift to us, and we each kept a journal and drew out a timeline where we'd plot out events and details we'd learned."

Dom's arm tensed where it rested against hers. She glanced over and noticed his jaw had tightened too. "I understand having a demanding father."

"Oh, he never demanded anything of us, except to have good manners and not run wild. Of course, Tristan ran wild regardless."

They exchanged a grin.

"But was it hard to live up to the example he set?" he asked her.

Tess frowned. "He never expected us to be as erudite about history as he was. In fact, when Tristan showed aptitude at mathematics, Father encouraged him to pursue it at university."

"And did he?"

"No." Tess shook her head at the memory of all the times their father had encouraged each of them to pursue various fields of study, only to find himself with two children as in love with the past as he was.

"I'm glad your father wasn't like mine," Dom said, a new gruffness in his tone.

"What was he truly like?" Tess asked softly, knowing a bit of the man by reputation alone but aware that Dominic wrestled with his father's legacy.

He lowered his head for a moment and then looked over at her. "He was a bit of a colorful blur, forever on the move, always on to the next adventure. Never content. And he was truly as fearless and charming as they say." She heard a bit of admiration in his tone, but also a thread of sadness.

"That sounds like what the papers say of you." Tess reached out and laid her hand atop his where he rested it on the wrought-iron rail. "But they don't have it quite right."

A grin curved his mouth, and he turned his hand palm up

so that he could lace his fingers with hers. "Are you saying I don't live up to the picture they paint of me?"

"Oh, you do, in some ways, but I've seen more. The Dominic Prince I see each day is fair, openminded, and hardworking. And willing to pitch in to save local cows."

He chuckled. "Only Daisy. She's the only one I'd risk it all for."

"I'm sure she'll never forget you."

He flashed her a blinding grin. "I'm glad you see those parts of me, Tess."

She adored those parts of him, but she hesitated to confess that much. Hesitated to let those feelings fully expand in her heart.

Looking out at the castle walls, she returned to safer territory. "However dissimilar our fathers were, they both loved history."

"Mmm. But your father simply passed on the love of it. Mine used it for gain." He arched a brow as he looked over at her. "And yes, you may call me a hypocrite for doing the same."

Tess stroked her thumb along his. "In truth, regarding the current dig, we are both doing the same."

"But for very different reasons."

A drop of rain landed on Tess's hand and trickled down to his.

"It seems the rain clouds have caught up with us. Perhaps we should head back," she suggested.

"We should . . ." he said, "but there's a matter we must settle first."

"Oh?"

"There was some talk of a prize, I believe."

They turned to face each other.

He ran his tongue along his lower lip, and Tess thought

how much she wanted to kiss that very spot. She leaned into him, both hands braced on his broad chest, and he stroked a hand along her neck to cup her nape.

Tess's stomach tightened with anticipation, but he didn't make her wait long.

After one hungry look at her as if he wished to devour her, he bent his head and swept his tongue against the seam of her lips. Tess gasped, and like the scoundrel he was reputed to be, Dominic slipped inside, tasting her, teasing her, all the while drawing her closer with an arm cinched around her body.

Like the night before, he braced her against him as if he knew that his kisses made her knees feel as if they might buckle.

With their bodies seamed together, she found herself arching into him, as molten and aching as she'd been when he touched her in the orchard.

"Dominic," she breathed when he broke their kiss and traced his lips along her neck, nipping at a spot near her ear that made her moan.

Then he lifted his head, smiling down at her as if quite pleased with his effect on her. He traced the shape of her lips with his fingertips and then bent to whisper in her ear.

"Kissing you is the real treasure, Tess. I relish each of them, and then greedily want more. I want an entire hoard."

She turned her head to look again at the castle walls because she felt something in her coming undone. The more she touched him, kissed him, the harder it was to keep up any defense at all around her heart.

And yet she couldn't seem to stop herself from wanting more of him either. This closeness that felt so right even as a far-off warning bell pealed inside her.

"We should go back."

"Tess, if I said something amiss—"

"You didn't." Reaching up, she drew her fingers along the hard line of his jaw. "But let's go home."

ON THE SHORT CARRIAGE ride back to Wiggenstow, Dom told himself that he had to tread more carefully with Tess's feelings. She'd told him what this would be. She'd laid down the rules and boundary lines of what would be between them.

It had always been enough for him in the past, but now it wasn't nearly enough. He couldn't pinpoint the moment, didn't know whether it had begun when she'd stormed into Lady Goddard's library, but somehow, at some point, everything had changed.

Dom could no longer imagine a future day, week, or even a year of his life that didn't include Tess.

He told himself to take what she offered as the gift it was. A few days or weeks with her was a bounty.

Yet no matter how much he told himself to keep to her parameters, to enjoy what she gave him, and focus the rest of his mind and energy on the reason he'd come to Norfolk in the first place, he couldn't deny that something inside him had altered.

They made the journey in silence. She seemed pensive too.

Dom feared they'd part ways in Wiggenstow, and he wouldn't see her again until the dig resumed the next morning, weather willing.

But as the road wound toward the village, she turned to him on the narrow cart's seat.

"Will you come back to the cottage with me?"

"Of course." Dom felt her gaze on him as she studied his profile before he tipped a grin her way. "I'd like that."

Any opportunity to spend time with her, he'd take.

"I haven't had time to take a proper look at Tristan's notes from yesterday's work at the site. I thought perhaps the three of us could make a plan for the coming week."

"Tristan won't be there," he told her. "He mentioned a trip into King's Lynn with a young lady."

"I see." Tess smiled and then shook her head. "Did he mention who?"

"A Miss Bromley, I believe." Dom wasn't entirely certain that Tristan would want his sister to know that detail, but he'd only asked Dom not to mention it to Bill Bromley.

By the time they arrived at Wiggenstow, their clothes were damp from a light drizzle that followed them back from Castle Rising.

"We'll have to light the fire. Mrs. Wells is visiting her sister in Norwich."

Dom took the initiative and had fresh fire flaming to life within a few minutes. When he turned back to Tess, brushing off his hands, he found her standing near the window, staring out with a fretful look.

"I don't know why he doesn't simply marry her," she said quietly. "If he breaks her heart again, Bill will surely have his head."

"Again?"

Tess turned back to him, her expression pinched with worry. "Two summers ago, they had a . . . romance. I'd never seen Tris so happy, and Justine is lovely and clever and kind. I expected him to offer for her." She shook her head. "Instead, he crushed her by ending things abruptly."

"Was there a falling-out?"

"No, Tristan says he's not the marrying sort." She turned back to the window after that declaration.

Dom suspected she thought the same of him. Hell, he'd told himself something akin to it for most of his life. Change was a fearful thing, especially when there was no promise that all would be well in the end.

"If he's with her today, then perhaps he's found the courage to be a different sort."

Tess approached him, coming to stand with him near the fire. "I hope so," she said with a wistful little tinge of longing in her tone. "I want to see him happy again."

Dom resisted reaching for her, though everything in him longed to.

"And what do you want, Tess?"

When her head came up and their gazes clashed, the look in her eyes caused the organ behind his ribcage to thud in a strange, unsteady way it never had before.

In his life, he'd gorged himself on adventure, fed himself on anticipation of what came next. But in that moment, everything seemed to stop short, balanced on a precipice.

It couldn't have been more than a moment that he waited for her answer, and yet his future seemed to hinge on it, so the world shrunk until all he saw was the lovely naked longing in her eyes.

"I want you."

That was all Dom needed to hear. Too quickly for her to utter another word, he stepped forward, took her by the waist, and lifted her against him. He kissed her with all he dared not say to her. Not yet. He kissed her with all the feelings that were so damned new, frightening, but too powerful to ignore.

She responded to him in kind, one hand tangling in his hair, the other gripping the muscles of his shoulder.

As he pulled back to look in her eyes, she reached for his hand.

"Come with me." She was a beckoning siren, and he needed no convincing.

She led him to her bedroom, and he shed his coat as she went to close the curtains on two windows that looked out on rolling green fields.

When she turned back to him, he caught a flicker of hesitation in her gaze.

Then she approached boldly, stopping just before him. With maddening slowness, she began to unfasten the tiny buttons that ran down the length of her blouse. Dom followed her lead and unbuttoned his own shirt too. It took him less time, and she smiled appreciatively when he shrugged the fabric from his shoulders.

Dom licked his lips when she dropped her blouse to the ground, revealing an ivory corset beneath.

Rather than unfasten it, she reached for the fly of her trousers, paused, and then arched one tawny brow as if waiting for him to do the same.

Dom made quick work of the buttons on his trousers, and then nearly lost his bloody mind as she inched the fabric down her gloriously long legs. Then she had her corset off a moment later, and the peaked tips of her lush breasts strained against the fabric of her chemise.

"Mercy." His mouth watered, and his thoughts scattered.

He tried to shove his own trousers off as artfully, but he was too eager, too starved for a glimpse of that heaven at the apex of her thighs, hidden only now by the thinnest cotton drawers.

"Mercy indeed," she breathed as she fixed her green gaze on his aching hard cock.

He shot her a shameless grin.

"Shall I help you with the rest?" Dom licked his lips and took a step closer, desperate to free her of every other bit of fabric between them. He reached for the pale-yellow ribbon at the top edge of her chemise.

One tug and the garment gaped wide enough for him to slip it over her shoulders and watch it glide down to her feet. Then he lowered himself to his knees before her. His hand trembled like he was a green boy as he unlaced the ribbon of her drawers.

Then he reached down and swept both garments aside.

Tess slid her fingers into his hair, and he groaned at how good it felt, how much he longed for her touch everywhere.

"These legs," he rasped, stroking his fingers from her calves up to her thighs as he got to his feet.

She shivered and then gasped when he bent to scoop her into his arms. Her gaze turned toward the bed, then she frowned when he walked her to the wall next to the fireplace.

Dom set her down gently. "I have another idea," he told her softly.

"Against the wall?" she asked confusedly.

"Only if you wish it, Tess. Only if you trust me," he whispered and knew he was asking for a great deal from a woman whose faith had once been abused.

She swallowed hard in the dimmed light of her room, nodded, and stepped back.

Dom held her gaze as he lowered himself before her once more. She watched him, a curious tilt to her head, as he stroked her leg again and this time urged her to lift it.

She nodded, giving him the permission he sought, and he settled her leg over his shoulder.

"You're so beautiful," he murmured.

Looking up at her again, he watched her eyes as he slid his fingers along her inner thigh, a stroke of delicious heat all the way to her curls.

Tess bit her lip as he touched her. His gaze never left hers, as if he needed to see her reaction, wanted to know what pleased her.

As his fingers slid into her heat, she bucked against him, then let out a moan when he found the spot where all her need seemed to center.

Reaching down, she slid her fingers into his thick hair, and he let out a low sound of pleasure that made her heart thrum inside her chest.

"Can I taste you, Tess?" His voice had dropped to a husky rumble.

The moment she nodded, he bent his head and stroked his tongue along the path his fingers had taken. Her body began to quiver as he licked her, and he lifted a hand to her hip, gripping firmly as if to assure her that he would not let her fall.

But he didn't stop tasting her, flicking his tongue in the most exquisite way, driving her closer to the edge.

When he slipped a finger inside her, she gasped at how good it felt, and he stilled, as if uncertain whether her exhale was one of pleasure.

"Don't stop," she whispered.

As if the words spurred him, his languid strokes turned hungrier, and his finger sought the spot that made her breath catch. Her body convulsed as her release caught her up, spinning her high. Her breath caught in her throat, her muscles tensed, and then she felt herself coming down into bone-melting bliss.

When she opened her eyes, he was there, holding her in his arms, looking at her as if she was the remarkable one when he'd just given her more pleasure than she'd ever felt in her life.

She cupped his jaw and kissed him. He smiled against her lips a moment before pulling her closer, until there was no space between them.

He stroked his fingers through her hair, then trailed his hand down to circle her nipple. Dipping his head to kiss her neck, he pulled back an inch. "How are you?" His breath gusted hot against her skin.

Tess laughed. "Can you not tell?"

He nipped her neck lightly with his teeth, and she gasped. "I need to know."

Tess found the edge of his jaw with her fingertips, lifting it until their gazes met.

"I'm dazed, in the best way," she told him, her voice a quiet rasp. "I want you, Dominic." Licking her lips, she added, "I trust you."

He swallowed hard. His eyes flashed as if with shock, then glowed with an emotion she couldn't name. "Maybe that tree is magic after all," he said with a grin.

Tess's throat burned. "That was your wish?"

He answered with a kiss that stole her breath, then cupped her face tenderly. "It was."

Tess reached down and clasped his hand in hers, then started toward the bed, looking back at him as he followed.

The hunger in his eyes made her heart flutter in her chest. "My siren."

She climbed onto the bed, then reached for him again, and he joined her, bracing his body above hers. Tess needed him closer and wrapped her arms around his shoulders, pulling him down for a kiss until he'd settled his body against hers.

The warmth and weight of his body was as soothing as it was maddening. She stroked down his back as she held him, tracing across the rippling muscles. She wanted this man with an ache she'd never felt before.

He hadn't cajoled her into this moment, hadn't promised her anything but pleasure and respect for her every wish.

And her only wish was to have him closer.

She bucked against him, and he looked into her eyes.

"Please," she whispered.

"Please what, Tess?" Yet he knew the answer because he shifted then and filled her with one maddeningly slow stroke. "Is that what you want?" He rocked into her, and she bent her knees, arching against him.

He bent his head to kiss her neck, nip at the juncture between her neck and shoulder. "Tell me," he rasped, even as he stroked deep inside her.

"Yes." The word emerged on a gasp.

He took her mouth, kissing her deeply, his tongue matching the thrust of his body. Need built inside her again, that delicious pull toward her release. She dug her fingers into his shoulder, and he pulled back, watching her as he took her to that peak.

She reached up, curled a hand around his neck, and he let her pull him into a kiss.

But then he lifted his head and fixed his gaze on hers again.

"I want to watch when you let go," he whispered, his breathing ragged.

And she did, gasping and moaning through the shudders, feeling the moment he built toward his own release. When he did, he dipped his head, groaned against her neck, and withdrew from her. At the loss of him, a little sound of protest welled up in her, and yet Tess understood he was protecting her. That brought a rush of warmth in her chest. He bent, his mouth against her cheek, his harsh breaths hot against her skin.

"Tess, exquisite siren," he murmured as he settled beside her and wrapped her in his arms.

She settled against him, feeling sated beyond anything she'd ever experienced. Nothing before had been like this. She felt safe in his arms, and that was the most exquisite feeling of all.

Chapter Sixteen

Tess woke, stretched, and let out a satisfied sound. Then she opened her eyes and looked over at Dominic as he lay on his side, tangled in her sheets, with an arm resting atop her middle.

He slept soundly, peacefully, and looked achingly handsome. His dark hair fell across his forehead and cheek, and the slightest smile softened the edges of his mouth.

That mouth. Mercy.

They'd spent a dream-like afternoon and evening, and her room had become a haven, where nothing mattered but the way it felt when they were together.

Being with him had been far more than Tess expected, unlike anything she'd experienced before. She thought she'd understood how things would be, but what they'd done was as far from what she knew as night was from day.

He'd touched her with passion, yes, but tenderness too. He'd made it feel good to be bold. To let go.

But she'd been wrong. Scratching the itch didn't resolve anything. She wanted him more now, and not just for a few weeks of lovemaking. The longer she lay looking at him, the further her mind spun with possibilities. Images of a future with him.

Then the contentment that seemed to saturate every part of her began to ebb. She laid a hand on her chest where her heart ached sharply. Though she hadn't moved an inch, her heart raced as if she'd run across a field, as if a cinch was being pulled tight around her body, stealing her air, ratcheting her panic.

Tess knew the cause. These feelings had assailed her before. A memory would come, or something would remind her of three years ago, and her body responded as if she was back there. The heartbreak was suddenly fresh.

In the past, deep breaths served to ease the ache in her chest and her racing pulse. She tried that, Dom's arm lifting slightly as she filled her lungs with air.

Tears burned, threatening to fall.

She hated that the past still held her in its grip. Would she never be able to know pleasure without paying some price?

Closing her eyes, she breathed deeply again, slowly drawing in a breath and letting it go. Then she turned her head to look at Dominic again.

The man had shown her nothing but care and brought her to a peak of pleasure she'd never known, and yet her heart felt as if she was lying beside the man who'd betrayed her.

It wasn't fair.

She didn't want to wake him, so she slid out of bed, carefully inching from beneath his hold. Scooping up her clothes, she dressed quickly, collected her boots, and then headed out Foxdene's side door that led to the field beyond the garden.

The land only rose and fell with the slightest of elevations, but working her muscles felt good. Rain had left the air feeling fresh and cool, and she drew in deep lungfuls as she waded through the damp grass.

This is different.

She repeated the words to herself, to her anxious heart.

Dominic had never lied to her. Never promised her anything.

And she wasn't wrong to hope. What was between them was more than mere attraction. She could read it in his eyes. And yet her heart felt trapped behind a bramble of thorns.

That protective barrier had served her well for years, but now she wanted to pull it down and didn't know if she could.

When she reached the stones—remnants of an old field wall—where she and Tristan used to sit to watch a sunset or the sunrise, she settled atop them and pressed a hand to her chest.

Her heart still raced, but less now, more from exertion than panic.

She hugged her knees and rested her chin atop them as she stared down from the small hill at the first golden fingers of dawn stretching across the horizon.

Regret, which she'd feared, wasn't any part of what she felt. Indeed, she couldn't think of a single moment they'd shared that didn't bring a smile to her lips.

What weighed on her was the thought of what would come next.

Each time they shared a bit of their past or their bodies came together in a kiss, she tipped a little more. Her heart listing in his direction as easily as her body seemed to whenever he was near.

If she let this go on—if she went back to the cottage and got into bed with him as everything in her wished to—she'd tip so far that she'd fall completely.

And some part of her, the part that he'd sparked from that first moment they'd met, wanted to be brave, to race back to him and allow whatever was between them to bloom.

Yet deep inside, far in the back of her mind, she couldn't resist imagining how it would end. And how, having fallen so completely, she'd break.

It had been hard enough to put the pieces of herself together three years ago. She didn't relish the prospect again.

Logically, she knew there was one clean, simple solution. End this now. Yesterday and last night had been perfect. Why crave more?

But she did. Heaven help her, she did.

As dawn lit up the sky, she stood to go back to him.

Tess felt no closer to knowing what the future held for the two of them, but she felt one thing deep in her bones. A firmer certainty than the fear in the back of her mind.

If she ended it now, she'd always wonder. And in that moment, with a gorgeous man sleeping in her bed, such a fate seemed worse than a broken heart.

DOM SMILED AS HE came awake. Tess's scent filled his senses and memories rolled through his mind. Then he opened his eyes and frowned at the empty space beside him.

Sitting up, he noted that the clothes she'd shed yesterday were gone. He listened but could hear no other sounds in the cottage beyond Tess's room.

Letting out a sigh, he ran a hand through his hair and then got out of bed.

Did she have regrets? Would she shut him out now?

As he collected and donned his clothing, there wasn't a single doubt in his mind. Last night had confirmed for him that he wanted Tess Hawthorne, and not just as a temporary lover. He wanted all of her, a place in her life, however she'd allow it.

He wanted to find her and tell her that, yet even as the thought formed in his head, questions came that he couldn't yet answer.

Marriage had never been among his plans for his life. At

moments, he'd thought that perhaps one day he'd settle into married life, but he'd always envisioned it as something he'd do when he was old and gray and prepared to calcify.

In truth, as much as he wanted a future with Tess, he didn't know the shape of what he could offer her. He didn't even live in his family's home in London out of a desire to live lightly, without trappings that might keep him in one place too long.

Could he give her the kind of life she deserved?

As doubts swept in to drown all his certainty, a knock sounded on Tess's bedroom door.

"Tess?" her brother called from the other side. "Are you at home? I saw the cart outside."

Dom opened the door and watched Tristan's face transform from shock to confusion to narrow-eyed anger.

"What the hell is happening here?" he demanded. "Where's Tess?"

"I don't know."

"You don't know?" He threw a hand toward Dom's chest. "You're standing half dressed in my sister's bedroom, and you don't know where she is?"

"She seems to have stepped out."

Tristan's frown deepened beneath a fall of blond hair a shade darker than Tess's. "Did you two have a row? Have you done something to her?"

Dom crossed his arms defensively as Tristan's pitch rose. "We did not have a row. We are getting along . . . well."

Tristan swept his gaze down Dom's rumpled clothing, stalling at his half-buttoned shirt. "I don't think I want to know the details. I just want to know where Tess is."

"Me too. I have no idea where she went."

Something in Tristan's expression seemed to soften at Dom's tone.

"If she merely needed time to herself to think, I suspect I know where—"

"Where would she go?"

Her brother held up a hand. "If she wants to be on her own, it's best to let her do it." Tristan sniffed. "There's a tip for you that you'll want to retain if this . . . between you is to go any further."

"Thank you."

"Though it seems to have gone quite far already." Tess's twin's eyes narrowed again. "Of course, I'm not entirely surprised."

"No, we did discuss the possibility."

Tristan nodded thoughtfully. "If I were at all an honorable brother, this is the moment when I would ask you what your intentions are toward my sister."

"Is that what you're asking me?" Dom lifted his brow.

"Yes," Tristan said, squaring his own shoulders.

Dom's mind stalled on the question, though it was a fair one and precisely the question he would have put to a man he found in his own sister's bedroom. Though he wasn't certain he'd be nearly as restrained as Tristan Hawthorne was managing to be.

Indeed, the man had an odd energy about him today.

"We set rules before this all began," Dom said, though he knew it wasn't the answer her brother deserved.

"Rules."

"Tess insisted upon them."

Tristan nodded again. "Understandable. She was trying to protect herself, no doubt."

"Yes, whatever happened before—"

"I told you. A rotter seduced her, promised her things, and then once he'd . . ." Tristan shot Dom a pointed look. "He told her it had all been a ruse for that very purpose."

"That's vile."

"Agreed." Tristan took a step closer. "But the question remains as to your intentions."

"I've never met a woman who I wanted a future with until I met Tess."

"You love her?"

Dom gave Tess's brother a firm nod, even as a sweat broke out on his body.

"Petrifying, isn't it?"

Dom brushed a hand across his forehead. "Is it supposed to feel like this?"

"For rogues like us, I suspect it is," Tristan opined. "You meet an extraordinary woman and suddenly wonder if you could ever deserve her."

Dom shifted uncomfortably, shocked at the man's insight. When he looked up again, Tristan was watching him.

Tess's brother immediately held his hands up, palms out. "I say that as a man who's always considered love a snare."

Dom frowned. "And the lady you went to King's Lynn with?"

"A gift I'm certain I don't deserve. She's forgiven me, so I'm determined to spend the rest of my days making it up to her." He all but bounced on his heels. "It's what I came to tell Tess."

"You proposed to her?" A twinge of something very like envy rushed through Dom.

"Better yet, she said yes."

Dom stepped forward and offered his hand. "Congratulations, Tristan."

He kept hold of Dom's hand as he assessed him. "I like you, Dominic. Wouldn't mind calling you brother."

"You're rushing ahead, man." Dom's eyes flared wider.

Tristan released his hand, then he lifted a slip of paper

from the pocket of his trousers and offered it to Dom. He glanced at the mantel clock.

"It's likely been long enough. Go and find my sister," he told him. "If she's where I think she is, it will be straight out the garden gate and along the field to an old stone fence on Fenbridge land."

Dom lifted the folded square of paper. "And what is this?"

"I found it affixed to the front door. A note from his lordship asking Tess to come to the hall and telling her to bring you along when she does."

"But it's Sunday, and we didn't dig yesterday. Why would he need a report this morning?" Dom had hoped to spend the morning with Tess, alone and free to perhaps visit some other local historical landmark. Or take her back to bed.

Tristan shrugged and reached for his hat where he'd hung it on a hook inside the door. "What the owner of the land we're digging upon wants, he gets, I suppose."

Dom watched as Tristan reached for the door handle.

"I thought you wanted to tell Tess your good news."

"Oh, I do, but I promised Justine I'd accompany her to speak to her brothers." The young man grimaced. "If you're the praying sort, a petition that I survive this meeting with Bill Bromley wouldn't go amiss."

"Shall I accompany you?" Dom asked him. "If I let her brother go to his death, I doubt Tess would ever forgive me."

"No." Tristan reached out and patted Dom's shoulder. "Go and find my sister."

As soon as Tristan left the cottage, Dom put on his boots and headed the way Tess's brother had directed.

Sunlight lit the horizon and there were patches of blue sky above his head. It seemed the late spring rain had passed for now, and they'd be able to return to work. Dom told himself the eagerness fizzing inside him should be about what they might find today. And the next day.

Yet it was all for Tess. And when he saw her in the distance, striding toward him, her long blond hair loose and whipping about her shoulders, he almost broke into a run.

He held back, tried for some of the control that had always been easy, at least where his heart was concerned. But he lengthened his gait, as did she.

"I came to find you," he called when the fact was blatantly obvious.

"And I was coming to find you," she replied with a smile, just as she had at Fenbridge Hall.

That smile loosened something in his chest.

"I'm sorry for disappearing without a word," she told him when they'd stopped and stood before each other.

"Your brother advised me to give you time to think when you need it."

"Tristan?" A pink-peach blush rushed over her cheeks. "Did he come home in the night?"

"No, this morning."

Both of her dark-gold brows winged high. "So, he knows."

"I think he can conclude . . ."

"It's all right." She ducked her head and laughed. "Tristan won't tell anyone."

"What matters most is that you're all right," he said quietly, stepping close enough to reach for her. Yet when he did, she cast a glance around as if to ensure no one from the village was wandering the same field.

"How could I not be?" she said a bit too lightly.

"Tess, last night—"

"Was wonderful," she finished with an earnestness that put him at ease.

"But you needed time to think." He didn't blame her for that. God knew his own thoughts were a jumble. "Did it help?"

"A bit."

Dom wanted to ask more, wanted to ask her for the same honesty she'd demanded of him, but something held him back. Something in her eyes—a hesitation, uncertainty. The last thing he wanted was to force her into some confession she wasn't ready to give.

"Tristan found a note on the door from Fenbridge," he told her instead.

"Oh?"

"It seems he wants his usual visit this morning, but he's asked that I accompany you."

She tilted her head as if confused. "That's curious." She took in his rumpled clothing, her gaze catching at the skin revealed by the open buttons at his throat. Then she glanced down at her own clothes.

"I'll go back to the inn and change and meet you back at the cottage."

For a moment, she looked as if she'd keep him with her, lifting her hand as if to touch him. So much was going unsaid between them, and yet they both seemed unable to articulate anything sufficient after the hours they'd spent together.

He was altered by it. That was his one certainty. "Will you come to the inn tonight?"

It was the plainest, simplest expression of how much he wanted the new closeness between them to continue.

"Yes." She wore an inscrutable expression, but he was too pleased at the thought of more time with her to worry overmuch.

Dom bent to kiss her quickly. Too quickly. Too brief a

taste, and then they parted ways. He crossed the field toward town, and she headed back toward Foxdene.

Tonight, he planned to tell her what he felt, even if he didn't yet know how she'd react. She needed to know that, to him, this wasn't just some temporary, rule-bound liaison. At least he didn't want it to be.

For the first time in his life, he wanted more, and yet he may be losing his damned cynical heart to a lady who wanted nothing more from him than any other had.

CHAPTER SEVENTEEN

Tess opted for her best day dress for the visit to Fenbridge Hall. She'd run out of clean trousers, though she'd borrow some of Tristan's, if need be, before they reopened the dig site.

After washing and dressing, she fussed with her hair, rather than being content with the usual practical knot she drew it into most days. Then she dabbed perfume on her skin from a bottle she hadn't touched in years.

Only when she opened the etched wooden box where she kept her rarely worn jewelry did she admit to herself that all of this effort was because of Dominic. Which was ironic, considering that he'd made love to her when she was at her most disheveled—hair mussed and curling from the rain, clothes rumpled and still damp.

And it wasn't so much that she was trying to be beautiful for him—though she did relish the way he looked at her as if he thought her a beauty—it was that her boldness and the way he had relished it made her feel confident in a way she hadn't in a very long while.

She glanced out the window to check for his arrival and caught him just as he made his way up the walk to the cottage's front door.

Stepping outside to meet him, she found herself as tongue-tied this morning as when he'd approached across the field.

"You look beautiful, though you always do," he said easily, as if it wasn't the grandest of compliments and was the simplest truth. "Ready to visit Fenbridge?"

"Thank you, and yes, I am."

He offered her his arm, though they'd taken walks together at the dig site or into the village throughout his time in Wiggenstow and had never walked so close.

Still, she took his arm. She found she couldn't resist.

"Any idea why he'd want me to come too?"

Tess had been wondering the same. "Yesterday was the first time I showed him something we'd found. The bit of metal and garnet. Perhaps he wants a better sense of what we've done and what we hope to find next."

"Did you tell him we have reason to believe it's a ship burial?"

"I didn't." She looked up at him. "Do you think we can confirm that now?"

"I do. There can be very little doubt."

Tess smiled. "Perhaps that will please him then."

"Your find didn't?" He frowned down at her, seemingly as confused as she'd been by Fenbridge's lack of interest in the dig's finds.

"Not a bit." She considered telling him what the nobleman had shared about her own personal history, but she hadn't even told Tristan yet. Indeed, she wondered if she should share it with anyone at all.

The whole tale cast her mother in a different light, whereas she and Tristan had idolized her. That was perhaps because they'd lost her when they were just on the cusp of ten.

"You're woolgathering," he said softly, laying a hand over hers where she held his arm. "About last night?"

Tess licked her lips. Even mention of the hours they'd shared sparked something deep in her middle. A flare of remembered pleasure and eagerness to experience it all again.

"No," she said with a smile, "though I have thought of it once or twice."

Dominic laughed. "Only once or twice. I find myself unable to think of anything else."

Tess tucked closer to him and whispered, "Then I'll admit it's been more than once or twice."

As they came into view of Fenbridge Hall, Tess slipped her arm from his. "His lordship already suspects there's something between us."

She sensed Dominic's displeasure when she stepped away, but he nodded. "Then we'll take care not to stoke his suspicions."

Tess stepped forward to knock on the hall's front door, and when the butler appeared, she immediately sensed that something was amiss. The usually stolid gray-haired gentleman looked harried today, his spectacles slightly askew, his upper lip dotted with perspiration.

"Hello, Teague, we're here to see his lordship."

"Of course, Miss Hawthorne." He focused on Dominic. "And Mr. Prince. You're both expected."

The man opened the door wide for them to enter, and Tess heard voices echoing in the house. That was unusual. Usually, the hall was quiet, even as the servants went about their work.

"Is his lordship entertaining visitors?" Dominic asked the butler.

The man took in a shaky breath and returned a tight grimace that may have been an attempt at a half-smile. "His lordship will wish to explain, Mr. Prince. Shall I escort you back?"

"He's in his study?" Tess confirmed.

"He is."

"Then we know the way. Thank you, Teague."

Tess made her way down one corridor and then another while Dominic followed, and they were soon outside the nobleman's study. As usual, the door stood cracked open a bit and Tess rapped once and pushed her way inside.

Fenbridge was on the far side of the room and turned as they entered the room. Only once they were inside did Tess note that the elderly nobleman was at the drinks cart. At shortly after eight in the morning.

"A cordial for my health, Miss Hawthorne, so you may remove that pinched look of concern from your pretty face." He sipped at a tiny glass as he faced them. "And good morning to you too, Mr. Prince."

Tess couldn't deny that whatever he was sipping put some color in the nobleman's cheeks.

"We've had a bit of a surprise at the hall."

"Visitors?" Tess asked.

Fenbridge grimaced. "Indeed. Uninvited. Unexpected. But they're here all the same, and I wanted you both here. To prepare you."

"Prepare us?" Dominic asked. "For *your* visitors?"

Fenbridge nodded with a strange solemnity. "The American and his heir." Fenbridge locked eyes with Tess. "I suppose he wants to see what he's purchased."

Tess's belly dropped into her boots, and she cast a look at Dominic, who looked as shocked and dismayed as she felt.

"We're only at the beginning. There's not much to show him," Dominic said, then cast a quick glance at Tess.

She wondered if he was thinking what she was. If their deductions were correct about what they'd found, there would likely be a great deal for him to see in the coming days, provided previous treasure hunters hadn't beaten them to it.

Tess's heart raced. She thought of what Dominic had told her before they'd begun the dig, that he'd ask Van Arsdale if some items could be kept in England. She looked up at him, wondering if he'd follow through now that the man was here in the flesh.

Dominic looked irritated, if not outright angry.

"Have you ever met him before?" she asked him quietly.

"Yes, once, on his first visit to London." He looked at her, his expression softening. "It was brief."

Fenbridge made his way back to his desk without the aid of the cane he usually used to assist him. He settled heavily into his worn leather chair.

"This visit won't be brief, I fear," Fenbridge told them before sipping again from his cut crystal glass. "The brazen man arrived last night, banging on my door, startling the staff. Apparently, the man and his heir had tried the local inn and found it wanting. Decided a suite at the hall would suit the two of them better."

"That seems rather presumptuous."

Fenbridge lifted his glass to her. "A far kinder description than I'd opt for, Miss Hawthorne."

"Should we speak to him now?" Dominic asked, his back straighter, shoulders squared.

Fenbridge exhaled a long sigh. "I would say yes, Mr. Prince, except that they're still breaking their fast in my dining room." He flung his arm out. "They've all but taken up permanent residence."

Tess's father had always taught her and Tristan to face the difficult tasks first. "Shall we go and speak to him?" Tess directed the question at Dominic.

He worked his jaw. "Perhaps we should discuss it first." He stepped away from her and went over to close Fenbridge's study door.

"What lies under that mound on your land, Lord Fenbridge, may be of greater historical value than we anticipated."

Tess stared at him wide-eyed. When he'd come to Wiggenstow, she'd been certain all he cared about was treasure. Now, as she'd confessed to him, she knew he was so much more than what the papers portrayed.

Fenbridge leaned forward, resting his hands on his desk. "Explain," he said, finally revealing a bit of interest in what the mound held.

Dominic fixed his gaze on Tess and arched one dark brow as if seeking her assent.

She nodded at him. If they could take anyone into their confidence, it was Fenbridge.

"This is likely a ship burial," Dominic said with such a low voice that it sparked memories of the previous night, of him whispering in her ear, against her skin. A little shiver ran down Tess's spine.

DOM WAS ALMOST PAINFULLY aware of Tess now. In order to think clearly, he first had to stop focusing on her sweet floral scent, her nearness, the desire to touch her.

The news that Van Arsdale had descended on Wiggenstow with no forewarning set him on edge. He and Eve had patrons in the past who'd attempted to keep them under thumb and manage every aspect of their efforts. It always hampered their progress, and those were inevitably the least successful expeditions.

Though excavation was more a science than an art, the freedom to make decisions on the fly always improved their outcomes. Thus, a large part of Van Arsdale's appeal had been his distance. Indeed, they had more correspondence with his men of business in New York and London than with the American steel magnate himself.

After staring at him a moment with a perplexed frown, Fenbridge glanced once at Tess and asked, "And what am I to make of that?"

"That it's a unique find," Tess put in. "It means we've most likely found the resting place of a nobleman. Perhaps even a king."

Fenbridge's eyes finally registered a bit of the excitement Dom had been feeling since they'd identified the ship's rivets. Until that excitement had been overtaken, of course, by his time spent with Tess.

"Van Arsdale will be ridiculously pleased with that," Fenbridge surmised.

Dom heard Tess make a little sound of distress, and she shot him a worried look. They hadn't talked much about the dig for the last two days. They'd been too caught up in each other to focus on anything else.

"This find could be an extraordinary discovery, my lord. And the historical value of these artifacts," she said, speaking a bit more loudly and forcefully, "may be so great that it would be a travesty to let them leave England." She took a breath after that impassioned declaration.

Dom wasn't at all surprised by her vehemence. She'd made her feelings clear before they'd sank a single trowel into the ground.

"So," he said, locking eyes with first Fenbridge and then Tess, "what should we tell Van Arsdale now, before we know exactly what we'll find?"

Fenbridge's face slowly softened into a mischievous grin. "That seems a very good question indeed."

"I'm going to make the same argument to him," Tess told Dom, as if he might have forgotten her thoughts on the matter. "If it's a significant hoard, some of what we find should remain in England."

"I know," he told her with a smile. "We can show him what we've found and tell him what it could mean." The American hoped for the grandest treasure they could unearth, but they didn't yet know what had already been plundered.

"Then let's go and speak to him," Tess said decidedly. Then she dug something out of the pocket of her skirt. A tiny box. Dom knew instantly what it contained. "Show him this if he needs proof of what we've accomplished."

Dom took the box, as small as a ring box, and closed his fingers over it. "Are you coming, Fenbridge?"

The old man waved them off as if eager to be rid of them. "To be frank, I've had enough of the Americans to last me a good long while."

Dom and Tess walked side by side, and he barely resisted reaching for her. She was all but vibrating with nervous energy.

"He's gregarious and rather loud," Dom told her by way of warning.

"That's just how I imagined him."

"Don't let him rattle you."

"I don't rattle easily, Mr. Prince." Her saucy expression heated his blood.

Dom wanted to stop her, brace her against the wall, and remind her how he could make her come apart in his arms.

Instead, he grinned and told her, "I'm well aware."

A housemaid directed them to the dining room, though

the lively conversation emanating from the room served as a kind of beacon.

The first thing Dom noticed when they stepped inside was that the table was all but bursting with dishes, far too much for two people to consume. The second thing he noticed was that Van Arsdale's heir was not a son but a daughter.

The young woman was garbed in an elaborate striped gown with enormous sleeves and wore jewels on every finger, around her neck and wrists, and even in her hair. She sprang up from her seat at their entrance, oblivious to the linen napkin that fluttered to the floor.

"Oh, I know who you are!" she said with too much enthusiasm. "The famous treasure hunter, Dominic Prince," she breathed with an awestruck American twang. She clapped her hands together and beamed at him, then turned her attention to Tess. "And you look a bit like his sister, Miss Eveline Prince, but you're not, are you?"

Tess laughed. "I am not, no." She stepped forward confidently. "I am Tess Hawthorne."

"Sofia Van Arsdale." The young woman held her hand out almost as a debutante would in expectation that a gentleman might take it and kiss it.

Tess clasped the young woman's hand and shook it.

"Darling girl," Van Arsdale boomed, as he dabbed a napkin at his lips and then tossed it aside as he stood, "I told you about the lady historian we hired in place of her deceased father."

Dom snapped his gaze to Tess at that. She maintained her pleasant expression, seemingly unfazed by the man's bluntness.

"You weren't expected, Van Arsdale," Dom told the man, who he knew he should attempt a bit more deference with.

"My dear girl here forced the issue, I'm afraid."

Miss Van Arsdale rolled her eyes dramatically. "What Papa means to say is that he forced the issue because he fancies a titled son-in-law." She grinned at Tess as if she might sympathize with her plight. "He's secured invitations for me to a dozen aristocratic soirees in London, but I refused to go until we came to meet the dashing Mr. Prince."

A demure batting of her lashes came after that revelation and then a brazen assessment of him from head to toe that her father, standing behind her, could not see.

Though Tess could.

Dom groaned inwardly.

He knew what was expected of him, like one knows the steps of a familiar dance performed again and again. And there had been a time when he would have relished it—stretching up to his full height, puffing out his chest, smoothing out his voice as he offered some brief, colorful tale of his exploits.

Now, none of it held any appeal. It felt a bit like a suit of clothes he'd long outgrown, and he took comfort in that realization, because it was a costume he no longer wished to wear.

"Stop fussing over Prince, my girl." Van Arsdale strode past his daughter, straight up to Dom. "Now, tell us, man, what have you found?"

"We've only just begun, Mr. Van Arsdale."

The tall, boisterous American's face crumpled. "Two weeks. Money for more than a dozen men. You must have found something."

Dom took a single step back, nearer to Tess.

The man seemed to relish using his booming voice and larger-than-life presence to overwhelm. Dom wasn't intimidated by the man, but he did value a bit of breathing room.

Except when it came to Tess Hawthorne. To her, he couldn't seem to get close enough.

Slowly, making sure to infuse it all with a bit of drama he thought the Americans would appreciate, Dom drew the box containing Tess's find out of his pocket.

"We have made some discoveries. Very promising discoveries. Including this." Dom lifted the box's lid, tipping it forward so that the metal and gem would catch the light.

"Ooh, Papa, let me see." Miss Van Arsdale rushed forward, one palm pressed to her chest, the other to her belly. "It's a gem," she said breathlessly. "An ancient ruby."

"More likely a garnet," Tess said factually. "But I believe the metal may be gold."

"Thunderation," Van Arsdale said, followed by a whistle. Though once he peered around his daughter's wide sleeves, his forehead puckered. "It's broken and very small."

"It's likely a piece of a buckle, or perhaps a brooch," Tess offered.

"Why is it broken?"

"My theory would be grave robbers," Dom told the man. "Perhaps within the last hundred years, or even contemporary to the burial."

"If we could find the matching piece, and there was another ruby, imagine what lovely earbobs they'd make," Miss Van Arsdale mused, peeking a glance at her father.

Tess sucked in an audible breath. Dom's stomach tightened with unease.

"We'll find you something much finer than a broken buckle, Sofie girl."

Dom glanced at Tess, who shot him a horrified look.

"They aren't truly thinking of wearing what we find, are they?" she whispered to him.

Dom hardly thought it the time to point out that his own family had earned their wealth and fame from the trade in antiquities—from frescos to wall hangings to gems and art. Though his father had finally refused the practice, there were even dealers who sold entire mummies to private collectors for the entertainment of party guests.

But he understood Tess's dismay.

"These items are to be secured in your museum, are they not?" Dom asked Van Arsdale, fully aware the man needed no reminder. "They'll be featured for their historical value."

"Of course." Van Arsdale glared at him, as if he'd caught the tightness in Dom's tone.

Van Arsdale cast a look Tess's way, and Dom immediately felt protective.

"You can tell us more of the history, yes?" the American said to her with a bit of a bark that set Dom's teeth on edge.

"I can."

Van Arsdale squared in on Dom again. "Take us out to the dig site. Sofia and I want to see what you've done." He gestured dismissively at the box. "I hope the next finds are better than this and preferably not broken."

"Whatever we find will be centuries old and likely greatly weathered if not broken," Tess told him, her tone surprisingly light.

And she was right. If the man thought this would be like pulling Egyptian relics out of an undisturbed tomb, he was greatly mistaken.

Miss Van Arsdale seemed to sense her father's growing ire and moved past him to draw next to Tess. "Whatever you find, I want to hear all the stories of the people who made it."

Tess nodded and offered the young woman a smile. "I can tell you about our theories of whose burial this may be, of course."

"Excellent." Miss Van Arsdale beamed, revealing dimples. "And can you make them colorful theories, Miss Hawthorne? Our guests will love that most of all."

"Guests?" Dom prompted.

"Oh yes, Mr. Prince, we've invited some of our friends in London to Norfolk for dinner tomorrow evening." She pointed a look her father's way. "Papa wants to let them all know of the glorious museum he's establishing in New York."

"Your dinner is to be hosted by Lord Fenbridge?" Tess sounded dubious.

Dom couldn't imagine it either.

"I'm hosting," Van Arsdale clarified, "with Fenbridge generously loaning us his dining room."

"You'll both come, of course," Miss Van Arsdale insisted. "And your brother, Miss Hawthorne. Papa says he's employed at the dig too."

"He is, and I'll be sure to invite him." Tess sounded as resigned as Dom felt about this impromptu social event.

"Now." Van Arsdale clapped his hands. "Give us a few minutes to prepare and take us to the dig site. We want to see what we're paying for."

Dom took the crass dismissal as an opportunity to lead Tess out of the dining room and into the hall's foyer.

She clenched her hands into fists and spun toward him with flushed cheeks and thunder in her eyes. "She wants to make earbobs out of a centuries-old relic," she hissed quietly.

"I'll speak to him privately."

"Why privately?"

Dom shrugged. "From the little I know of him, he seems a man who might be less prideful without an audience."

Tess scoffed and pitched her brow.

Though she'd hate for him to say it when she was so full of righteous fury, she looked beautiful when she was fierce.

"I could be wrong," Dom admitted in a soft tone.

He took a step toward her and his pulse jumped when she matched the movement, until they were within whispering distance.

"Promise me," she said in a hushed tone. "We'll make them understand the value of all we find amounts to more than gold and gems."

He understood why she was disturbed by the Van Arsdales and their attitude toward the antiquities they hoped to unearth.

Dom reached for her hand without thinking, needing the anchor of her touch. Tess let him, her fingers tightening around his, though her gaze remained stormy.

"I promise you," he murmured, his thumb grazing her knuckles. "We'll make them understand."

Her shoulders relaxed just slightly, but something flickered in her eyes. Fragile trust, maybe, or the hope that he would be the sort of man who wouldn't let her down. The weight of it settled in his chest, heavier than any artifact they might pull from the earth.

Before he could say more, the dining room door swung open behind them.

"Well then. Shall we?" Van Arsdale's booming voice shattered the quiet moment between them.

Tess pulled her hand from Dom's and turned, her expression composed once more. But Dom felt the loss of her touch like a frayed thread in a tapestry, unraveling something he wasn't sure he could stitch back together.

With every step toward the excavation site, he wondered

which would change everything first, the artifacts buried beneath the earth, or the feelings unfolding between them. Last night hadn't just been about becoming lovers. She'd offered him her trust. Yet her walk this morning—her hesitance when he met her in the field—made him wonder about her doubts.

Chapter Eighteen

By the time Tess reached the dig site after stopping at home to change, she found that the Van Arsdales had been delivered by Fenbridge's carriage and coachman and were just descending.

Van Arsdale stomped down first, then his daughter waved helplessly at Dominic to assist her. Shockingly, Miss Van Arsdale still wore jewels and a pastel frock that Tess feared would be ruined as soon as she stepped around the muddy site.

The young lady placed her hands on Dominic's shoulders, her smile warm as he gently lowered her to the ground. She said something to him, and he returned her smile—it was his charming smile. The one that could stop hearts. The one that left ladies breathless.

Then, as if he sensed her watching, he turned and locked eyes with Tess.

A new smile curved his lips—a bit lopsided, wider, one she almost believed he reserved only for her. But a moment later, Miss Van Arsdale tugged at his arm, and Dominic turned, responding to whatever question she'd posed.

"You must guide me, Mr. Prince," Tess heard her say. "I'm terribly curious about every little thing."

Tess turned away, trying not to let the Americans' presence and the young lady's command of Dominic's attention irk her.

He was not hers to feel possessive of, at least not in the

long term. They were each other's for now. She knew that; understood it from the very start of whatever this was between them. Yet the arrival of the Van Arsdales felt like a pointed reminder of the distance that should exist between them, a distance she had once told herself was necessary. If they were to work together with clear minds, she could not afford to let herself become so deeply entangled.

"Excuse me, Miss Hawthorne." Mr. Townsend approached, his hat in his hand. "There's no sign of Mr. Hawthorne. Is he unwell?"

Tess hadn't even noticed that her brother wasn't among the workers already gathered at the site. "Not that I'm aware of. Let me ask Mr. Prince. He saw him this morning." Tess felt her cheeks flame at that admission and turned to wave a hand toward Dominic.

He'd begun leading the Van Arsdales on a promenade around the trench's perimeter but broke away immediately and strode toward her.

"Are you all right?" he asked with a furrowed brow and genuine concern in his tone.

"It's Tristan. You said you saw him this morning, but he's not shown up at the site."

"That's not a good sign."

"How did he seem this morning?"

He hesitated. "He has news that I suspect he won't wish me to share."

"You and my brother are keeping secrets from me now?"

"No, not at all." He reached for her arm, his touch gentle. "I just know that he'd want to tell you himself."

Normally, when Tristan was in dire trouble, Tess felt an odd sense of unease herself. A strange twin phenomenon that neither of them could explain but both accepted. She didn't have that feeling, and there was an amused twinkle in Dom's eyes that told her it wasn't bad news Tristan needed to share.

He scanned the dig site. "Are the Bromleys here?"

Tess lifted her hand to shade her view from the bright morning sun. The younger Bromley was down in one of the segments where they'd found metal fragments, excavating carefully alongside one of the other village men. But she didn't see Bill.

"There they are," Dominic told her, pointing toward the lane that led toward Fenbridge land.

Tess turned to see her brother and the much taller Bill Bromley walking down the lane in jovial conversation. Even from a distance, the men's laughter carried on the breeze.

"Good heavens," Tess breathed. "It's like witnessing a miracle."

Dom chuckled behind her and then drew closer. She could feel the heat of him at her back and resisted leaning into it. "Perhaps people can change after all."

Tess glanced back at him, catching a flicker of wistfulness in his eyes.

"We have visitors?" Tristan called from a few feet away.

Tess strode toward her brother and Bill. "I trust you two can explain why you've become bosom pals."

"Later, Tess," Tristan told her. "And I promise the wait will be worth it."

Tess narrowed her eyes at her twin and saw something in his expression she hadn't seen in years, something very like joy.

"This has to do with Justine," she guessed, half worry, half hope.

Bill winked but said nothing.

"Very well, if you're going to drive me mad with wondering, then I must advise you both to be on your best behavior since our patrons are visiting."

Both men turned to gape at the Van Arsdales, who seemed stuck in place where Dominic had left them, as if marooned without his guidance.

"What exactly are they going to do at the site?" Tristan's skepticism matched Tess's own.

"Observe," Dom put in. "Though I'd wager they'll get bored soon enough and return to Fenbridge Hall."

But just then Miss Van Arsdale's voice, bright and loud and youthful, peeled across the site. "I say, Mr. Prince, can you give me one of those tiny shovels so that I may dig too?"

Tess bit down so hard her jaw throbbed.

"It'll be all right," Dom whispered. "I won't let her do any damage." Then he brushed his hand along her back with the lightest touch before marching back toward the Americans.

Tristan stepped closer until they were shoulder to shoulder. He assessed Tess as she stared at the madness unfolding across the trench—Miss Van Arsdale stepping down into the dirt, trailing the ruffled hem of her stylish gown along the ground.

"If you could breathe fire, I suspect we'd all be singed at the moment," Tristan told her in a teasing tone.

"I'm glad you're happy." Tess reached out to take hold of his arm. "But I just want to get through the day. Between waiting to learn your secret and whatever these two plan to do to the dig site, it will be extraordinary if I do."

"Justine and I want to tell you together."

"Good heavens, what have you done?" Tess turned wide eyes her brother's way. "Is she with child?"

Tristan let out one of his deep, full-throated laughs. "It's even more shocking." He leaned in. "Wedlock," he whispered.

"Oh, Tris, that's lovely news!" Tess embraced him, holding

him tight, smiling so wide her earlier ire started to melt. A little. "And I promise to pretend to be shocked when you tell me together." She pulled back to look at him. "I am shocked."

"I am too, a bit." He looked chagrined, but it didn't dim any of the brightness in his eyes.

"Well, you're both invited to dine at Fenbridge Hall tonight."

"Are we?"

Tess gestured toward the Americans. "They've commandeered the place and Fenbridge is allowing it. Apparently, there's to be a formal dinner this evening with London visitors and all."

"Well, I guess Dominic was wrong. They're going to stay a while." Tristan's comment wasn't about the dinner, but about the fact that two footmen approached across Fenbridge's field carrying chairs and umbrellas. There could be no doubt who they were for.

Tess groaned. Tristan put a comforting arm of allegiance around her shoulders.

"If only the old curmudgeon had allowed us to dig, he could have saved us all this fuss. Though we would have been a bit poorer."

"Exactly. We couldn't have afforded all these men," Tess admitted, "but, yes, point taken. It's still a mystery why he refused us and then allowed . . . this." Tess waved toward the sight of Mr. Van Arsdale marching down the length of the trench, expecting the workmen to part before him like the Red Sea.

"I wonder what we'll find today." Tristan rolled up his sleeves. "That's what matters, Tess. Not them. It's the story of the people who built this ship, who put it into the ground, and whoever they meant to honor by its burial."

It was very like what their father's sentiments might have

been but spoken in Tris's playful style. It resonated inside her chest.

"Yes. You're right." Tess rolled up her sleeves too. What mattered was what they'd find. Not the Americans' meddling, not even the yearning she felt every time she looked Dominic's way.

Because he would soon walk out of her life, but what they dug out of the mound would endure. Displayed in an American museum, perhaps, but the history they recovered would be better understood. Tess suspected Eveline Prince planned to write about their finds, as she had with other Prince expeditions. Still, Tess couldn't help but think how their discoveries might bring a fresh depth to her father's Norfolk history.

She needed to stop replaying last night in her mind and remember: the dig was what mattered today. Everything else had to wait.

THE VAN ARSDALES WERE hardier than Dom had given them credit for. Even as the sun climbed high in the nearly cloudless sky and the temperature rose, they remained seated in their chairs under umbrellas, partaking of the various drinks and foodstuffs Fenbridge servants delivered to them every couple of hours.

Dom had the gut-twisting feeling he always did during a dig when they were on the cusp of something big. It had rarely failed him, though as the day progressed, his attention was drawn again and again to Tess. Whatever they were about to unearth mattered to him more because they'd find it together.

"Dominic!" Tristan was down in the lower middle end of the trench with three other men, and Dom made his way down the dirt shelf at the edge of the trench to where the three worked.

"What do you make of these?" Tristan cupped his dirty hands together, displaying five coins, gold coins.

"There are more here," Townsend said quietly, still crouched down, gently unearthing what seemed a purseful of coins, though the container itself had long since decomposed in the soil.

Dom took one from Tristan's hand, rubbing gently at the dust to make out the engraving.

"Tess," Tristan called. "Come have a look."

Even the sound of her name being called set off a little flutter in Dom's chest, and he watched her approach with a too obvious eagerness. They'd both been so intent on their work that they'd not spoken to each other for the past couple of hours.

"What do you see?" Dom asked, offering her the coin he held.

"It's gold," she murmured, then looked up at her brother. "Papa was better with coins than either of us."

"But you know who's mentioned there," Tristan told her.

"Dominus Noster . . ." she read and then looked up, locking eyes with each of them in turn. "Roman Emperor Justin. Sixth century. Are there more?"

Dom felt a bit dizzy, and he had a sudden wish that Eve was with him. She loved the finds that gave them indications of hard fast dates.

Tristan crouched down and Townsend handed him half a dozen more coins. All gold, from the looks of them.

"An ingot?" Dom reached for a rectangular lump of gold. It was common practice to include coins with royal or special burials, often with the notion of paying a ferryman or paying for whatever the soul might need in the afterlife.

"What have you got there?" Van Arsdale called from the packed dirt ledge above them.

They'd all been too caught up in their find to notice his approach.

"Gold coins," Dom told him.

"In good condition?"

"Excellent condition, sir," Townsend put in.

"That's what I want to hear," Van Arsdale said, seemingly uninterested in the finer details. "Find me lots more."

Dom approached Tess once the American made his way back to his chair.

"Breathe," he whispered to her.

She'd closed her eyes and seemed to be holding her breath. At his urging, her eyes opened and the frustration he saw there made the excitement of the last moments fade.

"I'm going back to the front to work," she told him, then offered the Justinian coin they'd found to him. "This tells us that the burial took place after the sixth century, and that would fit with the theory that it could be Redwald or one of his sons."

"It's a good theory."

"Not that Van Arsdale will care much about the details." She stared down at her mud-covered boots. "It's an odd feeling. I want to find more and yet I don't."

Before Dom could reply, she turned and made her way back to the spot where she'd been working for much of the day.

He glanced over at Tristan, who was bent over his field notebook, documenting each coin as well as sketching the spot where they'd discovered them.

"Let's move a few more men to this area," he suggested.

"Agreed," Tristan told him. "I'll see to it as soon as I have this all down."

"I'll take care of it." Dom stepped up to the perimeter of the trench and directed a few men in a corner section to move down toward the middle, closer to where the coins had been found.

As he made his way back to Tristan, he heard a gasp and turned quickly back to Tess.

She and the younger Bromley brother were hunched, their heads almost touching, as they stared down into the depression they'd excavated.

"Easy now," Dan Bromley murmured.

Tess nodded and swiped gently with her brush. "It's extraordinary."

Dom glanced up at the Americans, who seemed to be in excited discussion, perhaps about the find of the gold coins. He climbed down to where Tess and Bromley were on their knees.

"What is it?"

When Tess looked up, her eyes were glassy. "It's beautiful, but I'm not sure what it is." She kept her voice quiet, and he understood.

Crouching beside her, he spotted what she'd found, and his mouth went dry. Gold and ornately carved, the object was in perfect condition.

Dan tapped the handle end of his trowel against the edge and a clump of dirt fell away.

"I think it's a buckle," Tess breathed, brushing eagerly. She used her fingers to peel away a bit more of the top sediment and the whole piece became visible. It wasn't the tiny fragment she'd found earlier. This was massive in comparison.

With care and patience, she lifted it free of the soil and laid it in her palm. It filled her hand from her wrist to the tips of her fingers.

"This was a wealthy person," she said softly. "The workmanship is breathtaking."

It was without a doubt one of the most beautiful artifacts he'd ever seen, the kind that would cause gasps of delight for years. The kind that the papers would display in sketches and photographs. The kind that would be a centerpiece of a museum display.

Dom swallowed hard as he noted the shift of interest from the Van Arsdales.

Tess held his gaze, and it felt as if she was willing him to keep the find between the two of them for as long as possible.

A shadow passed over them, and Tess curled her fingers around the buckle, as if to shield it, but it was too late for that. Even the other workers on the dig were gathering around, sensing the excitement in the air.

"What do we have here?" Van Arsdale's voice was almost breathless, seemingly edged with the thrill of acquisition. He crouched beside them, peering at the artifact with the sharp eye of a man weighing worth and ownership, rather than history.

Tess hesitated. Dom felt it as much as saw it.

"It's a belt buckle," Dom said, then cleared his throat of the lump that seemed to have formed there. "Gold. Perhaps made for royalty, given the craftsmanship."

Van Arsdale whistled. "A true treasure!" He reached an arm out and slapped Dom on the back. "You'll be in the papers again, Prince. Your father would be proud."

Dom flinched at the words he might have savored weeks ago.

That kind of praise was what he'd sought; it had fueled his restlessness. He'd once relished notoriety as much as his father had. *Like father, like son*, he'd often been told.

But now, looking at Tess and the emotions swirling in her eyes, that legacy felt like a weight, pulling him away from who he truly was and what he wanted.

Tess's gaze on him held steadily. She said nothing. Expressed no anger. Made no demands. If she'd pleaded in that moment, he would have given her whatever she wanted.

Yet her eyes held something that shook him even harder than tears or anger. Something far more dangerous—hope. As if she trusted him to fight for her.

She reached for his hand and let the magnificent buckle slide from her palm into his.

"Let me have a closer look," Van Arsdale demanded.

Dom closed his fingers over the intricately carved gold. It should have been an easy choice. Two weeks ago, it would have been. For the first time in his life, Dom didn't care about the story of his exploits of the glory of this find. He wasn't determined to follow an already-trod path carved by his father. He wanted something more. He wanted her.

Yet he knew what he'd agreed to, that his work and his finds on this dig had been bought and paid for by the Van Arsdales. The battle couldn't be won in this moment.

So he stood, turned toward his patron, and held out his hand.

But he glanced back at Tess.

She didn't look away. Didn't try to hide her disappointment, but there was no condemnation in her gaze. As if she knew the inevitability of and expected the choice he'd make.

And, somehow, that was worse.

Chapter Nineteen

The crowd dripped with jewels. Diamond chokers, bracelets flashing with rubies and sapphires, stick pins glinting with emeralds. Their gowns and dark evening suits were equally elaborate, and the very air seemed thick with wealth and refinement.

Tess had dug out her single ball gown, a green velvet relic that, though lovely, felt painfully out of date among such extravagance. She felt underdressed, certainly under-adorned.

Perhaps that was why she kept accepting glasses of champagne from the Fenbridge footmen, who appeared agog at the spectacle around them, taking in the dramatic display taking place in Fenbridge's enormous drawing room, which likely hadn't been used in years.

Each glass of champagne seemed to dull the sharp edges of her anger, her confusion about Dominic, her frustration that she'd let herself fall so far.

Her eyes kept drifting around the gathering, searching for Dominic, though she'd promised herself she wouldn't.

Van Arsdale had whisked him away, according to Tristan, to charm a few aristocratic collectors eager to contribute to his growing museum. It was hard to keep bitterness at bay as the Americans seemed to claim everything—Fenbridge Hall, the treasures in its mounds, and now Dominic.

Without Dominic in sight, what continually drew her eye was the centerpiece of the evening—the gold buckle she'd found.

Her discovery. It felt like a real, tangible accomplishment at a time when she felt increasingly uncertain about everything else.

Van Arsdale had somehow, in a very short time, arranged for an elaborate display for the artifact. It sat atop a pillar on a platform covered in deep burgundy velvet that adorned the gold to perfection.

Guests swarmed around the find, some reaching out to stroke the buckle's delicate curves. Tess flinched every time someone touched it and then called herself a fool for caring so very much, for her sense of possessiveness. The long-dead Anglo-Saxons might argue that she had plundered it from its rightful resting place just as the robbers of old had stolen from the burial site, but it still stung to see it treated as nothing more than a pretty bauble.

Her glass was empty, and a servant approached a moment later to exchange it for a full one.

"Slow down, sister dear." Tristan appeared beside her and plucked the glass from her hand, taking a sip himself.

Tess turned to find him looking every bit the polished gentleman with Justine on his arm, radiant in a deep pink evening gown.

Tess's heart swelled. "I'm so happy for the two of you," Tess rasped as she hugged each of them in turn. Her joy for her brother and Justine was the only feeling she was utterly certain of tonight. Everything else felt like a murky quagmire.

"This is a bit much," Justine said quietly, voicing what all of them seemed to feel.

"Can't believe Fenbridge is stomaching this." Tristan scanned the room. "Where is he?"

"I haven't seen him at all," Tess said, her voice tight. "It's as if he's forfeited his home as well as everything dug from his land to the Americans."

Just then, a ripple of murmurs swirled through the drawing room, followed by applause. Tess's stomach lurched as she turned toward the sound.

Sofia Van Arsdale had climbed up onto a dais that Tess hadn't even noticed at the edge of the room. She held a glass of champagne raised high in her hand.

"Tonight," the young lady called out, "we celebrate my father and his brilliant museum, which grows with wonders by the day." A round of applause followed. Then she gestured out into the crowd. "And, of course, we honor the famous Dominic Prince for finding this extraordinary artifact today!"

She waved toward him, urging him to join her on the dais. Tess's heart was in her throat as she watched him take his place beside the heiress.

"Hip-hip hooray to Mr. Prince," Miss Van Arsdale said and then lifted her glass as if to toast him.

Dom raised his hand, and the cheers faltered. "There's been a misunderstanding." His gaze found Tess again, locking with hers. In that instant, the world seemed to still. "I didn't make this find."

Tess's pulse quickened.

He looked directly at her, his admiration so palpable, she felt it as something physical. A warmth that rushed through her from her cheeks all the way to her toes. His eyes softened and there seemed to be a message in them, meant only for her.

"Tess Hawthorne found the extraordinary piece on display this night." His deep voice carried across the room and seemed to echo in her chest. "She deserves all your praise."

He lifted his glass and the crowd turned to find her.

"Who is she?"

"Is that her?"

"Come, Miss Hawthorne," Miss Van Arsdale called. "Let us celebrate you properly."

She waved her forward, and Tristan put a hand on her shoulder. "Go, Tess, you deserve it."

Tess felt woozy as she wended her way through the overheated room. A swell of scents, perfumes, and pomades washed over her, and just as she was stalled by an elaborately garbed couple, he was there.

Dominic had stepped down from the dais to cut through the crowd and reach for her. She took his hand and felt instantly steadier. Then he wrapped an arm around her to escort her to the dais, and she had to remind herself not to lean into him too freely, not to bury her face against his neck, as the deepest part of her wished to.

Miss Van Arsdale was still on the dais and reached a bejeweled hand down to help her up. She clasped the young woman's hand with her free hand but was loath to let go of Dominic. He understood and ascended onto the dais with her.

It was a tight fit with the three of them, and he rested a hand on her lower back—that warm point of comfort kept her from bolting when all gazes turned her way.

She'd never liked being on display or being the focus of so much attention. The last time she'd felt so many eyes on her had been after her ruin. Her scandal.

"To our treasure seekers!" Sofia Van Arsdale said before sipping at her drink.

Tristan now held Tess's drink, but she watched as Dominic took a sip. Then he offered his glass to her.

She took a smaller sip than she had all night, and Dominic's expression turned heavy, hungry as he watched her swallow and lick her lips.

The crowd went back to murmuring, back to circling around the gold buckle she'd found.

And Sofia departed the dais, leaving them to stand facing each other.

"Why did you do that?"

He blinked as if confused by her question. "I only told the truth."

"But all of this will be your achievement."

"That's nonsense," he said, almost affronted by her claim. "I won't ever claim credit for your finds."

"But I work for you. We all do on the dig."

He took the glass from her hands and downed the rest in a single swallow. "Are you determined to argue with me? Are we back to being at odds like the day we met?"

"I'm not arguing, just being precise." Part of her wanted to row with him. It would make it all so much easier.

"You're maddening." He stepped closer. "From the moment I met you, you have been." His voice had dropped low, quiet, just for her ears. "And I've wanted you from that moment to this one." His breath gusted against her cheek as he bent further to whisper in her ear. "The question, darling Tess, is what do you want?"

His nearness made her feel as if she was going to tip off the dais, and she reached for him, a hand against the heat of his chest.

Immediately, he laid his hand over hers. "Tell me you feel as I do." There was a thread of desperation in his voice.

Then a deep-toned bell rang somewhere in the house, quieting the conversation in the room.

"Dinner is served," a footman announced loudly, and as a wave the bejeweled and richly garbed crowd moved one after the other from the drawing room toward the dining room.

"We should go in to dinner," Tess told him because this wasn't the time to say more.

"I'll escort you." He offered his arm, and she took it.

"Will you sit by me?" She wasn't sure why she asked, but she wanted it all the same.

"Yes, if you want me to. Do you?"

But even as he asked the question, Sofia Van Arsdale rushed up to them and grabbed him by the arm.

"Come, Mr. Prince, you must be meet Lord Gowring. He says he's followed your career and knew your father."

He held fast to Tess, where she had laid her hand on his arm. But she knew he was in an impossible situation and slipped her hand free.

"Go on," she told him. "Find me after dinner."

Tess watched him go and then followed the last of the guests into the crowded dining room. Van Arsdale sat at one end of the long table and his daughter sat at the opposite end. Fenbridge was, once again, missing from an event in his own home.

Tristan waved from the near side of the table. "Sit with us," he called to her over the din of conversation.

Tess approached, nearly colliding with a footman who'd already begun serving. "I'll be back in a bit."

He frowned, but before he could stop her, she headed out of the dining room in search of a member of Fenbridge's staff. She found a harried-looking maid in the hall.

"Could you direct me to his lordship, please?"

"I believe he's in his study, miss."

"Thank you." Each step Tess took away from the dining room and the clutter of guests, she breathed a bit easier, thought a bit more clearly. Though she didn't feel at ease.

Everything about the night, barring the moments with

Dominic and the pleasure of seeing Tristan and Justine together, felt wrong. And she was determined to solve the mystery of why the garrulous Fenbridge was behaving like a kicked dog in his own home.

The study door was closed over, but she twisted the latch and found it unlocked. When she stepped inside, it was as if she'd entered a separate world from the noisy, gem-crusted one of the Van Arsdales.

His study was lined with bookshelves along one wall, polished wood paneling on all the rest, and lovely landscape paintings which she'd always admired. Tonight, he had his window that looked out on the garden open, letting in the breeze. He sat in his enormous desk chair with his boots propped up on the window ledge.

"Thought you might come find me," he said without even looking at her. "Imagined your brother would revel in all of it, but you'd tire of it soon enough."

"Did you see what I found?"

The desk chair creaked as he turned to face her. He had a brandy snifter cupped in his hand, and his cheeks were bright enough to tell her it wasn't his first.

"Pour yourself one if you like," he said, noting her attention on the glass.

Tess did, though only a small amount. The champagne was beginning to wear off, and now that she was with Fenbridge, the anger burned fiercer.

She approached the front of his desk and sipped the brandy. It was smooth and its bite sharp in the back of her throat.

"Why did you deny me?" she asked when she thought she could do so without her voice breaking.

Fenbridge's silver brows dove closer as he frowned. "What do you mean?"

Good God, had he forgotten? "I asked to explore that mound. Tristan and I came to you with a plan, and you refused us."

"Ah," he said and then lifted his glass for a drink.

"You sit in here as if you can't bear the Americans, and yet you let this happen. You signed the agreement and took his money."

He simply stared at her.

"Have you nothing to say?"

Tipping his head, he told her, "No, I'm waiting as I suspect you're not finished."

Tess narrowed her eyes. "Is it that you only care about the money?"

Fenbridge burst into laughter. A raucous yet bitter sound. "My dear Miss Hawthorne, you're too clever for such a hypothesis. Have I ever sought your rents on Foxdene?"

Dropping her gaze, Tess twisted the snifter in her hands. The overdue rent was yet another point of shame to add to her others, but what he said was true. He'd not even sent a notice of eviction or mentioned the matter during her meetings with him each morning since the start of the dig.

"Then why?" Her voice came out plaintive, full of all the frustration she felt.

"Your father."

Tess snapped her head up, locked gazes with the old man. "What does that mean?"

"Did he never tell you that he wanted more for you?"

"More?" Her father had urged Tess and her brother to pursue their interests.

"He wanted you both to move beyond Wiggenstow, both literally and in terms of your ambitions. Though perhaps you were staying for him, and he didn't want that."

"We were staying for him." Tess had once considered going

to a lady's college in London, and Tristan had almost been convinced by their father to study mathematics at university. But as their father's illness progressed and he grew weaker, leaving seemed unthinkable.

"So, he was right."

"Yes, but when we came to you, it was because we wanted it. Father didn't care if we dug up the mounds. He was content to write his book."

"There are six mounds on my land." He took a swig of brandy and seemed to savor it a moment. "Now that you've found treasures in one, the others will draw interest too. This is a project that will take years."

Tess slumped into the chair in front of Fenbridge's desk. "Are you saying our own father thwarted us?"

Fenbridge sat forward. "I hope you don't see it as such. He mentioned it out of love, out of hope for your futures." He lifted his bearded chin. "But the decision was ultimately mine, so you may blame me if you please."

"Oh, I do."

The nobleman winced at that, then he settled back in his chair with a heavy sigh. "I denied you the dig because I thought it might spare you a life's obsession over this corner of Norfolk, and yet here you remain."

"You made a mistake to deny us permission." Tess would not waver on that point, even if she adored her father and his desire for more for his children. "Do you regret it yet?"

He arched a brow at her. "Letting those bloody Americans trample over my land and home? What do you think?"

"Then renegotiate your agreement with Van Arsdale. Send him away."

"And let you and Mr. Prince finish the job?"

"Yes, I'd much rather work for you than for them."

Fenbridge groused and waved his hand. "You assume my coffers are as flush as the Americans' and can easily fund so many salaries. Sadly, Miss Hawthorne, they are not."

"I'd still rather be employed by you than them. Even if we had to take the project more slowly."

"And would your *gentleman friend* feel the same?"

Tess stiffened at his tone. "You once said you did not judge me, my lord."

"It's not judgement. But I do wonder. Do you love him, Miss Hawthorne?"

"We're talking about the dig and Van Arsdale," she told him, her whole body tensed, defensive, at the change in topic.

"If you do, perhaps you should tell him."

"I haven't come here to discuss Mr. Prince."

The old nobleman shook his head, hunched down in his seat as if defeated. When he looked up again, his eyes were glassy. Tess didn't know if it was the brandy or emotion that caused them to glitter.

"You remind me so much of your mother. And why we never would have suited." A ghost of a smile softened his expression. "She was stubborn, as you are. As I am."

Tess stood again and crossed her arms. "Forgive me, Lord Fenbridge, but I don't wish to hear about you and my mother."

He nodded. "Then let me speak only of myself. Take me as your example, Miss Hawthorne . . . of what not to do."

Tess blinked and frowned. "I beg your pardon?"

"I've lacked courage, but you seem a braver sort." He nodded again as if warming to his subject. "Love is always a risk. I was a coward, but I trust you won't be."

"You could prove your courage now and challenge Van Arsdale."

They stared at each other for several moments, then

Fenbridge lifted his glass out to her as if in a toast. "Touché, Miss Hawthorne. I shall speak to the American. You go find your treasure hunter."

Tess didn't relish Fenbridge as a matchmaker, but she departed his study to find Dominic.

THIS DINNER HAD BEEN far worse than the one Dom had endured at the Walcotts' party. Tonight, Tess wasn't seated far away from him. She wasn't even in the bloody room.

After the first course was served, he excused himself. The Van Arsdales were so thoroughly in their element that he doubted they'd notice his departure. And Tristan Hawthorne shot him a wink as he stood, as if fully aware of Dom's intention to find his sister.

He checked Fenbridge's library first, as that's where she found him at the Walcotts' party. Then, since he wasn't entirely sure of the hall's ground-floor layout, he checked inside every unlocked room. When he exited the third, he heard footsteps and turned to see her striding toward him.

"Were you looking for me?" she asked as if there might be any other answer to explain him wandering the hall.

"Of course. There hasn't been a moment to speak to you, not truly, all day."

She cast her gaze back over her shoulder and then down the length of the hall behind him as if wary of others hearing them. Dom didn't give a damn if they did.

"Why don't we step outside?" he asked her.

With a single nod, she stepped past him, and he let her lead the way. Toward the back of the house, she pushed open two French doors that led toward a paved terrace. Someone had lit lanterns for the guests' benefit, and Tess stopped near one.

"It feels as if days have passed since this morning."

"An eventful stretch of hours for certain." The smile she wore held no real amusement.

"Tess," he told her softly, "I need to know what you're thinking."

He drew closer and it seemed a victory when she didn't pull away. His breath caught in his throat when she reached out to run her finger along the buttons of his shirt.

"I'm thinking that something I told myself could be simple is now very complicated." Her eyes glowed in the lantern light, but Dom could only see a stew of emotions he was afraid to interpret. "I was a fool to think it."

"It needn't be complicated."

"Of course it is. My feelings for you are more than I wanted them to be."

Dom smiled. "Forgive me if I'm quite happy to hear that." He reached for her then, cupping her cheek. "Tess, you may believe I'm the man that all of them believe I am—"

"You know I don't. I've already told you as much. You're more than that." She smiled up at him. "A great deal more."

"And you are the only woman who's made me want to be more than some ridiculous caricature of my father." He drew in a breath because he felt suddenly at sea, unsure of how to say all that was weighing on his heart. "I hardly remember the man I was before I met you."

She looked into his eyes, studying his features as if weighing his words. "We said this would be temporary," she whispered.

"I don't want it to be. Do you?"

"No." She shook her head, then looked away from him. "But I can't fathom how it would work. You'll leave. Go off on the next adventure."

"Not without you." He cupped her face in both of his hands, bent until their lips were a breath apart. "You are my first thought when I wake and in my dreams all night. You say you cannot fathom how it would work. I cannot fathom my future without you in it."

He kissed her, praying she'd respond as eagerly as she had every other time. Yet it was more than every other time—more hunger, more passion, more need—as if both of them had been waiting to unleash the feelings they'd held at bay.

Dom clasped her nape, aware he'd dislodged pins, though neither of them seemed to care. She slipped a finger between the buttons of his shirt, as if desperate to touch his bare skin, and he took full of advantage of the low neckline of her gown, licking, tasting, nipping the softness of her neck.

"Dominic," she moaned when he tugged at the edge of her gown so that he could kiss the swell of her breast.

Fingers sunk in his hair, she urged him closer.

"Ah, there you are," Sofia Van Arsdale called from the terrace doors.

If it weren't for the perfection of having Tess in his arms, he would have growled his irritation at the interruption. He kept his back to the American, helping Tess to right her gown, then turned, sheltering her as well as he could from Miss Van Arsdale's view.

But the young woman was already striding right up to them.

"Ah, and Miss Hawthorne." She glanced at each of them, and it was obvious the moment understanding dawned. She let out a little chuckle. "I see. I'm not sure what my father will make of this."

"If your father takes issue with how I conduct myself, then let him say as much to me," Dom told her. What was between him and Tess was none of the Americans' business, and it had not impacted their work on the dig in any way.

"I have something I must say," Tess said and then stepped

out to face Miss Van Arsdale. "I'll forestall any concern your father might have. I hereby leave my post as advisor to your father's treasure hunt. Neither of you seems to care much about the history anyway."

"Tess, you needn't—" Dom started.

"No, I want to. If I can't stomach their treatment of the artifacts, then I shouldn't be taking their money."

He wasn't sure if she was saying he should do the same, but he understood how she felt.

"I'm going home," she told him. "Enjoy the rest of your evening."

"I'm coming with you."

Tess flashed a soft smile, and he started toward her.

"But my father wants you back in the dining room, Mr. Prince," Miss Van Arsdale called. "He sent me to find you."

"I don't have much of an appetite." The only thing he needed was more time with Tess. "I'll bid you good evening, Miss Van Arsdale."

"You can't just walk out when my father's asking for you," Miss Van Arsdale said, her voice full of shock that he'd dare to do other than Van Arsdale's bidding. "Surely, you don't mean to forfeit your position too."

"Don't," Tess said softly, reaching out to clasp his hand. "Don't make some hasty decision because of me. Go back and do what you must. We can talk in the morning."

"I can come tonight, or you could come to me," he whispered.

"I've had too much to drink, and it's been an eventful day. Let's talk in the morning." She arched up onto her toes, pressed a hand to his chest, and kissed his cheek.

His heart thudded hard as he watched her walk away.

Chapter Twenty

Tess barely slept a wink despite how exhausted she'd been when she returned to the cottage.

She had listened in the dark as Tristan and Justine tiptoed in hours later, and some part of her settled at the sound. They had made it back safely, and that was something, at least.

She smiled to think that her brother had finally found the courage to give his heart to someone. What she asked herself over and over was whether she had the courage to do the same.

Dominic had spoken of them making a life together, and yet nothing underscored the differences between them more sharply than Miss Van Arsdale's voice, clear and commanding, calling him back to join the adoring crowd who wanted to think of him as some dashing treasure hunter.

Regret sat in her chest like a weight. She had given up her spot on the dig, but that didn't mean she was finished. If Fenbridge challenged Van Arsdale and took back control, she'd happily work all the hours of the day to continue excavating. Yet in the cold light of day, it seemed a tenuous possibility—Fenbridge had signed a contract, and the Van Arsdales would not let the dig go without a fight.

She feared her choice had put her and Dominic on opposing sides too. At the least, it put him in an awkward position, especially if Fenbridge did challenge the Van Arsdales as she hoped he would. She hadn't meant to do that to him, hadn't even considered it in the moment.

If he was forced to choose, she could not blame him for choosing his livelihood. His reputation. Even his family's reputation. All could be at stake if he walked away from Van Arsdale's patronage.

His words from the night before, so tantalizingly full of hope for their future together, played in her mind, made her heart fill with warmth. But whenever she tried to imagine a practical means of making it happen, she couldn't.

Even if she knew he was more than the man in the papers, he was that man too. People like Van Arsdale would insist upon it.

As the first rays of daylight peeked through her curtains, she sat up in bed and rubbed at her tired eyes.

To her surprise, she heard movement in the cottage's kitchen.

After dressing quickly in a simple day dress—there would be no need for trousers if she wasn't employed on the dig—she left her room to find Tristan warming a teapot of water on the hearth.

"Couldn't sleep?" he asked without looking up.

"I might ask you the same. It's five in the morning."

He huffed a rusty laugh, then scraped a hand through his mussed hair. "Justine decided to return home rather than stay. Propriety. Her brothers. All that. So, no, I didn't sleep well."

Silence settled between them, broken only by the clink of porcelain as he prepared two cups of tea.

"I quit the dig, Tris," Tess admitted as she sought some comfort by wrapping her hands around the warm ceramic.

He froze, the teacup midway to his lips. "What? Why on earth did you do that?"

Tess bristled at his tone. "Can you not guess? Did you not see how they treated the buckle? How they see it all as—"

"Baubles?"

Tess frowned. "It doesn't disturb you?"

"Did you really expect anything more? They're paying a ridiculous amount of money for the dig, and then they'll pay through the nose to transport it all back to New York, where there are already fine museums." He looked at her expectantly, as if astounded she'd missed some crucial detail. "It's a vanity project for Van Arsdale. That's always seemed obvious."

"And that's all right with you?"

He shrugged. "I thought you'd be happy for the chance to dig. You wanted it so much for so long."

"Tris," Tess said quietly, "I thought we both did."

He sipped his tea and stared into the steaming cup as if looking for his next words. "I wanted you to be happy. You threw yourself into it after . . ." He looked up at her bleakly. "After Shaw. After we lost Pater. It put a sparkle in your eye when nothing else did. So I sure as hell was going to support it."

Tess felt as if all the air was slowly being drawn from her lungs, leaving her hollow. Her mind spun. Over the last few days, she'd learned that so much she believed wasn't true at all.

Her parents' love story hadn't been a simple romance. Fenbridge's refusal to let them dig hadn't been a simple cruelty. Tristan's support of her goals hadn't been a simple shared dream.

And her feelings for Dominic? They weren't simple either. They were enormous, complicated, ready to consume her if she gave into them.

"I don't think I can quit the dig, Tess," Tristan said quietly. "Not with the wedding approaching."

"I wouldn't ask you to." She bit her lip. "It seemed right last night, and I don't wish to do this under the Van Arsdales' control . . . but I have to admit I still want to go back out there and continue searching."

"Then have Dominic speak to Van Arsdale. He can convince him to bring you back on board. I know it." His lips twitched into something like a grin. "Besides, we both know Dominic Prince would do anything for you."

Would he? Even if he tried, she wasn't convinced the Van Arsdales would let her set foot on their dig site again after her snappish comments to Miss Van Arsdale.

"There's more," Tess admitted. "Miss Van Arsdale found Dominic and I . . ."

Tristan arched a dark-gold brow. "Oh, I see. Do I need to call him out?" he asked in a teasing tone.

"Don't be ridiculous." She gave him a playful shove. "I merely mentioned it to explain why her father may not wish to have me on the dig any longer."

Tristan scoffed. "That's hypocritical if they keep Dominic on. And he would argue as much too, I suspect."

Tess wanted to believe that. She wanted to believe in him. In the two of them together. But how could she when she wasn't certain she could even trust herself anymore?

She'd been wrong about so many things.

The only time her doubts faded was when she was in Dominic's arms. No questions. No second-guessing. It was just . . . right.

DOM WAS UP, DRESSED, and ready to seek out Tess by seven. He hesitated a moment at his door, fearful it might be too early, but the thought of waiting was unbearable. He'd barely slept for how eager he was to resume what Miss Van Arsdale had interrupted.

He understood trust was hard for Tess. But her kisses, the

way she touched him, the way she always pulled him closer. That was real. Her feelings were real. He felt it in his bones.

The notion of scanning the dig site all day and not seeing her there, working with methodical care, gnawed at him all night too. He respected her decision to leave the Van Arsdales' employment, but he also wanted her, needed her, as his partner in this endeavor. Hell, she'd found the most significant artifact they'd yet dug from Fenbridge's field, and she'd even found the first one that proved they were on the right track.

He wouldn't pressure her to return, but he would damn well make sure the Americans took her back if she wanted it.

As he latched his room door and headed down the stairs, he was stopped cold by the sound of voices below. The bloody Van Arsdales. They were downstairs, speaking in boisterous terms to Mr. and Mrs. Randall.

He had a wild thought of climbing out the window of his room just to avoid them. The drop might be worth it.

Instead, with a sigh he felt bone-deep, he made his way to the lobby to face them.

"And there he is," the innkeeper's wife, Mrs. Randall, said cheerfully.

Whatever the Americans had said seemed to please her. They either appalled or charmed Wiggenstow's inhabitants. There was no in-between.

"Mr. Prince," Miss Van Arsdale called, her gaze bold. "Your expression is so fierce this morning." She plumped out her lower lip as if pouting might change his mood.

"I'm on my way to pay a call," he told them, nodding politely. "I hope you'll excuse me."

"We need to talk, Prince." Van Arsdale's booming voice

made clear it was a command more than a request. "Perhaps that table in the corner will do."

The taproom was quiet, all but unoccupied. Dom didn't relish stopping to speak with them at all, but they'd positioned themselves in front of him as if they'd tackle him bodily if he tried to escape.

"Very well. I can spare a few minutes."

Van Arsdale's brow jumped at that.

Once they were all seated, Mrs. Randall appeared with a tea service and a serving girl deposited a tray covered in pastries. None of it boded well for Dom's hopes for short conversation.

"Do you miss London, Prince?" Van Arsdale asked after taking a large slurp of black tea.

Dom frowned. "Not particularly." Anytime he thought of London, it brought back memories of the day he'd met Tess, but Tess was here, so Wiggenstow was where he was content to be. "Why?"

Miss Van Arsdale leaned both elbows on the table and propped her chin on her hands, beaming at him. "We're departing today and want you to join us."

A flicker of pleasure lit in his chest. They were leaving. No more meddling. No more ridiculous social events. No more suffocating oversight of the dig.

"I've spoken to Mrs. Randall," Van Arsdale added, "and she'll retain your room. I've paid up for the next fortnight. If the dig takes longer, I'll extend it."

Dom narrowed his eyes. "Retain my room?"

"You're coming with us, dear Mr. Prince," Miss Van Arsdale gushed. "Oh, can I call you Dominic? And will you call me Sofia? Papa says he approves."

Dom offered the young woman a tight smile and picked up his cup, swigging down tea rather than letting loose the curses that were threatening to spill from his mouth.

"It's not a good time to leave the dig." He managed to keep his voice even. "It's a crucial moment. My departure now is impossible."

Van Arsdale raised a finger, stabbing into the air. "Already assumed as much. Already have a solution." He yanked a slip of paper from his pocket and slapped it onto the battered wood of the inn table.

Dom leaned in to see a telegram from his sister: *Will arrive Wiggenstow Mon PM as requested. Eveline Prince*

She hadn't written him. Dom suspected she hadn't had time and that the Van Arsdales had sprung this on her much as they had him. He only hoped they hadn't forced her to abandon something important at her Berlin conference.

"I need to speak to my sister."

"Surely you can when we return." Miss Van Arsdale tipped her head. "It's only a couple of days, Dominic. Papa has engaged several reporters. You must meet with them and explain the marvelous discovery of the buckle."

Dom stared at her a moment intently. She knew exactly who'd found that buckle and the last time she'd encountered Tess.

"This is in your contract, Prince," the American titan reminded him. "Your availability, at our pleasure, to speak with the press about the dig, its progress, and its finds." Van Arsdale pointed a beringed finger at the tabletop. "We must do this now before rumors about what we've found begin to spread. Never let whispers get ahead of you."

For a brief, reckless moment, Dom considered ending it all. Breaking his contract with the Van Arsdales. Walking away from the dig. Reshaping his life into something new. A life with Tess at the center of it.

But would she want that?

Her own scandal haunted her. Could he drag her into another? Because he felt certain the Van Arsdales wouldn't just let him go. They'd make it ugly. They'd pull her into it. How could they not? She had found the buckle they prized so much.

He ran a hand through his hair, gripped the back of his neck, forming the words. Deciding how he'd tell them he wanted nothing more to do with their brand of treasure seeking.

Then he dropped his gaze to the telegram staring up at him from the center of the table.

Eve. They'd been partners for years. Any choice he made would touch her reputation too. And she deserved the chance to be a part of this excavation. It was already proving to be exactly as valuable as she'd suspected it would.

"I need time to prepare before I depart."

Van Arsdale scoffed. "Do you have so very much to pack for two days away?"

"I want to visit the site. Speak to my foreman—"

"Make it quick, Prince," Van Arsdale put in before Dom could finish. He gestured for his daughter to hand over a ticket. "We'll see you at the station in an hour."

Miss Van Arsdale plucked a slip from her reticule with dramatic flair and offered it to Dom. "Don't be late, Dominic."

Dom nearly burst out of the inn's door and decided to walk the distance to Foxdene Cottage. He needed air. He needed to burn off the frustration that any interaction with the Van Arsdales seemed to spark.

No other patronage had ever made him feel so owned. So much as if he was little more than a puppet pulled by another's strings. But it also made it abundantly clear to him that he would be replaceable in the Van Arsdales' minds. They didn't value his experience, his knowledge, his passion for the past. They valued the legend. The caricature.

He needed to speak to Eve almost as much as he wanted to talk to Tess.

He decided he'd pen her a note if he had time for the Randalls to give to her upon her arrival.

As the bright pink and purple primroses that lined Foxdene's front path came into view, the irritation in Dom's chest began to ebb. When she appeared, everything else faded.

Tess stepped onto the cottage's front path, bonnet in hand, her honey-blond hair catching the morning light.

She turned and spotted him, her lips curving into something that seemed like relief.

"We have this habit," she said as he approached. "Of always seeking each other out at the same time."

"I'm fond of it," he murmured. "Let's keep doing it." Every day, if he had his way.

"Shall we walk?"

"Of course. Do you have a destination in mind?"

"I was going to speak to Lord Fenbridge, but I'm not on any timetable." She pointed toward the field where she'd gone to think just the previous morning. "Let's just amble in that direction."

Dom offered his arm. When she took it, something in him slid satisfyingly into place. As if Tess was the missing piece that made everything else make sense.

"I realized this morning how I'd put you in a terrible position," she said when they were wading through the tall grass. "I didn't think it through."

"I know." He glanced at her, exhaled, and felt the last of

the tension in him unravel. "They were at the inn this morning when I came down."

She closed her eyes. "Because of me?"

"No," he said firmly. "You did nothing wrong. We did nothing wrong."

Tess watched him, her brow furrowing. "Why were they there?"

Dom slowed his steps, gaze fixed ahead, as if the horizon might offer an answer. But there was only the open field, the wind stirring the tall grass, the hush of morning settling between them.

He didn't want to say it.

Not now. Not when she was beside him, her arm resting so easily against his, like she belonged there. Like they belonged together. Not when there was so much left unsaid between them. He worried distance would cause her to doubt again.

But there was no sense in delaying the inevitable.

"I have to go to London." His voice came quiet, but firm. "With the Van Arsdales."

Tess stopped walking, withdrew her arm.

He felt the absence of her touch like a coldness creeping over his skin.

"Oh." Her voice emerged as a soft exhale.

There was no anger. Just that one syllable, almost as if she'd been expecting this moment. And she had, of course. Hadn't she insisted he'd leave?

But that wasn't what this was, and he needed to make her understand.

Dom turned to face her fully. "It's only for a couple of days. Nothing will change, and we'll pick up right from this moment when I return."

Tess held his gaze, a flicker of doubt in her green eyes.

She swallowed hard. "You don't sound as if you want to go."

"Of course I don't. Hell, I didn't even want to part from you last night." He held his breath a moment. "But my contract—"

She glanced away, toward the field where she'd stood the morning before, no doubt questioning everything. When her gaze met his again, her expression was carefully composed.

"I do understand, and a couple of days isn't long."

It would certainly feel like it to Dom, and he feared she'd erect barriers in the meantime. He already wanted to tear them down.

He wanted to say, Forget the goddamned contract. Forget the Van Arsdales. Forget London. I'll stay.

But Eve deserved this dig. And Tess deserved more than being pulled into whatever scandal and censure that might result from him breaking with the Van Arsdales.

"It won't change anything between us, Tess. It won't change what I feel for you."

A flicker of something crossed her face. Hope, he thought. But then, just as quickly, it was gone.

Tess gave him a small, aching smile. "I fear I've put us on opposing sides now."

"You haven't. I understand why you don't wish to take their money or dig under their auspices. But Eve and I are bound to them, and they've funded all our work thus far."

"There's more though." She hesitated, bit her lip, and then admitted, "I've urged Lord Fenbridge to break with them. To take control of the dig himself."

Dom didn't think that could happen. Van Arsdale's lawyers were legendary, his contracts were notoriously entangling, and they'd already claimed ownership of the most valuable piece yet uncovered.

"You don't want Fenbridge to?" she asked, one tawny brow arched as if in challenge.

"I don't think it's possible for him to, Tess."

She stepped back, and Dom had the sudden, gut-wrenching realization that she was already pulling away. It wasn't because of the dig; she was preparing herself for some break between them that she'd always foreseen.

"I should go," she said softly.

He wanted to stop her. To tell her that her leaving the dig and his trip to London were irrelevant. He wanted *her*, regardless of all the rest. He wanted to tell her that he was going to London with every intention of coming back to her, and he'd count the hours until he did. This wasn't goodbye.

But she'd tell him not to overpromise. Promises wouldn't reassure Tess. He needed to prove himself with actions, and regardless of what he said, he had to part from her today. Only when he came back would she know, and God, he prayed she'd believe him and let him love her.

So he let her go.

As she turned and walked away, the wind carried the scent of primroses, and Dom had never hated the smell of spring more.

Chapter Twenty-One

The Van Arsdales had paid for a room for Dom at The Metropole where they'd secured an entire top-floor suite. But after his first meeting with a reporter from one of the London dailies, he left the hotel and made his way to his family town house in Manchester Square.

Since their marriage, his youngest sister, Alexandra, and her husband, Detective Inspector Benedict Drake, had taken up residence. It made the town house feel like the family home, and Eve and Dom were thrilled with their decision to make it their own.

Though he had no real sentimental attachment to the house, he yearned to see Allie, and as the hansom cab dropped him outside, he hoped he'd find her at home.

Lottie, the maid who answered the door, looked shocked to see him, but she dutifully led him to one of the sitting rooms, where Allie was settled behind a desk clacking away at her typewriter.

He spied a pile of her books on a side table too.

"I'd like one of those books of yours before I leave," he told her by way of catching her attention.

"Dominic!" She flew from her seat to embrace him, and he swung her around as he used to when she was a girl. It made her giggle, and that made him smile.

It was good to be with his sister. To be home, if only because she was here. And that was a sentiment he'd rarely let himself savor.

"What ever are you doing here? I thought you were in Norfolk."

"I woke up there this morning, but our patrons wanted me to join them in London for a couple of days."

He'd never told Tess that his youngest sister was also a historian like she was, having made a study of lady pirates. Now he was looking forward to gifting her one of Allie's books.

"Come sit. Tell me everything. How is the excavation progressing?"

Dom settled into one of the room's delicate-looking damask-covered chairs and found it shockingly comfortable. He waited until Allie had taken the matching one opposite him.

"You'll no doubt read it in the papers soon, but we've found something extraordinary."

She immediately leaned forward, her eyes blooming wide. "Tell me," she breathed with the same eagerness he and all his siblings had when it came to finding historical treasures.

"It's a ship burial, Allie."

"That's marvelous." She clapped a hand over her mouth. "Do you have any idea who it is? Have you found remains?"

"No, but we've found beautifully crafted metalwork that would likely only be reserved for the very wealthy or royalty." He swallowed as thoughts of Tess rushed in. God, how could he miss her so desperately after only a few hours apart? "The historian who's helping us on the dig . . ." *Was helping, dammit.* "She believes it may be King Redwald or one of his sons."

"Oh, Dom . . ." She shot up from her chair and rushed

to the bookshelf along the pastel-papered room's back wall. Running her finger along one row, she finally stopped and plucked out a volume. "Bede the Venerable wrote about them, of course. Thank heavens for Bede. What would we do without him?" she said as she came back to her chair.

Dom chuckled at Allie's references to an English monk who'd died over a thousand years ago as if he was a dear friend who'd done them all a grand favor.

"What were his sons' names?" she queried as she flipped pages.

Dom heard Tess's voice in his head. "Eorpwald and . . . Sigeberht, I believe. Tess would be able to tell you all about them, no doubt."

Allie's head snapped up. "Tess?"

"Tess Hawthorne." Dom shifted in his seat. "She's the historian I hired to assist in Eve's absence. She's lives in the village." He couldn't help a chuckle. "She's beloved there in Wiggenstow, though she thinks they see her as a scandal. She's wrong, of course. Beautiful, stubborn, wrongheaded woman."

He realized all of a sudden that Allie had stopped sifting pages, stopped moving, held still and stared at him, slack jawed. "It's finally happened."

Dom narrowed his gaze at his baby sister. "What's finally happened?"

"You've found her." She bit her lip and then beamed. "The woman who makes you ramble. Who makes you look"—she pointed at him—"like that."

"Like what?"

"Like you're madly and wildly in love."

"It's terrifying."

Allie put her book aside and leaned toward him again. "Tell me everything."

He let out a belly-deep laugh at that. "Some things I'll keep to myself."

She blushed and fussed with the ribbon at the front of her gown. "Very well. But do tell me about her. Does she know you adore her? Does she feel the same? Have you proposed?"

"Slow down." He held up a hand but couldn't keep the smile from his face.

"Then at least tell me why it's terrifying."

"She's determined to run away from it, I think. What's between us."

Allie's expression immediately crumpled, and she slumped against the back of her chair. "So she doesn't feel the same? Heavens, I never thought you'd meet a woman who could resist your charms."

"Hey now, I didn't say that. I believe she feels the same, but she's been . . . burned, as her brother says."

Allie let out a heartfelt sigh. "Of course. A man hurt her. Bastard," she bit out.

Dom arched both brows. As far as he knew, Allie'd never had a blackguard break her heart, but she seemed to empathize with Tess thoroughly.

"Tell me about marriage," he said, trying for a light tone.

Allie started to speak and then chuckled. "I never thought I'd hear you say that word either."

"Yes, all right. I've been a cad about town. But I'm not that man anymore." He sat up straighter in the diminutive chair. "At least I don't want to be."

"I recommend it wholeheartedly," Allie said, her lips curving into the loveliest grin. "You take your vows, you pledge your troth before others, and then it's just the two of you, deciding on everything together. And with each other's best interest always at heart."

Dom sat forward and reached for her hand. "It does my heart good to see you happy, little sister."

"And it would make mine burst to see you happy." A stark, pained look entered her eyes. "You haven't been for a while, if you don't mind me saying so."

"No," he whispered. "I haven't been."

"But now there's Tess." She tipped her head and studied him. "And such a glint in your eyes."

"How do I convince her that I'm the man I want to be and not the one I have been?"

"Marrying someone takes courage, Dom. In lots of ways, it's an enormous act of hope and faith."

Hope. Faith. They weren't principles he'd had much interest in over the years. He believed in luck. In a treasure seeker's instincts. And in all the historical facts Eve dug up before an expedition.

"And trust." His voice emerged rough, the feelings in it raw and deep. "How do I make her believe she can trust me?"

"Trust takes time."

Time. He hated it. He was a man of action. Of impulse.

If he gave her time, what if she walked away again? What if she decided it was easier to live her life as she had before he'd come along?

His gut clenched at the thought.

God, he'd wasted so many years chasing what didn't ultimately mean a thing—adventure, the next thrill, the next distraction. And yet now he knew what mattered, what he couldn't live without—Tess—and he feared his impatience might make her too afraid to trust him.

Dom settled back in his chair, stared at the pretty pastel wallpaper he'd never really noted before, the pile of books his sister had written, the steady ticking clock on the mantel. There was such comfort in this room, in the life she and Drake had made.

That's what he wanted with Tess. Not a brief liaison. Not a fleeting affair. A life.

He met his sister's perceptive gaze, and something must have given him away fully because she smiled softly.

"You've already decided, haven't you?"

Dom nodded. "I'm going to ask her."

Saying it aloud made something spiral high inside him. And then his thoughts brought the soaring sensation crashing down all at once.

What if she said no?

"If she's afraid to trust, you may have to prove yourself, Dom. You may have to fight for her."

"Tess is worth any fight."

Allie ducked her head and nodded. "Then you'll know what to do. Think first of her best interest, and it will guide you."

As Dom sat in that cozy room, bolstered by his sister's faith and encouragement, an idea began to form in his mind. The rough outlines of a plan took shape. And, shockingly, if his plan worked the way he hoped it would, his two days in London, away from the woman he missed with a physical ache, would prove a godsend.

"Allie?"

"Hmm?"

"What's the name of that chap you know at the British Museum?" He looked around the sitting room. "And where are the newspapers? Does Eve still order the New York newspapers from America to keep tabs on the Van Arsdales?"

"I believe so. Lottie would know better." She pursed her

lips and looked at him mischievously. "What are you concocting?"

"A way to prove myself to Tess. A way to fight for her."

ON THE SECOND DAY without the dig to occupy her and Dominic gone, Tess settled into her father's old chair in the cottage's study. The creak of the old leather and the scent of aged paper brought a wave of nostalgia.

For the first time in months, she pulled out her father's manuscript pages. She decided to read through it from the start and soon found several changes she could make to improve the early chapters. Facts she'd uncovered in her own studies, phrasing that would make it more accessible. Her father, though a wonderful tutor, did tend to write in an opaque way.

He also tended to focus on the achievements of men. And though Tess was well aware that was the fashion of most histories, she also knew better. Women had been key and influential in shaping the world too. She tended to focus on women's actions whenever she read historical texts, and over the course of the day she'd penciled many of those details into her father's manuscript.

By afternoon, she'd also pulled out her typewriter and begun transcribing the early chapters. Her father had written everything in his distinct loose italic style. The curves were as familiar as his voice in her head.

Intermittently, she stood to stretch, refresh her tea, and stare out past the old oak to the fields of Fenbridge land. She couldn't see the dig site from the cottage, but she imagined the others and Tristan working there.

Dominic's absence felt like a tangible thing. A hollowness in her chest.

She wanted to believe he'd come back, but some dark fear

whispered that he wouldn't. That she'd driven him away. That her own fear of being hurt again had kept her from any kind of happiness and might always do so.

A knock at the cottage door pulled her from her sad musings.

Mrs. Wells was due to return today, though she wouldn't bother knocking.

Tess tidied her hair and went to answer the door.

Priscilla Walcott stood on the doorstep, the afternoon light catching the sheen of her fine silk sleeves. She carried herself with her typical confidence, yet her smile was unfamiliar based on their previous interactions. She looked downright... friendly. She'd never paid a friendly visit to Foxdene.

"Hello, Miss Hawthorne." Priscilla hesitated, looking a bit uncertain. "May I come in?"

"Of course you may." Tess stood back to admit her.

She was garbed in far finer clothes than Tess's simple day dress, and her rich perfume was so different from the scent of old books and wood smoke in the cottage.

"If you have a seat, I'll prepare a tea tray," Tess told her.

"Thank you. That would be lovely."

When Tess returned to the drawing room, Priscilla was standing near the mantel, studying the photographs and knickknacks. She seemed fixed on a drawing Tristan had made of their father.

"He was such an excellent teacher," Priscilla said almost wistfully.

"He was." Though their father had encouraged her and Tristan to pursue passions of their own, his love for history had been so infectious that Tess had fallen in love with it too. "And he was always impressed with your abilities."

Priscilla looked taken aback. "Was he?"

"Oh yes. Some questioned why he took on a girl tutee to study history and geography and Latin and French, but he'd simply tell them that you excelled at those subjects."

"He told my mother much the same," she said with a little hint of bitterness. "She thought I should take up watercolor and piano. My father championed academic subjects for young ladies." She smiled at Tess. "As did yours."

Once they were settled on the face-to-face settees in the middle of the drawing room, Tess began to pour.

"Sugar and cream?" Tess didn't even know Priscilla well enough to know how the young woman took her tea.

"Yes, please."

Tess handed her cup over and tried to find something in her seemingly guileless gaze. Some hint of why she'd come. A nagging feeling told her it had something to do with Dominic.

"You're studying me as if I've committed some crime and might reveal a clue."

Tess huffed out a chuckle. "Forgive me, but you must admit this is unusual."

"I consider it long overdue."

"Do you? Then why did you wait to come and call?"

Priscilla stirred her tea, eyes fixed on the steaming liquid. "Embarrassment, I suppose."

Tess's own fingers tightened on the handle of her cup. She set it aside lest she break the dainty porcelain. She could feel perspiration on the back of her neck and had an overwhelming urge to stand and stride from her own house to avoid this conversation.

"I can see from your reaction that you feel as I do. It's not a pleasant topic. That is why I haven't come before." She drew in a sharp breath. "Even speaking the man's name seems as if I'm giving him some power he does not deserve."

"I try to avoid any thought of him too."

"And does that work well?"

Tess shot her a sharp look, one that Priscilla seemed to understand. She nodded. "It doesn't work well for me either. So I thought perhaps the avoiding is what gives it power."

Tess tipped her head back, staring up at the exposed beams of the cottage's roof. It had always been a place of safety and comfort. She let out a slow breath and dropped her gaze back to Priscilla.

"Perhaps you're right. I'm sorry that we share a similar history in that regard."

"As am I." Priscilla tipped her head as she looked at Tess. "Though I think you've taken a great deal more blame onto yourself than you should."

"I was foolish. Impulsive. I let myself be ruined."

"No." Priscilla shook her head vehemently. "You were lied to. Seduced. Taken advantage of by a man who preyed on your trust."

Tess didn't disagree, but she knew the part she'd played. The warnings she'd ignored. The choices she'd made.

Priscilla shocked her by standing. Tess thought perhaps she meant to depart. Instead, she came around and settled on the settee next to Tess. Without a word, she took Tess's hand. The gesture was gentle and completely unexpected.

"May I be potentially rude?" she asked softly.

Tess laughed. "Well, when you ask so nicely, how can I refuse?"

"I heard that Mr. Prince has left Norfolk."

Tess's heart leapt a little at the mere mention of his name. "Yes, for a brief time, he says."

"Oh good." Priscilla gave Tess's hand a gentle squeeze.

"That pleases you?" Tess asked, side-eyeing the young

woman who'd flirted with him rather mercilessly the day they'd met.

"Oh, not for my sake, silly. For yours." She hesitated. "I thought perhaps you'd . . . pushed him away."

Tess frowned and pulled her hand away. "I'm not certain why that's your concern, Miss Walcott."

"Oh, please let me explain."

Tess searched again for any hidden agenda in the young woman's eyes but found only seeming sincerity.

"Say what you've come to say."

Priscilla squared her shoulders and cleared her throat in the most quiet, ladylike manner. "Do you know how many suitors I've had since . . . Shaw?"

Tess frowned and shook her head. "Of course not." Though looking at Priscilla's pretty face and imagining the size of her dowry, she guessed. "Quite a few, I suspect."

"Six."

Tess blinked, yet it wasn't an unbelievable sum considering her beauty and wealth. "None of them suited you?"

She closed her eyes a moment and then looked up as if she'd bolstered herself. "One did quite well. I can admit now that I loved him. Truly loved him." Her voice broke and a tear slipped down her cheek.

Tess dug in her pocket for a kerchief, but Priscilla produced one she'd had tucked in her sleeve.

"I knew I'd need one," she said with a chagrined smile. "I realized in the weeks after I'd refused Robert's proposal that I made a terrible mistake." Biting her lip, she looked out the same window Tess loved looking out, where the old oak stood protectively watchful. "I thought I was guarding my heart, but it cost me a chance at love."

Tess knew then. Priscilla had come with a cautionary tale, and it hit her with all the impact she'd likely intended.

She reached for Priscilla's hand as the young woman dabbed at her eyes with the other.

"Could you not reconcile with him?"

Priscilla sniffed and shook her head. "By the time I learned how to overcome the fear, he was engaged to someone else."

Tess tried, for the flicker of a moment, to imagine Dominic proposing to someone while he was back in London and immediately felt as if she'd cast up her accounts.

"I'm sorry. He should have had more patience," she told Priscilla vehemently.

"I never told him about Shaw. He didn't understand why I pushed him away." She gave Tess a wry smile. "But yes, I often wished he would have tried just a bit harder. Or that I'd been a bit braver."

Tess understood that desire entirely. "You will be the next time."

Priscilla took a shuddery breath. "That's what I tell myself too."

For a moment, they simply sat together quietly.

Then Tess asked, "How did you overcome the fear?"

Priscilla gripped Tess's hand tighter. "I wanted a chance at joy more than the comfort of all the ways I told myself I was protecting myself. And . . ." She turned and focused on the photograph of Tess's father on the mantel. "Did you know your father had me read Aristotle?"

At the swift change of subject, Tess shook her head. "It's not surprising. He loved Aristotle."

"I'm going to bungle this but . . . 'the courageous endures fear and dares the deeds that manifest courage.'"

Tess understood. Her father had written out his favorite quotes from ancient philosophers and pinned them to the wall next to his desk.

"One builds courage by daring to do things in spite of fear. That's how I always interpreted it." Priscilla watched Tess, her gaze fierce, as if willing her whatever courage she could.

"Thank you for coming and teaching me a lesson." Tess grinned. "My father would have loved that you managed to work in a bit of Aristotle."

They both laughed. Then they drank their tea and talked of Tristan's news, of Priscilla's father's investment in a new publishing venture that interested her, and, finally, of the train times to London and that the fastest train was from Norwich.

Chapter Twenty-Two

Dom remained at the Prince town house on his first night in London. He'd slept in the rarely used bedchamber set aside for him because he loathed parting from Allie and Benedict.

Not only were they a heartwarming example of a thriving marriage, they were eager to hear more about the dig, the challenging Van Arsdales, and, of course, Tess. And he could never tire of talking about her.

Allie was half convinced she should accompany him back to Norfolk just to meet her, but he vowed that if all went as he hoped, she and Tess would be more than acquaintances. They'd be sisters.

The following day, he made his way back to The Metropole to speak with another journalist the Van Arsdales had contacted. The bespectacled young man awaited him in the elegant, high-ceilinged lobby of the lavish hotel. He was accompanied by a sketch artist, and the young lady sketched him as he answered questions about the Norfolk dig.

It all felt familiar. Dom knew what to tell them, how to phrase it for maximum dramatic effect, and made sure to mention Tess as the one who'd found the buckle. To his shock, the lady sketch artist had already produced a drawing of it, having met with the Van Arsdales the day before.

He wasn't aware they'd transported the find with them to London.

"Thank you for your time, Mr. Prince," the young man

said after nearly an hour. "May I call on you again when you make more progress on the dig?"

"Certainly." Dom took the man's card and slid it into his pocket.

After the two had departed, Dom approached the wide stairwell to head up to his room and prepare for his departure back to Norfolk in the morning.

"Mr. Prince." One of the young men who worked at the hotel's front desk approached. "There's a note for you from Mr. Harcourt. A messenger delivered it not an hour ago."

Dom took the envelope from the young man. "Thank you."

"And there is also the matter of the lady, Mr. Prince."

"The lady?"

"I advised her to wait in the lounge until you concluded your meeting, but when I checked, she'd departed again." The young man's gaze flickered over Dom's shoulder. "Oh, there she is now."

Dom knew before he turned. He felt her like a sweet breeze across his skin, even though it made no sense. Then he turned toward The Metropole's front doors, and she was there.

Tess looked wind-blown and magnificent. A few strands of hair tumbled to her shoulders, and her cheeks were flushed as if she'd been walking in the sun.

Dom smiled so wide his cheeks ached.

He barely registered the hotel employee retreating. All his attention was focused on Tess, standing just inside the hotel's grand entrance.

"Tess," he breathed, closing the distance between them a few long strides. "How—"

"I came to find you." She swallowed hard. "I took the train from Norwich." She clutched her gloved hands together in way that told him she was nervous. "I had to see you. Tell you—"

"Let's sit," he said, offering her his arm.

She didn't hesitate to loop her hand around his arm.

He led her toward a quiet corner of the lounge, past potted palms, velvet settees, and well-dressed guests sipping cocktails. Late afternoon light poured in from the tall windows, casting a buttery glow over the gilt moldings. None of it shone like the gleam of Tess's sun-kissed hair.

They took seats facing each other. Dom leaned forward, forearms on his knees.

"Tell me," he said softly.

She exhaled. "Priscilla Walcott came to see me."

His brows lifted. It wasn't at all what he'd expect her to travel a hundred miles to tell him.

"She . . . gave me some advice." Her eyes lit with amusement and something he dared not name until she did. "Very wise advice."

A hotel staff member approached, no doubt to offer them refreshment, but Dom kept the young man away with a slight shake of his head.

Tess took the moment to slip her gloves off, then clenched them tightly in her lap.

"She reminded me that fear keeps us from joy." Tess nodded as if speaking the words aloud solidified something in her mind. Then she reached for him.

Dom stroked his thumb across her palm, savored her softness and how her touch always felt so right.

"I don't want to let it keep me from what's between us anymore."

A warm pressure built in his chest—like a fire that burned bright.

"Then don't." He barely resisted pulling her into his arms right then and there, in front all of the well-heeled guests.

She let out a soft laugh. "You make it sound simple."

"Isn't it?" He searched her gaze. "You're here. You came to me. Whatever caused you to board that train, it brought us to this moment. Together."

"I don't want to be a coward."

"Tess, you never were." He reached out and stroked a finger along the satiny curve of her cheek. "You're the siren who led me into an apple orchard and had her way with me," he whispered so no one but her would hear. "That took courage."

She smiled and then straightened her spine, pulling her shoulders back as if bolstering herself, summoning the courage she'd spoken of.

Then she tightened her grip on his hand.

"I love you, Dominic."

The words knocked the air from his lungs, and he edged closer to her.

"Tess." He whispered her name, infused it with all the awe he felt in that moment.

"I was afraid of admitting it to myself." Her expression was open, her eyes glistening. "But the truth is that I loved you even when I couldn't say it. I think I loved you from the moment you climbed down from that ladder at Lady Goddard's. I hated watching you walk out of that room."

"As soon as you stepped into that room, everything changed. As if my world tilted on its axis." He lifted her hand and laid a kiss across her knuckles. "Or maybe it was set aright."

He stroked his fingers along hers. "What would you say if I told you I thought, even then, that you might have felt it too?"

Her breath hitched. "I did. I knew it was impossible, but I hoped I'd encounter you again. Somehow." She dipped her head. "And you found me in the village lockup."

Dom chuckled. "I was never happier to see anyone in my life." He licked his lips. "But that's honestly how I feel every time I see you."

"It's a mutual feeling."

"Then what would you say if I told you I love you too, Tess Hawthorne?"

Tess's laugh burst out of her, softening her posture, revealing a dimple in her cheek as she smiled wide. "I was rather hoping you did."

Dom couldn't resist anymore; he stood, still holding her hand, and she did too.

He put an arm around her, drew her close.

"I'm going to make sure you never regret it," he vowed to her.

"That sounds suspiciously like a promise." She stroked his hand as she said it, and he wondered if she was debating whether promises weren't such awful things after all.

"When you start thinking about forever with someone, they sort of bubble out of you."

She laughed and the sound wound a ribbon of pleasure through him that settled somewhere in his chest.

"In that case," she said with an enticing grin, "I shall allow it."

DOMINIC'S ROOM IN THE Metropole was sumptuous and yet not intimidatingly so. The curtains and coverlet on the spacious bed were a rich, deep yellow, and the walls were a comforting pale green. Fresh flowers sat in vases dotted throughout the room.

"This is beautiful." Tess turned back to him and found he'd stopped after closing the hotel room door and stood watching her take it all in.

"I suppose it is. I slept the first night at my family home."

"It must have been nice to be home."

He strode forward then, and Tess's pulse kicked up. "Actually, I rarely sleep there. I stay above the family shop."

"Why?" Tess huffed out a little laugh and then her breath caught as he reached up and began removing the pins in her hair.

"I didn't want to get too comfortable in any one place. I wanted to force myself to keep moving."

As soon as he had her hair down, Tess reached up to push his suit coat from his shoulders. Then she reached for his neckcloth, but he was already removing it.

"Do you still want that?" Tess's fingers stilled on the second button on the front of his shirt. Her heart seemed to stall in her chest as she waited for his answer.

"No, not at all," he told her with a smile. Then he stroked her cheek, running the backs of his fingers down along her jawline and then to the buttons of her bodice. "I want a home. I think I always did, but I wouldn't allow myself to have it."

"Did stopping for a while frighten you?" Tess had a sense he'd done all he could to keep chasing his father's reputation.

"Yes." He worked her buttons deftly, so quick it left her breathless. "I thought I'd lose the chance to be like my father. He wasn't a man who ever sat still for long."

Tess had gotten to the final button of his shirt and even as he worked the last one, she couldn't resist kissing his chest. His skin was golden in the dusk light filtering through the curtains.

"And now," she breathed against his skin before kissing it again, flicking her tongue out to taste him.

He pulled her up and took her mouth in a searing kiss that made her clutch at his shoulders, moan as he cupped her backside and pulled her flush against him.

"Now," he said when he lifted his head, breathing as hard as she was, "I only want to be where you are." He reached out to unfasten the hooks on her skirt and petticoat and slid them from her hips. "I only want to be as close to you as I can be."

He immediately pulled up her chemise, then found the opening of her drawers. "God, I've missed you," he told her.

Tess pulled his head down and kissed him again as his fingers found her, wet and warm and aching for him. He stroked her until she was begging, so lost in sensation that she continued kissing him, hungrily, more demanding than she'd ever been, as he freed her from her corset, chemise, drawers.

Then he broke their kiss and lifted her into his arms.

She made a little sound of protest, and he chuckled in the near darkness.

"My impatient siren."

He laid her back on the velvet coverlet and then shed the rest of his clothing. Tess's blood pounded in her ears, and every part of her body felt as if it was stretched, waiting, desperate for him to touch her again.

Then she felt the bed shift as he climbed atop it. Tess reached for him, wanting him in her arms, but he knelt before her, stroking lines of heat along her thighs before pushing them gently apart and settling between them.

"Oh," Tess gasped when his tongue swept against her, then again and again. She reached for him, fingers in his hair, hips bucking of their own volition.

He murmured against her core. She didn't catch all of it. Just individual words. Hot gusts of his breath before his tongue made her tremble. Sweet. Delicious. Mine.

The *mine* made her shudder. Pulled her toward that peak that he'd taken her to before. He stroked a finger inside her, curling to find that spot that made her shatter.

She cried out. Sparks flickered behind her eyes, and she wasn't certain if she was saying his name or if it was simply repeating over and over in her head.

"I'm here, love," he whispered as he lifted over her, then settled between her legs. "I'm not going anywhere."

He bent to take her aching nipple between his lips as he thrust inside her, setting a rhythm that made her gasp with each stroke. He filled her completely, his body fitting against hers as if they were two pieces of a puzzle finally put back together again.

Tess grasped at the shifting muscles of his back, gripped his nape to pull him down for a kiss. That's when his perfect rhythm faltered and his strokes became more wild, pushing them both to the edge.

"I love you," she told him against his lips.

Their eyes met, his body straining against hers. "I love you, Tess."

He let go. His mouth crashed onto hers, his groan of release echoing through her as he lost himself in her.

He held her close as they came down, their breath returning to normal, their heartbeats easing into a steady pace.

Then, to her great shock and dismay, he eased himself away from her and got off the bed.

"Dominic—" She was ready to demand he return and hold her, but then she got caught up watching him move. He was beautifully muscled, lithe and strong. And he seemed a man on a mission. He lit the lamp near the bed, then found his suit coat and dug inside a pocket.

Then he shot her one of those breath-stealing Dominic Prince smiles as he strode back to the bed.

Tess lifted her arms, so eager to have him beside her, atop her, below her, or any way she could have him again.

But he just held that maddeningly seductive smile on his lips and knelt beside the bed.

"I suspect propriety would dictate—" he started.

"We've trampled propriety almost from the moment we met."

He chuckled low and deep. "We have, haven't we?" He drew in a breath. "Very well. Then I can't wait any longer."

Tess swallowed against a lump in her throat, suspecting what came next, wanting it so desperately something pinched in the center of her chest.

He lifted a black velvet box, then sprung the latch and opened the hinged top.

A gorgeous emerald glinted among a rectangle of diamonds.

"Tess, will you do me the very great honor of being my wife?"

Tess licked her lips as she stared into his eyes. There wasn't an ounce of anything but sincerity, hope, love, in his dark amber gaze.

"Yes!" She reached out and clasped his shoulders, pulling him up, pulling him into bed again. He settled beside her, and Tess bent over him to kiss him. "Yes," she whispered again.

He'd freed the ring from its case and lifted her hand to slide it onto her finger.

"It's beautiful."

"Reminded me of your eyes," he told her, and he lifted her hand for a kiss. Then his gaze met hers, his brow slightly furrowed. "It's not an antique. I considered selecting something for you from Princes. Something with a grand history."

He stopped, licked his lips. "But I decided I wanted something that was uniquely ours and with a fresh history that we could write ourselves."

"It's perfect, Dominic." Tess's heart felt as if it would burst out free of her ribs. "And I love the idea of writing our own history."

"I thought you might." He bent and took her lips, then his hands were on her hips pulling her closer.

Tess settled over him, her legs on either side of his hips. She braced her hands on his chest, then bent to kiss him slow and deep.

She felt safe, loved, cherished, and as much as she adored history, her heart thrilled at the fact that their love story had just begun.

Chapter Twenty-Three

Dom woke early, scratching out a quick note to the Van Arsdales, informing them of his immediate return to Norfolk. They wouldn't be pleased, but they could hardly quibble overly with him returning to the task they'd hired him to do.

More importantly, he wouldn't risk Tess being put in an uncomfortable position where they were concerned.

By half past eight, they'd checked out of The Metropole and were aboard the train, the countryside rolling past in the pastel hues of early morning light.

Tess's bare hand fit perfectly in his, her thumb tracing idle circles against his skin.

"Should I speak to them?" she asked.

"The Van Arsdales?"

She nodded, glancing at him. "About my post on the dig. Perhaps I was hasty—"

Dom squeezed her hand and shook his head. "I understand why you made the choice you did."

"But I regret it now," she admitted, eyes searching his. "I want to be back out there."

"So do I," he told her, watching the way the sunlight made her green eyes glow. "I want us working together."

She nodded, a bit of tension in her posture seeming to loosen. "Then I'll speak to Mr. Van Arsdale when he returns to Norfolk."

"What if we both speak to him?"

Her lips curved him an amused smile. "Tristan did say you could convince the American to take me back."

"Actually . . ." Dom started, then shifted to face her more fully. "I have another idea."

Tess's burnished gold brows winged up. "Oh?"

"Have you ever been to the British Museum?"

"Of course." Her face softened at some memory. "Father took Tristan and me many times. I once fantasized about working there. It's a favorite place of mine."

"I thought it might be." Dom grinned, feeling the pleasure of knowing her well enough to guess at what the place might mean to her. "I know you spoke of a museum in Wiggenstow—"

A sigh gusted out of her, and she settled closer to him. "I realize it won't ever happen. Tristan's right. The Americans won't leave anything truly valuable behind in Wiggenstow."

She curled her arm around his and leaned close, kissing him softly on the cheek. "I appreciate that you offered to try, but we both know what they'll say."

Dom leaned closer, savoring that fleeting warmth of her lips on his skin. "They'd refuse outright because it would gain them nothing. But what if there were a way to persuade him it was in his interest to leave the finds in England?"

Tess shot him a skeptical look. "Do the Van Arsdales strike you as particularly magnanimous?"

Dom chuckled. "No, not unless there's self-interest involved." He reached into his satchel and pulled out a folder. "But they do like good press."

The folder seemed to pique her curiosity; she leaned in as he sifted through the clippings.

"That was the whole purpose of bringing me to London," he explained. "They met with twice as many journalists as I did. Wined and dined them. All for colorful write-ups in the papers."

"The gold buckle is just the beginning."

"Exactly." He pulled out one particular clipping and handed it to her. "Have you ever heard of T. T. Aldridge?"

Tess frowned, examining the article. "I don't believe so. Should I?"

"Theodore Tiberius Aldridge," Dom told her, excitement building in his chest. "Van Arsdale's greatest rival. Their wives are rivals too. Always trying to outdo each other in New York society. And the two titans are forever attempting to one-up each other in terms of wealth and success."

"Sounds exhausting," Tess muttered.

Dom laughed deeply. "Agreed, but it might work to our advantage." He tapped the clipping.

Tess's breath hitched as she read. When she looked up at him, her eyes were alight with the anticipation he felt.

The article detailed how Aldridge had recently donated an impressive collection of prehistoric bronzes to the British Museum. A generous act, for certain, but it had also earned him resounding transcontinental praise, with glowing articles in both the London and American newspapers.

"You think Van Arsdale might do something like this?"

"If he saw the benefit, the opportunity to outdo Aldridge. A ship burial and all its riches donated to the British Museum? The press would be agog. Wouldn't that tempt him?"

Tess pursed her lips, considering. "That seems too much to hope for."

He nodded. "It's ambitious." And there was no certainty of success. "But we can assemble allies."

She turned toward him, gaze sharp, curious. "Allies?"

"Fenbridge will likely be in favor of this idea."

Tess scoffed softly. "Based on how the Van Arsdales took control of Fenbridge Hall, they haven't much respect for his lordship."

"True." Dom squeezed her hand where it rested on his arm. "But Fenbridge knows the right people. As do I. Nobles. Respected collectors. Some of them museum donors."

"And they respect you. An antiquarian. A Prince of Princes of London."

He gave her a rueful smile. "They like my father's panache, perhaps."

"And yours," she insisted.

He let out a harsh breath. "Van Arsdale sees me as someone he's bought and paid for."

Tess turned his hand, laying her hand atop his and lacing their fingers. "Then we call on those collectors you know. Anyone particularly estimable?"

Dom studied their entwined fingers, then looked into Tess's eyes. So bright and beautiful. Just like her. His chest filled as if it might burst with the love he felt for her.

"I have a few ideas," he told her, then bent to steal a too-quick kiss.

"You know this is a great risk for you," she said quietly. "Van Arsdale might withdraw his patronage."

Dom nodded, shifting in his seat. "We'll need to speak to Eve, though I have every reason to think she'll agree. When she hears of how they've behaved . . ."

"I'm eager to meet her."

"She'll be pleased to meet you."

"How can you be so sure?" She pushed at him playfully.

"My sister Allie said it best." He reached out and cupped her cheek. "She said I look happy and haven't in a long while."

This time Tess leaned in, pressing her lips to his in a kiss that made him groan.

"If you don't mind the risk, then I'm with you." She drew her finger along his jawline, a stroke he felt wend through his body, making him ache for her and the next time they could be alone.

As the train carried them north, he tried to keep from pulling her into his lap and ravishing his bride-to-be in a public train carriage.

They talked about their plan and how best to approach Fenbridge. Their whole scheme took shape—one that might change everything.

"I suppose this is all my fault," Eveline Prince said as she stood in the drawing room of Foxdene. "I'm the one who asked you to visit Lady Goddard's that day."

Dominic's sister was not happy with the plan to persuade the Van Arsdales.

"Yes, and we'll be sure to tell our children that Aunt Eve played a part in our first meeting," Dom told her with a wink.

Miss Prince rolled her eyes. Then she looked over at Tess and her expression softened.

"I mean no offense to you at all, Miss Hawthorne. I'm thrilled for both of you." She approached until they were almost toe-to-toe. "Thank you," she said more quietly, "for being the reason my brother seems more himself than he has in a very long time."

"He's done the same for me."

"Congratulations," she said with a warm smile, "again. Please know none of my reservations are about you."

"I understand." And Tess did. The dig mattered to Eve Prince. She could see it in her eyes, the excitement in her voice when she spoke of what they'd found before her arrival and what had been discovered in the last two days.

A silver bowl in perfect condition had been recovered, along with silver spoons that indicated they may have been Byzantine in origin due to their design and inscriptions.

Miss Prince turned back to her brother, who sat on a settee next to Tristan.

"You understand what I'm afraid of."

Dominic nodded. "I do. Of course, I do. But it's a risk worth taking."

Tess cleared her throat, drawing everyone's gaze her way. "As much as I don't want to create enmity between siblings or with you, Miss Prince, since I'm very much looking forward to having you as a sister . . ." She hesitated and took a breath. "I know that I am the reason Dominic is determined on this course of action."

"That's not entirely true." Dominic stood and approached her, taking Tess's hand gently in his. "Do you think it didn't bother me to see the way they treated the dig, the artifacts? The notion of them all being shipped to America never sat right with me."

"Nor me," Miss Prince put in. "But it is what we agreed to. Van Arsdale could fund a dig of this scope when others wouldn't. We can say whatever we like about them, and they probably deserve it all, but he is generous when he's determined to succeed."

"The man has more money than he knows what to do with. Of course, he treats it lightly." Tristan spoke, and everyone turned his way as he'd remained mostly quiet. "I wasn't bothered at first. I knew Tess's goal was to excavate that mound, and if Van Arsdale could be the means, then I was content with whatever the consequences might be."

"And the thousand pounds he offered," Tess reminded him.

He managed to look momentarily abashed. "It was convincing for both of us," he reminded her in turn.

"Agreed." Tess had to acknowledge that she had signed Van Arsdale's contract like the rest of them, even if it made her stomach knot. "It was their arrival that changed everything."

Eveline Prince nodded, though she hadn't been present to witness any of it. "Tristan filled me in." She cast a gaze at her brother and then Tess. "Do we know where the gold buckle is now?"

"We don't," Dom told her. "We assume they're traveling with it. Hopefully safeguarding it."

"And showing it off to everyone they meet," Tess couldn't help adding.

Miss Prince crossed her arms and paced on the pale floral rug all the way to the edge of the room and then back again.

"So, the happiest outcome is that Van Arsdale wants to surpass his rival and gain fame from a donation to the British Museum?"

"Yes, that's what we're betting on." Dom shot Tess a smile.

Tess knew her own smile was weak and uncertain because hearing it spoken aloud in Miss Prince's sharp, firm tone reminded her that they were putting a great deal of hope in Gordon Van Arsdale believing acclaim would come from giving this find to a British museum rather than creating his own.

"And the worst outcome," Miss Prince went on, "is that he fires all of us, hires new excavators, and ships it all back to America anyway." She turned a look her brother's way. "And the papers will report that the Princes were dismissed from one of the most extraordinary finds in English archaeological history."

Tess had been standing, her back to the window and the old oak, but now she made her way to the settee opposite her brother and Dominic and slumped down.

"I don't think the odds are in our favor," she admitted in a low tone, loath to say it and yet determined to get the words out. "And I hate thinking that this might tarnish your family's reputation or future opportunities. It seems too great a risk."

Lifting her head, she looked first at Tristan and then the man she'd fallen completely in love with. "I think perhaps the best course of action is continuing on the dig under the terms we all initially agreed."

"But you're not on the dig anymore," Tristan pointed out. "I suggest we rectify that at the very least." He turned toward Dominic. "You can arrange that, yes?"

"Of course, but—" Dominic stood up from the settee and then approached his sister. "What was that play you saw last year and adored?"

Miss Prince arched one brow at him, then frowned as if she was beholding a madman. "Mr. Wilde's play? *The Importance of Being Earnest*. How can that possibly be relevant?"

"Yes, and it is relevant because despite the title, everyone is pretending to be something they're not to get what they want."

"The point of the play is that it was a bad idea, Dominic."

"Nonsense. It was a comedy and it all worked out in the end."

Miss Prince's eyes narrowed to slits. "I'm a terrible liar. You know that."

"We've both held our noses with clients and even with Papa when he did something dreadful through the years."

"I still don't understand."

"We can part ways on this. You and I." Dominic glanced at Tess, and there was such hopefulness in his eyes that Tess felt it too. "We'll attempt our idea. If you like, you can tell Van Arsdale that you disagree wholeheartedly." He tipped a crooked smile. "Which, in some ways, you do."

"I don't." Miss Prince shook her head. "I just don't think it will work and that it will cost us this opportunity."

"Right, but my idea is that it need only cost one of us. You needn't even disagree. You must only remain staunchly in favor of whatever the Van Arsdales want." Dominic shrugged. "If it goes our way, you'll tell them how beloved they'll be for their donation. If it doesn't, assure them that your preference was always to see their American museum established."

"You're asking me to betray you?"

Dominic placed a hand on his sister's shoulder. "Eve, it's not betrayal. It's an insurance policy. One of us must continue on this dig. And you, most of all, have spent years suspecting we'd find a hoard here."

"You won't be happy walking away from this dig, Dominic. I know you better than that." She slid a glance at Tess and smiled. "But I also know there's now something far more important to you."

Tess watched him as his expression remained decisive, unwavering, and then he fixed his gaze on her. Though they weren't standing next to each other, she felt that look of his as a cascade of love and warmth that washed over her.

"And you, Miss Hawthorne," Miss Prince added, drawing Tess's attention away from Dominic. "What will you think of me if I side with the Van Arsdales?"

Tess approached and twined her arm with Dominic's. "I agree with your brother. One of us—" A thought struck Tess and she turned back to Tristan.

"I'd prefer to stay on the dig too," he told her, as if he could read the unspoken question.

"Then we divide." Dominic's voice had taken on a firmer tone. "At least as far as the Van Arsdales are concerned. And then we can be sure that at least part of our soon-to-be-joined families can be a part of this historic dig."

"We just have to hope Gordon Van Arsdale believes siblings would oppose each other this way."

"He'll believe it." It was the one aspect of their plan that Tess did not doubt. "Van Arsdale thinks everyone is motivated by money. If anything, he'll realize that Miss Prince and Tristan no longer need to divide their payments."

Eveline Prince eyed her brother and then smiled softly at Tess. "I am hoping the two of you succeed and we can all take part. I truly am."

"So are we," Dominic told her and then bent to press a kiss to Tess's forehead.

She felt it to her toes. And though they'd all just agreed to divide, she felt they'd gained allies.

Next, they had to inform Lord Fenbridge of their plan.

Chapter Twenty-Four

"You two look as if you're full of the joys of spring," Fenbridge said as he stood behind his mammoth desk and eyed them through a pince-nez.

Dom stood next to Tess, their arms warming each other's, hands clasped, as they allowed for the old man's inspection.

The gold-framed lens dipped down as he examined the ring glinting on Tess's finger. She stepped forward and proudly lifted it for his perusal.

The old nobleman whistled. "Quite a gem that is. Convinced her quickly, Prince, didn't you?"

"I didn't require a great deal of convincing, my lord," Tess told him pertly.

He lowered the handheld lens and squinted one eye at her. "Just courage, eh? Which I knew you had in abundance."

Dom couldn't help a swell of pride. "She is a lady of courage, and I'm the luckiest man in England." He stepped forward because, whether the grumpy nobleman knew it or not, he'd given them the perfect segue.

"What of your courage, Lord Fenbridge?"

The nobleman visibly bristled, then pulled at his cuffs. "What are you on about, Prince?" He locked gazes with Dom and then Tess, his face pinched in a scowl as if that might cause them to cower.

Dom wondered if he'd tried it on the Van Arsdales.

"If this is regarding the Americans and how they—"

"Took over Fenbridge Hall as if it was their own?" Tess asked sharply.

"I took the path of least resistance to save my staff and myself. Do you know that half the staff and all the food for those days was ordered in by them from Norwich or London?"

"And now they're coming back," Dom reminded him. "Will you allow them to take over again?"

Fenbridge grabbed a cane and stomped over until he was in front of Dom.

"You are in their employ, Mr. Prince. Are you suggesting I be less than courteous to your employers?"

"We're suggesting precisely the opposite, Lord Fenbridge," Tess told him. "We're suggesting that you host a soiree to celebrate their return."

Fenbridge stared at her a moment and then burst into a chortle of laughter. "Do you not recall who you're speaking to, Miss Hawthorne? When have I ever wished to host a soiree?"

"What if we did all the planning?" Dom asked him. "We'll handle the guest list, help the staff with the menu, even pay for the expense, just as the Van Arsdales did before their departure."

Fenbridge strode a few steps closer, glaring at each of them. "What nonsense are you two concocting?" He tipped his head at Tess. "You're an honest young woman, aren't you, Miss Hawthorne? I'd hate to think the man you've promised yourself to has drawn you into some deception."

"It's not nonsense," she told him, notching up her chin an inch. "It's a marvelous solution that will allow what's found in that mound to stay on the island where it lay for a millennium."

Fenbridge shook his head and looked at her indulgently, as a parent might with a whimsical child. "It's a very fine notion, but you've met Mr. Van Arsdale. He won't retreat." He stuck out a finger toward his desk. "And I signed the damnable contract."

His shoulders slumped in his finely tailored coat. "I'm sorry, Miss Hawthorne." He looked up, his gaze fixed on her face. "Though I explained last time we talked, it wasn't a sufficient excuse. I should have given you permission to dig."

Tess let out a little gasp and pressed her lips together. "Thank you for acknowledging that, my lord." She stepped a bit closer to the old nobleman. "But if you truly have any regret, then help us with this." For a moment, she hesitated.

"We know our plan may fail," Dom admitted. "Please help us try."

"This is a moment," Tess told him quietly, "for courage."

Fenbridge turned away from both of them and made his way back to the long window behind his desk. He stared out onto the garden for a long moment.

Dom reached for Tess's hand, and she squeezed his, then nodded slowly. She believed the nobleman would relent.

Then, after a stretch of silence, he did.

"When will this . . . event take place?"

"We'd like it to happen this evening," Tess told him. "They'll arrive any moment from London, and we think they'll like the notion of a dinner hosted to celebrate their return."

"And we have a few important guests expecting to travel to Wiggenstow to attend," Dom added.

Fenbridge spun, both brows arched high. "Out with it then, the two of you might as well tell me your plan."

Dom and Tess exchanged a quick smile, savoring their success, if only this part of it.

And then they told him their plan.

"We couldn't have pulled this off without you." Tess approached Mrs. Wells and wrapped an arm around her shoulder. "Thank you."

Wellsy drew in a deep breath. "It's not even begun yet, my dear."

"No, but the food looks marvelous, and that will matter to the Van Arsdales."

Mrs. Wells had returned to Foxdene, and Tristan had filled them in about the plan to host a party where the Van Arsdales might be persuaded to be magnanimous.

The Fenbridge staff had panicked a bit when Tess went to the kitchen to explain what they hoped to accomplish. It was very short notice, and Mrs. Wells's oversight helped them greatly. They'd settled on a somewhat simple menu, but with rich flourishes and a sumptuous dessert, which the Van Arsdales had favored earlier in the week.

Now, they'd secured the Van Arsdales' agreement to attend the meal and the staff had put the finishing touches on the dining room setup.

The Van Arsdales were out at the dig site with their chairs and umbrellas. Dom had been out with them part of the morning, then made his excuses, claiming he had to speak to Fenbridge. Tristan had promised to keep them there in the afternoon following a lavish lunch to prevent them from interfering with the dinner arrangements.

Tess looked up when she heard the thud of footsteps in the hallway and let out a big exhale of relief when Dominic appeared in the doorway.

"I've met with our guests. They're gathered at the inn. I've offered to put them all up for the evening, and the Randalls were happy to accommodate them," he told her and Mrs. Wells.

"Even the guest? The most important one," Tess asked him.

Dominic swallowed and shook his head. "He won't be coming."

Tess's heart fell.

"But," Dominic said as he strode toward her and handed her a slip of paper, "he sent this."

Tess looked down at the telegram and grinned. It was perfect. Not quite as perfect as the powerful nobleman banker's appearance in Wiggenstow would have been. But Lord Rothschild's influence couldn't be dimmed by his absence. His words on the telegram would make an impact on Van Arsdale. The only question was whether it would be enough.

"We should change," Dom reminded her.

They'd both brought clothing appropriate for a formal dinner, though for Tess that meant she was donning the same purple gown she'd worn to Priscilla Walcott's again. Lord Fenbridge had insisted they take one of the guest rooms to make their preparations.

After giving their dear housekeeper Mrs. Wells a peck on the cheek, Tess made her way with Dominic upstairs to their borrowed room.

As soon as they stepped inside, Dominic took her in his arms and kissed her. He tasted her deeply, licking into her mouth, tangling his tongue with hers as he lifted her off her toes and backed her against the closed door.

Tess pushed his coat from his shoulders, and when he broke the kiss, she turned so that her back was to him.

"Help me with my buttons?" she said breathlessly.

He did, and she could feel his breath coming fast against her nape, then his lips were there as he kissed and nipped at her skin.

When his hand came around to cup her breast through the fabric of her corset and chemise, she bucked back against him.

"The fact that I don't have time to make love to you properly right now is criminal."

Tess laughed as she turned and twined her arms around his neck. "We'll have time afterwards."

"You make it sound as if I am a patient man."

She chuckled again. "The anticipation, though"—she arched up onto her tiptoes and drew her lips along his sharp jaw—"is delicious."

"You, love, are delicious." He started to inch her gown up, and she wanted him to taste her and make her shatter as much as he clearly wanted to. But they didn't have time.

"I want to," she told him, then bit her lip. "But I want to savor it."

He bent until his forehead rested against hers. "Good God, I've found myself a logical wife."

After pressing a kiss to her forehead, he stepped back and then went to retrieve her purple gown.

"This reminds me of our first kiss, so you'll be driving me mad all evening in it."

Tess approached and reached up to stroke her fingers through his thick, dark hair. "We'll be driving each other mad." She drew in a breath. "I just hope this works."

"Me too, love."

They got busy dressing then, Dom in his formal evening suit and Tess in her old violet gown. The dress accentuated her waist and décolletage, and she smiled when she noticed

Dominic watching her wolfishly. Then voices below stilled both their movements. Loud, boisterous voices.

"They're here," he said, and they strode toward each other, clasped hands, nodded, and made their way downstairs.

By the time they reached the ground floor, the Van Arsdales had headed up to their own borrowed rooms to wash and change, just as they'd anticipated they would.

The Fenbridge staff had been instructed not to breathe a word to the Van Arsdales about the plan unfolding. They only knew that a dinner was being prepared to celebrate their return.

Right on time, the guests that Dominic had invited began to arrive.

First, the Duchess of Norberry, who had donated an enormous collection of historic ceramics to the British Museum ten years ago. Next came Lord Julius Montague, Marquess of Ashbourne, a trustee of the museum, and the man who most often met with, or even persuaded, prospective donors to part with their collections. Finally, Richard Wrothley, an American steel magnate who'd married an English duke's daughter and built a vast estate for them in Surrey.

Tess gathered them into the Fenbridge dining room where she and Eve and Dominic greeted them personally and thanked them for coming. Then, to her utter delight, Fenbridge strode into the room soon after to mingle with the distinguished guests.

Half an hour later, a maid signaled to Tess, and she left Dominic and Eve to keep the guests in the drawing room occupied.

The Van Arsdales swept down the main staircase. Miss Van Arsdale wore an exquisite pale pink beaded gown that glittered as she moved.

"Miss Hawthorne," she said, her gaze narrowing slightly. "What a surprise to find you here. Were you invited?"

"I was," Tess told her with a smile. "Mr. Prince invited me."

"Gads, girl," Van Arsdale barked, "you two are determined on a proper scandal, aren't you?"

Tess held her smile, refusing to be baited. "As he is my betrothed, I doubt there will be a scandal."

Miss Van Arsdale blinked and then her lips curved. "My, you do work quickly, Miss Hawthorne. Perhaps I should ask you for some pointers when I go back to London to snap up a duke."

Dominic strode out of the drawing room, baiting the Americans' attention before Tess had the time to decide whether Miss Van Arsdale was being sincere or simply cutting.

"We've invited a few special guests tonight, Van Arsdale. I hope you won't mind."

Van Arsdale seemed utterly unfazed and even a bit intrigued by that news. "More's the merrier I always say." He waved an arm imperiously. "Introduce me."

Dom led the two of them into the drawing room and did precisely that. Eve, who seemed to know the collectors as well as he did, acted as a sort of intermediary, jumping in to add little details to link each guest to British archaeology or the London museum.

Tess watched from a distance, seeing Van Arsdale's eyes glitter when he was presented to the duchess and then the fellow American who'd secured a blue-blooded wife, much as he was hoping to find a noble-blooded Englishman to add to his family tree.

When Lord Ashbourne stepped forward for an introduction, Tess noted a flash of interest from Sofia Van Arsdale. He was a tall, lean, classically handsome young man with burnished blond hair, a winning smile, and striking blue eyes.

Van Arsdale seemed intrigued when he shook the young man's hand. He wasn't the duke the American titan was seeking for his daughter, but he would be one day.

"I hear you've made a marvelous find." Lord Ashbourne leaned in as if they were speaking of state secrets. "An extraordinary gold buckle of Anglo-Saxon origin, is it?"

"It's the prettiest thing you've ever seen, I assure you, Lord Ashbourne," Miss Van Arsdale gushed.

He grinned at her. Tess almost expected him to disagree and claim she was the prettiest thing he'd ever seen, but the astute young man knew who he had to convince and focused all his attention on Gordon Van Arsdale.

"Have you considered donating any of the dig's discoveries to the British Museum?" he asked Van Arsdale almost casually. "The duchess there recently bequeathed the most impressive collection."

"We're building our own museum," Van Arsdale boomed. "You're all invited to come and see it in New York."

"Oh, but we'd hate to see British history leaving our little island, Mr. Van Arsdale," Ashbourne said smoothly, his voice rich, his accent pure aristocratic haughtiness. "Tell me, Miss Van Arsdale, is there anything we could do to persuade him?"

Sofia Van Arsdale let out a throaty laugh and ran her fingers over the diamond choker at her throat. "Perhaps you should persuade me first, my lord."

Tess felt Dominic come up beside her and turned to find him watching the unfolding flirtation with as much interest as she was.

"This wasn't part of the plan," he told her quietly.

"I didn't realize how handsome Ashbourne was."

Dominic slid an arm her waist and stepped a bit closer. "Find him handsome, do you, my bride-to-be?"

Tess grinned and nudged her hip surreptitiously against his. "I only meant objectively speaking. He's handsome if you like that blond Greek god kind of beauty."

"And do you?" he asked, his hold hot and firm against her waist.

"No," Tess breathed, then looked up at Dominic. "I prefer the dark-haired, dark-eyed, devilishly handsome sort of beauty."

"Thank God for that."

They both chuckled. Tess clutched his lapel when the dinner gong sounded, and Ashbourne offered his arm and led a seemingly smitten Sofia Van Arsdale into dinner.

"This may work for a reason we hadn't even considered," she told him excitedly.

"Mmm, but Van Arsdale still needs to be persuaded."

"The man may not have a single bit of real respect for history, but I think he'd give his daughter anything she wants."

As they strode into the dining room together, Dominic bent to whisper, "The question is whether he'll settle for a marquess for her."

This time, Tess made sure that she and Dominic were seated together, and by some bit of serendipity, Sofia Van Arsdale and Ashbourne were seated near each other too.

Mid courses and on a prearranged cue, Wrothley piped up and asked Van Arsdale if he'd heard about Aldridge's enormous donation to "the local museum."

Van Arsdale's hands tightened around his cutlery at the

mention of Aldridge's name and even Sofia, who'd been happily chatting away with Ashbourne, quieted.

"Of course, I've bloody heard of it. Man's forever grandstanding and getting in the papers."

"You should come see the Aldridge bronzes once they're on display," Ashbourne put in casually. "They're thinking of calling it The Aldridge Room." Ashbourne swept his hand through the air as if imagining the American's rival's name etched on a plaque.

"Oh, goodness," Tess said after a charged look from Dominic. "I almost forgot to say that we've had a telegram from the one guest who could not attend."

Tess's hands shook slightly as she took up her glass of wine and looked at Dominic.

"Won't you read it out to everyone?" she asked him.

"Of course." He pulled the telegram from his waistcoat pocket and lifted it with dramatic flair as if he'd learned a great deal from the Americans in the past days. "Lord Rothschild apologizes that he could not attend, and says . . ." Dominic paused and looked down, reading directly from the telegram:

"I hear you are planning to donate your finds to the British Museum. I commend you heartily, Van Arsdale."

"It would be an extraordinary act of philanthropy, Mr. Van Arsdale," Duchess Norberry said with genuine emotion. "One for which the English public and I daresay the American too would remember you forever."

"We'd be pleased as punch to have a Van Arsdale Room," Ashbourne said, offering his wine glass in toast as if the deal had already been done.

"Oh, Father, wouldn't that be magnificent!" Sofia Van

Arsdale said, her eyes glittering, not at Van Arsdale, but at the handsome marquess seated next to her. "Would you see to it all yourself, Lord Ashbourne?"

"I would see to anything that would please you, Miss Van Arsdale."

Tess was shocked to see that the young man's interest seemed genuine, though with a young lady as pretty and wealthy as Miss Van Arsdale, the nobleman's quick interest seemed natural.

Van Arsdale swigged down his wine and cast a look around the table. Everyone, even Fenbridge, watched him expectantly.

Finally, he locked his gaze on the Marquess of Ashbourne. "I want more than a room, Ashbourne."

The young nobleman arched one aristocratic brow. "Oh?"

"I want a whole goddamned wing."

The duchess and Wrothley exchanged a surreptitious smile. Tess gripped Dominic's hand under the table, where it had been resting on her thigh.

"Sounds very grand," Fenbridge said, though he'd been quiet throughout dinner. "A toast, then, to our esteemed American guests, and to their future generosity to the British Museum."

Van Arsdale still looked a bit stunned at the turn of events.

But as each guest at the table lifted their glass toward him and then the duchess began a round of *hip-hip hooray* that everyone joined, he smiled under his neatly trimmed mustache, seeming to bask in the attention and praise.

Later, after dessert had been served, the guests made their way back to the drawing room for port.

"We did it," Tess whispered to Dominic as they stood together near the unlit fireplace. She slid a hand along his chest, curling her fingers around his lapel. "You concocted a marvelous plan," she told him after glancing around to ensure no one might overhear.

"Honestly," he said, tipping a glance to where Ashbourne sat on a settee and Sofia Van Arsdale sat in a nearby chair, leaning toward him, a lovestruck look in her eyes, "attraction did a great deal more than I was anticipating."

"I can't disagree. And they do make a charming couple."

"We still need to get you back on the dig."

Tess wasn't worried. "I don't think that will be a problem. I can apologize to Mr. Van Arsdale. And to Miss Van Arsdale, if it comes down to it, and I suspect she'll be in a forgiving mood."

Dominic arched a brow skeptically.

"Look how happy she is," Tess pointed out.

"I'll convince them one way or another," he assured her.

"I know you will." Tess smiled up at him. "You're very convincing."

"Am I?" He bent to whisper in her ear. "Then let me convince you to come up to bed with me. Now."

"As you once said to me," she told him, fingers tightening around the fabric of his lapel, "I'll follow you anywhere, though people may talk."

"Let them talk." He turned, bracing his hands on the mantel on either side of her, standing scandalously close. "I care about what you think. What you want." He dipped his head. "I want you. Always. Forever."

He was making promises. Soon he'd be making vows, and she'd be making them too. Yet Tess wasn't scared of promises anymore. She wanted them because she loved and trusted Dominic Prince with her heart.

"Always," she whispered. "Forever."

EPILOGUE

Thirteen months later
June 1897

As the omnibus rolled into Bloomsbury, Tess clutched Dominic's hand in both of hers. The museum came into view as they turned onto Montague Street, and she felt the excitement fluttering in her middle.

Tristan and Justine were set to join them within days, and Dominic and Tess had arrived the day before and settled into the Prince town house for their visit.

Meeting Dominic's sister Allie again had been as lovely as the first time they'd met when she and her husband had come up to Wiggenstow for their wedding. They discussed their research, writing, the challenge of being a woman who wished to publish in a field that had long been dominated by men, and a few other matters out of the hearing of their husbands.

Tess had a secret she planned to divulge to Dominic at some point during their visit.

To match her own happiness and excitement, the whole city seemed to be full of anticipation as preparations were made for Queen Victoria's diamond jubilee, which would take place in but a week.

Dominic had been concerned they'd get caught up in the crush of all of it, but Tess was determined to see the Van Arsdale collection laid out in all its splendor at the British Museum.

"Perhaps you were right about the crowds," Tess told him as they stepped off the omnibus and she spied the queues near the museum.

"It's to be a grand celebration over two days, apparently," Dominic told her, his hand on hers where she held his arm. "If you want to wait, we can."

She quirked an eyebrow at him. "Who are you? My husband is not a patient man."

Dominic laughed the deep, full-throated sound that never failed to make her smile.

"I am patient only for your sake. I don't want you overheated or crushed by the crowd."

The weather was lovely and warm, though they'd had some late spring storms in the first few days of their visit.

"We're here now. I don't want to turn back."

They headed for the queue and Dominic stroked her back in delicious circles as they waited. Though they'd planned their visit for weeks, they'd decided to take each day as it came, but Tess told him of a few sites she wanted to visit.

"And Princes, of course."

He smiled. "Of course."

Tess had yet to visit the famous antique shop, but she was eager to, not only to see the beautiful historic pieces they carried, but also to understand more about Dominic's family history. She even wanted to see the famous "bachelor lodgings" he kept upstairs.

"There's a jeweler's shop we should visit too."

"You've spoiled me enough."

Since their wedding, her wardrobe had grown by dozens of fashionable, beautiful gowns, and her small wooden jewelry box could no longer contain the earrings, bracelets, and necklaces he'd gifted to her.

"Oh, I haven't," he assured her, "but I'd also like to pay a visit. They're the family of a friend I lost a while ago."

"I'm so sorry, my love."

He bent and pressed a soft kiss to her cheek. "He was far too young for such a loss, but I think he'd be proud of the turn my life has taken."

Tess reached up and cupped his cheek. "I'm eager to meet his family."

A few moments later, they were admitted to the museum and broke off from the main area to find the collection they'd come to see. A collection they'd worked to excavate, clean, document, and study.

In the end, Van Arsdale didn't get a few displays or a single room. His donations got an entire wing.

After passing through several corridors, they found *The Van Arsdale Bequest*. The displays were artfully done, and the panels behind the artifacts contained historical details, some of which Tess had provided.

On a wood pillar and set upon a rich green velvet pillow sat the golden buckle. It had been cleaned and polished to a high sheen, and Tess felt tears well as she took in its incredibly detailed knotwork and remembered the awe she'd felt the day she'd pulled it from Fenbridge's field.

The silver bowls had been polished too, and the coins they'd found looked like a true treasure as they lay assembled together.

Though scholars disagreed on whose burial they'd discovered, and there was nothing among the finds to know definitively, all agreed it was likely a royal personage and one deemed worthy of great honor.

"An incredible accomplishment," Dominic said as he stood

beside her, reading one of the panels for which she'd contributed verbiage.

"So many people had a hand in this. I can't wait for Tristan to see it." Tess turned to him. "We should ask Fenbridge if he'll allow us to host an anniversary dinner and invite all the workmen and their families."

They'd held one last autumn to celebrate, though there were so many in attendance that they had to bring in extra tables and chairs to accommodate everyone.

"That's a wonderful idea," he told her. "Let's speak to him when we get back. It's plenty of time to prepare."

"Even if we have quite a bit else to prepare for too?" Tess asked him, her voice full of joy she could barely contain.

Dominic frowned. "Autumn shouldn't be terribly busy. We're going to tackle that barrow in Little Greeling this summer. I estimate the project will only take about a month or two."

They'd agreed to a small excavation at a mound in a village south of Wiggenstow.

"I think so too, but . . . we'll have our own project to prepare for as well." She placed a hand over her belly that had begun to gently swell over the last few months.

Dominic beamed at her, then pulled her into his arms, ignoring the glances of other museumgoers.

"What would you say," he whispered near her ear, "if I told you that I already suspected?"

"Did you?"

He led her to a corner of the room, where they were slightly sheltered by a display.

Then he cupped her face in his hands. "I wanted you to tell me in your own time." He offered her one of his genuine, slightly crooked smiles. "But thank you for telling me today. It was bloody agonizing to be patient."

Tess laughed and wrapped her arms around her husband, holding him close, feeling his love. She smiled as she laid her cheek against his chest, and he kissed the top of her head.

"I love you," he whispered.

"I love *you*," she murmured back, smiling, knowing what their child was in for.

Two parents who were mad for history, each other, and making a life filled with love for them too.

Acknowledgments

Thanks to my editor, Alessandra Roche, for your encouragement, understanding, and helping me make this book better. Thanks also to the whole team at Avon Books for helping bring this book to readers.

About the Author

Fueled by Pacific Northwest coffee and inspired by multiple viewings of every British costume drama she can get her hands on, *USA Today* bestselling author **CHRISTY CARLYLE** writes sensual historical romance set in the Victorian era. She loves heroes who struggle against all odds and heroines who are ahead of their time. A former teacher with a degree in history, she finds there's nothing better than being able to combine her love of the past with a die-hard belief in happy endings.

Discover more swoon-worthy books from Christy Carlyle and Avon Books

Princes of London

Love on Holiday

 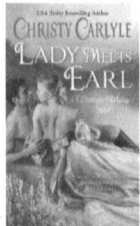 

The Duke's Den

 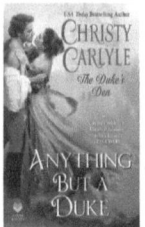 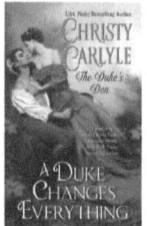

Romancing the Rules

DISCOVER GREAT AUTHORS, EXCLUSIVE OFFERS, AND MORE AT HC.COM

www.ingramcontent.com/pod-product-compliance
Ingram Content Group UK Ltd.
Pitfield, Milton Keynes, MK11 3LW, UK
UKHW040237250426
12048UKWH00043B/1567